Larry Brown is a retired business executive living near Lake Keowee, Seneca, South Carolina. After a successful business career, he began to pursue writing. This will be his third novel. His goal is to continue writing.

This book is dedicated to my wife of 48 years, Marsha. She is my toughest critic, but also my biggest motivator. She is also the love of my life.

Larry Brown

SUDDENLY SINGLE

AUSTIN MACAULEY PUBLISHERS™

LONDON • CAMBRIDGE • NEW YORK • SHARJAH

Ordering Information:
Quantity sales: special discounts are available on quantity purchases by corporations, associations, and others. For details, contact the publisher at the address below.

Publisher's Cataloging-in-Publication data
Brown, Larry
Suddenly Single

ISBN 9781643785929 (Paperback)
ISBN 9781643785936 (Hardback)
ISBN 9781645368274 (ePub e-book)

Library of Congress Control Number: 2019919329

www.austinmacauley.com/us

First Published (2020)
Austin Macauley Publishers LLC
40 Wall Street, 28th Floor
New York, NY 10005
USA

mail-usa@austinmacauley.com
+1 (646) 5125767

Thanks to Charles Bassos, Cliff Barlow, and Jan Dickson, who helped me stay motivated and on track.

Chapter 1

The old man was shaking uncontrollably. His sobbing was so deep his chest hurt. He didn't even notice the blood that was on both his hands and now beginning to show on his shirt and pants.

He had taken her body off the glass coffee table in front of the stone fireplace in their great room, where she landed after the shotgun blast had opened up her chest. The second blast had killed their dog, Belle.

He had awkwardly moved her body onto the sectional leather sofa where they had been watching TV only minutes ago. He sat on the floor beside her trying to close her blouse that had been ripped open by the shotgun blast. He placed his arm around her, put his head on her shoulder, closed his eyes and tried to compose himself.

He said out loud, "Oh God, my God, how could this happen?" Now he was mad. Not at God, he was a man who loved God; they were a couple who loved God. No, he was now furious at the two men who had invaded their home.

He got up and picked up his Ruger .38 revolver which he had laid it on the glass table beside her. A small amount of blood had leaked onto the handle, but it didn't matter as his hands were both covered with blood.

He walked to the hallway which led to their bedroom and stood over the body of the first dead man, who had received two of his .38s. He screamed an obscenity and shot the dead man in the face. Now he walked back to the great room then onto the porch and the porch entrance to their bedroom.

The other dead man lay in the entry among the glass shards and wood pieces of the ruined door frame. He stood over the dead man and shouted the same obscenity again and shot him in the face. This seemed to calm his rage.

He walked back into the great room, placed the Ruger on the glass table, and sat down in his big leather recliner. His sobbing and shaking had stopped even though his hands still trembled. Suddenly his body felt numb. He knew he needed to call someone, but he wasn't sure he could pick up his cell phone on the table next to his recliner.

What just happened? They had been talking about food to be bought for their daughter and her husband's visit. He had interrupted her and told her to wait while he went to get a sweater. She always kept the temperature so cold.

As he started down the hallway to the bedroom, he heard the crash of wood and glass as it exploded. He looked back to see two men in ski masks charge into their entrance. One had a shotgun, the other a handgun. From that point, his instincts took over.

His shotgun, always loaded and in easy reach in the hall closet, was his first stop. He grabbed it, then entered the bedroom and pulled open the nightstand drawer, where he kept the Ruger. That may be the thing that saved him; they probably didn't know there was an entrance to the back porch from the bedroom. As he grabbed the Ruger, he heard two shotgun blasts. With no forethought, he charged onto the back porch and then to the great room.

Maggie was draped half on the glass table, her chest pouring blood. Belle was lying by the fireplace, a mass of white hair and blood. The two men were gone, and he knew they were in his bedroom and would soon be at the porch door which he had left half open. When the first man stepped into the porch entrance, he fired both barrels of the 12-gauge coach gun, blowing the man along with glass and pieces of the door back into the bedroom. He quickly stepped into the great room from the porch and crouched behind the big TV stand. Setting the shotgun on the floor, he aimed the Ruger at the hallway entrance. The man stepped into the great room and seemed momentarily focused on Maggie's body. From his crouched position, the old man fired two .38s through the man's chest.

As he sat and leaned against the wall, he knew he didn't believe in coincidences. It was no coincidence that he had gotten cold and had gone for a sweater. For whatever reason, God did not want him to die that day. But, why Maggie? Why poor little Belle? Why us? He then remembered the box of gold coins. He picked up his cell phone and dialed 911.

Chapter 2

The town of Lakeview, SC, was in Polk County and on the perimeter of Pine Lake. Polk County was on the far western side of the state with two pieces of the county bordering North Carolina and Georgia. Lakeview was the largest town in the county and the headquarters of the Polk County Sheriff's department.

Sheriff Clay Hardaway had lived in Polk County his entire life. He had been in the department for 30 years, the head man for the last 20. The sheriff was a big man at 6'5" before he put on his brushed leather cowboy boots. He weighed about 250 pounds with a pink to red complexion. He had always worn his hair in a flat top cut, and you could hardly notice the white hair now mixing with his blonde. He was an intimidating figure, even at age 56.

Sheriff Hardaway's team of 10 included three dispatchers and one administrative assistant, all females. Four of his six deputies were under 35 years old and had done tours in the military special forces in the Middle East as did the one female deputy. His sixth deputy was 65-year-old Al Johnson, the former sheriff, and Clay's best friend.

It was 10:50 pm when the 911 call was received at the sheriff's office. According to procedure, any call that involved gunfire with people down gets the highest priority. If there were not a deputy on patrol, one was immediately dispatched to the location. The second call went to the sheriff, wherever his location was at the time. EMT dispatch received the third call.

On this night, the call went to the sheriff at his home, a cabin on Pine Lake. The location would take about twenty to twenty-five minutes to reach from the office, but Hardaway could be there in ten minutes from his home. He had just cut a big red apple into slices when the call came. When he heard the name and address, he was shocked. He had just been at a reception in the county auditorium honoring Harry Blake and his wife, Maggie.

They were older than him but full of life and energy, and he had enjoyed meeting them both. He felt like they were genuinely nice people. He remembered thinking how much Maggie had reminded him of his wife, Louise. Louise would have liked the couple. She had died of breast cancer six months ago, about the same time the Blakes had moved to Polk County and the lake.

The reception was to celebrate the literary award Harry Blake had received. He had been a successful businessman, retired and began to write fiction. His first two books received the American Literary Association's Craft Master Award. Not only was the recognition national news, but it also contained the grand prize of $125,000 in gold coins enclosed in a gold inlaid box. The box and coins were on display at the reception, and all of the mainstream media outlets had pictured the prize. It was awe-inspiring.

His mind shifted back to the dispatcher's remarks, "apparent home invasion." They didn't have home invasions in Polk County. Maybe a drunken husband or boyfriend in a gone-bad relationship, but that was about all they had to deal with in that regard. And three dead bodies, *Oh my God,* he thought, he couldn't remember the last time he had dealt with something like this. He and his team had talked about the unhealthy things that were happening in the county, and they all had hoped it would be later than sooner to come to Polk County. He hoped this was not the beginning.

Traffic around the lake at this time in the evening was non-existent. As the sheriff turned onto Ridge Road where the Blakes lived, he lit up the colored lights on his black four-wheel-drive Tahoe. He turned down the driveway that was long and steep. He could see a faded blue panel van, with both front doors open, parked close to the front door. It was entirely out of place unless you were loading or unloading. He pulled up close, blocking the van.

It was dark outside; only the lights inside the house gave illumination. He took his 12-gauge pump shotgun from its rack, opened his front door cautiously and stared carefully at the half-open front door. About that time lights came on everywhere around him. Floodlights from the house corners and over the doors of the three-car garage lit up the driveway and the generous parking area. Then the front porch light came on, and the door opened all the way. The 12-gauge went instantly into the shooting position.

Harry Blake stepped out holding both hands in the air, "It's okay, Sheriff, it's all over."

"Are you alright, Mr. Blake?"

"Physically, yes. I was not shot." Harry had moved toward one of the stone columns on the porch, so he could hold on to steady himself.

Hardaway realized how shaky Blake was and ushered him back into the house. As they passed through the foyer into the great room, Hardaway grimaced as he saw the devastation. Ahead were the bloody bodies of Maggie Blake and the dog and a bloody glass coffee table. To the left in the hallway was another body. He felt Harry shudder and choke up when he looked at Maggie again. Hardaway guided Harry to a stool in the kitchen and out of sight of the carnage.

"Mr. Blake, can I get you something? Maybe some water?"

"Sheriff, please call me Harry."

"Only if you call me Clay."

Harry nodded affirmatively.

"Sheriff, sorry, I mean Clay, would you mind going to the bar and getting me a glass and a bottle of Buffalo Trace?" he pointed to the bar at the entrance to the dining room. "Join me if you will," asked Harry.

"Wish I could, but I am working. Maybe later."

After pouring Harry's crystal glass half-full, Clay excused himself and began his inspection. His first stop was at Maggie's body and the immediate area. He now realized that the TV was on, and he found the remote by the big recliner, ending the game show that was in progress. The silence was now deafening.

Something caught his eye, and he realized a woman in pajamas and a robe, with a dog on a leash, was starting up the front steps. He rushed to the door to make sure the woman did not enter or see anything. Before he could open his mouth, she spoke.

"I'm Ms. Turner from down the street. I was walking Pookie when I saw your flashing lights. Are the Blakes okay?"

"Ms. Turner, I'm Sheriff Hardaway; I have just arrived. I'll have an update a little later. Would you mind going back up the driveway to the street and ask the other neighbors to please stay away until we can sort things out here?"

"What things?"

"Ma'am, please let me do my job, now please go."

"I'll go, but I do think you should tell me something."

Clay stared at the lady with his most serious face and pointed up the driveway. She grunted and left, shaking her head. He closed the front door and went back to the kitchen to check on Harry. He looked around the opening to the kitchen, hoping not to be seen. No Harry. He was gone. The light was on in a room on the opposite the big kitchen. He walked to the door; it was Harry's office. Harry and the Buffalo Trace were at his desk.

"Come in, Clay. A little more comfortable in here."

"Not yet, just checking to make sure you're okay."

"Clay I'm exhausted; I feel like I've been up for a week."

"Adrenaline, you probably got such an overdose of it, that may take a while to recover. Do you mind if I ask how old you are?"

"No, I'm 72."

"Damnation, you should be tired. We'll talk when I'm through."

Clay went back to work; his next stop was the body of the intruder in the hallway. As he bent over the body, he heard the front door open.

"Clay, everything okay?"

Clay stood up and met Morris Canady, the oldest of his young deputies. Morris was 35 and black.

"We got a mess. A damn sad mess."

Clay motioned Morris to follow him back into the hallway. They both bent over the body; the obvious thing was two gunshot wounds in the chest. Morris had put on a pair of latex gloves and started removing the black ski mask when Morris said, "Shit, look at this. Shot in the face and at fairly close range, I would say." When the mask was removed, and they could clearly see the face, Morris said, "Tee Watson, a Milltown boy." He had been arrested several times: drugs, fighting, nothing good in his public life. "And I got five bucks says I know his partner. There's two of them, right?" asked Morris.

"Yeah, let's check on the other one."

They continued down the hallway and into the master bedroom. The French doors from the bedroom to the back porch had been blown apart, and the body lay in a pile of glass, wood, and blinds. His whole front had been blown apart.

"Double hit," said Morris.

"No question. Still, think you might know who it is?" asked the sheriff.

"Big Moe Jones." Canady was sure; he had grown up on the eastside and knew most folks in Milltown.

"Look," Morris said as he started to remove the mask, "another face shot at fairly close range. What's that about?"

"I don't know but let's keep that quiet until we hear Harry's story."

They walked out onto the porch and back into the great room as the EMTs arrived. Clay put a finger to his lips to keep the EMTs quiet. He walked over to them and explained that they had two dead guys and one victim, and under no circumstance did he want the lady placed in the same vehicle with the bad guys. Everything is on hold until Jesse Corbin, the coroner, gets here and does his work.

Clay asked Morris to call dispatch and get them to wake Al and have him come over. Clay went back to Harry's office. "Can we talk?"

Harry nodded yes.

Clay closed the door and sat down across from Harry. "I know you haven't had time to think about these things, but have you a choice for taking care of Mrs. Blake?"

"No, we are so new here and haven't been spending any time thinking about dying. Who is the best?"

"When Louise died, I called Arthur Dobbins. I've known Art forever. He was the only one I considered to take care of Louise."

"Okay, I'm sorry, I had forgotten. We had heard your wife had died. Cancer, right?"

"Yes. Would you like for me to call Art for you? He'll handle everything tonight, and you can go see him tomorrow."

"Thanks, Clay, I appreciate all you're doing."

"I'll be right back."

Clay left the office, and from the kitchen used his cell phone to call Art Dobbins.

When the arrangements were made, he went back to Harry's office.

"All set, Arthur said anytime tomorrow you can come by and work through everything. If you can, I would like to talk to you about tonight."

Harry drained the last of the bourbon in his glass and said, "Fine."

"Let me tell you what we know. The two men are bad guys, long records. What I don't know is why. Why you? Why this house? What's the motive?"

Harry interrupted, "I think I may have the answer." Harry stood up and motioned to Clay to follow. They walked out of the office through the kitchen to an open area between the dining room and great room. As a break between the two spaces, there was a large walnut table with antique porcelain candle holders on each end. The centerpiece of the table was a golden box with a glass centerpiece revealing large gold coins; it was the prize from the Literary Association. The box and coins were worth $125,000.

"Clay, this has been in every newspaper and on every TV station in America. All the local news folks covered the reception at the county. Probably not many people in the county that don't know about this."

Clay placed his big left hand over his mouth, raised his eyebrows and stared at the box. He finally looked at Harry, "I'm sorry, I had assumed the coins would have been in some secure place. But you're right, strong motive."

The two men looked up as Deputy Morris Canady, and a new deputy, much older, walked up to the table.

"Harry, these are my deputies, Morris Canady and Al Johnson. Al was the former sheriff and is now my assistant."

"Gentlemen, the motive," and he pointed to the golden box.

The deputies nodded affirmatively, and Harry said, "Why don't one of you pick it up."

Morris pointed at Al and said, "Age before beauty."

Al leaned over, put one hand on each side of the box and did not move it.

"What the heck, it's fastened to the table."

Harry smiled, "I assure it is not."

"Move, old man," Morris said as he grabbed the box and moved it about an inch.

"Gentlemen, everything but the glass is solid gold. Do you know how much it weighs, Harry?"

"I'm told close to 100 pounds."

The two deputies were speechless.

"Morris, stay in charge out here. Make sure we get plenty of pictures. When Dobbins gets here, let me know. Harry, would you mind if Al sits with us while we talk?"

"Fine."

The three men went back to Harry's office.

"Harry tell us what happened here tonight."

Chapter 3

It was two in the morning, and the house was finally empty. Harry was flat worn out and felt very alone. The times that Maggie had traveled without him, there was always Belle as his constant companion. The only time he could think of, that he had been entirely alone, was when she took Belle to the vet.

The hard fact of the matter was he had better get used to being by himself because he was more than likely going to be by himself until he died. He just could not go back to their bedroom now. He loved his big leather recliner, so many good naps there. Then his thought was maybe a second bourbon would be in order. He retrieved his glass, filled it to the halfway mark and sat and leaned back as far as the chair would go. He closed his eyes. He truly was exhausted, but he could not sleep.

He thought about his kids. Should he call them now? No, let them sleep. It was going to be a hard day when they found out she was gone. Sally and her husband Troy were already planning to be here anyway. Sally was their youngest and their only natural child. His mind jumped to when they first married and put their two families together. He had two boys, four and six, and she had a boy, six and a girl, eight. Their commitment to each other was, there would never be his or hers; they would always be ours. In spite of many other issues in their marriage, they had done a pretty good job with their children. None ever in any real trouble, no drugs, alcohol in moderation, and best of all, they were all believers. All five were settled, married, and doing well, even though three were in second marriages. The kids' choices, the second time around, were far better than their first.

He wanted to sleep; it just wouldn't come. His mind was racing. Clay Hardaway, he really liked the man. He was considerate and kind, but there was never any doubt about who was in charge. Respect, you could see he had it not only from his employees but also the EMTs, the coroner and even the man from the funeral home. Maggie, my Maggie. What a life we have had! How our relationship had evolved over our 46 years of marriage. His mind wandered, Clay had lost his wife, so they had one thing in common. He had to go to Clay's office today and to Dobbins Funeral Home. Maybe he would wait on Sally before he went to Dobbins. They were low on food. They were going to shop this morning before Sally arrived. Could he get that done? They would need more now. Everyone would be coming, Johnny, Paul, Pete and, of course, darling Millie.

Those sons of bitches who came in and killed Maggie and Belle. All they had to do was ask, and I would have given them the gold and anything they wanted. Just ask and go and leave us alone. But no, scum bags, no thought of life. Damn, I wish I could shoot them again. One reckless act is going to cause so much pain. Bastards. He sat up and drank about half of his bourbon. He leaned back again, closed his eyes and slept.

The back of the house faced his gazebo, docks, and Pine Lake. When the sun started rising over the trees on the other side of the lake, its bright early morning rays came through his porch and enveloped his recliner. He slowly opened his eyes and realized that all of his joints ached. With great effort, he stood and thought, *Where is Maggie?* Then the events of the night before hit him. He needed coffee. The Keurig in the kitchen was his quick answer. He needed coffee before he made his first call.

Halfway through his second cup, he called Sally. She was devastated. Once she regained her composure, she said she would repack and that they would be on the road within the hour. He was crying again. He would need more coffee and some time before he called Millie. He needed to be strong for his family. *So, stop the damn crying.* After a few minutes, he called Millie. She was stunned, but more in control than Sally. Millie asked if he knew where her mother was, and he told her, Dobbins Funeral Home.

"No, Dad," she replied, "she is with our dear Lord." He didn't know why, but he could not control himself. He began to sob. Neither one could speak, they just cried together for what seemed like a long time. She finally spoke.

"Dad, I have things to do, but I will be there by dark. I love you, Dad."

He tried to tell her he loved her too, but it was lost in his moan.

Millie had agreed to call Pete and Johnny. Sally was calling Paul. He knew his phone would be ringing soon, so he poured more coffee and took a quick shower, hoping to regain his composure. The problem was, at every turn, her things were there. Everything appeared the same except she and Belle were gone.

For some reason, the damages to the house began to weigh on him. They had to be repaired and quickly. When he and Maggie had moved in, they had met a handyman named Ed Tuttle. He was a short man with a big barrel chest and thinning grey hair which was almost always covered by an 'NRA' baseball style cap. Ed was in his mid-fifties and was more than competent in carpentry, plumbing, electrical and most things that might need to be done in a house. He had done a lot of work for them and had spent much time in their home. Ed and Maggie had bonded. He had to call Ed.

"Ed, Harry Blake."

"You up mighty early, ain't you, Mr. Harry?"

"Got some bad news, Ed." He then proceeded to give Ed the details of the previous night.

"That ain't very funny, Mr. Harry."

"I'm not kidding, Ed, it's true."

"Naw, naw, not Mrs. Maggie, No, Mr. Harry, no!"

"Ed, I need your help. My front door is blown all to hell so is the porch door to the bedroom. I don't want my family to see it longer than they have to. I hate to ask because I know how busy you are, but is there any way you could handle this quickly for me?"

"Consider it done. I'll be at y'all's house within the hour."

"Ed, I have things to do in town. If I'm gone, you know what to do. As always, everything first class. I trust your judgment."

"Yessir, Lordy, I can't believe Mrs. Maggie's gone!"

In the next thirty minutes, he talked to all three boys. After their calls, there were just no more tears. He felt drugged. His phone was ringing again. This time neighbors. He did not answer; he wasn't ready for those calls. He needed to get out. He headed for Clay Hardaway's office.

Chapter 4

Polk County had one big county government building. All the county government offices were there, including the sheriff's office and the county jail. Harry pulled into the parking lot and saw the big black SUV in its reserved parking place. He and Clay had arrived at the same time.

Clay escorted Harry into his office while they exchanged nods. Neither man spoke. Clay left and came back with Al Johnson and coffee. Al closed the door and spoke first, "Mr. Blake, we have typed a statement recapping what you told us about the events of last night. We would like for you to read and sign if you agree it is true and accurate. Why don't you read it, but before you sign, we have one other point we need to talk about."

Harry read the statement, laid it on the desk and said, "I think this is fine. Now, what else do we need to talk about?"

Al looked at Clay, waiting for him to speak. "Harry, we didn't mention this last night, but Jesse, the coroner, said the families of the two men might question this." There was a pause, but Harry did not speak.

"The shots in the face at point-blank range, could you explain?"

Harry stared at the floor with a blank expression on his face. He finally raised his head and looked right into Clay's eyes. "When it was over, I moved Maggie off the table, and I saw how bad the shotgun had violated her body. I went to each one of the bastards, and I screamed obscenities and shot each of them in the face. I wanted whoever saw them know they had been violated the way they violated my Maggie. As I have gotten older and have seen how this world has evolved, I have begun to hate evil with a passion. I used to think it was bad, but it didn't bother me the way it does now. I hate it. If someone wants to sue me over it, screw them. Bring it on. Then I can say what's on my mind. The evil bastards didn't ask for the gold. I would have given it to them plus everything else they wanted. No, the evil sons of bitches killed my Maggie and Belle without even trying to get what they wanted without killing. Clay, Al, I would have given it to them." He was sobbing again, not for sadness but mad again. "I wish I had reloaded the shotgun and blown their heads off. They took my Maggie for no cause. May they rot in hell forever." Harry stood up walked to the window in Clay's office and tried to stop shaking and regain his composure.

After a few minutes of silence, Clay spoke, "Al, you have any more questions?"

Al stood up, stared at Harry, "None, Mr. Blake. I understand." He left the office.

Clay stood up, "Coffee has gotten cold, Harry. I'll get some fresh; be right back."

Clay returned in a few minutes with fresh coffee, and Harry spoke first, "Clay, I want to apologize. I lost it. I'm trying to figure out how to deal with this. I'm not doing real well with it so far. Anyway, I'm sorry."

"No apologies necessary. I think you are doing fine under the circumstances. Why don't you sign the statement and let's move on. This should be the only thing you have to do. You are not charged with any crime. The intruders have been taken care of, at least there is nothing else my office can do. What could I do to help you?"

"Clay. Nothing. You have been very kind. My family is on the way, so some sad days are ahead."

"Harry, what did you do with the box of coins?"

"Nothing, still where you saw them last night."

"How did you secure your front door?"

"I didn't, but Ed Tuttle is coming out to replace or fix everything."

"Harry, we need to talk about this. There are more than two bad guys in this county, and everybody knows about the gold."

"You may be right, let's talk after the family leaves."

"If I can do anything for you or your family, let me know."

"Thanks."

When Harry got to his car, his phone rang; it was Sally. They were 30 minutes out, and they agreed to meet at the funeral home. At the funeral home, the arrangements were made. Maggie's body would not be ready until that evening, so the decision was made for a family viewing only on the following day. Maggie had insisted on cremation and family viewing only.

With the arrangements made, Harry, Sally and her husband left to do a big grocery shop with the rest of the family on the way.

They were surprised when they stepped into the funeral home parking lot to find two different TV vans plus a half dozen of reporters, all wanting to get interviews with Harry. It was a reminder of the publicity he had received with the literary award he had won. The award ceremony had been covered by all the networks and cable news. He had actually appeared on one of the morning business shows.

Sally turned to Harry and said, "Dad, you and Troy go to your car and let me handle this." Sally was a VP for one of the big tech companies and was comfortable dealing with the press. Troy and Harry trotted to the car, while Sally called all the reporters to gather round. "Please respect the privacy of my father and our family during our time of grief. He will provide a statement to you within a few days. I will not be taking any questions at this time. I am Sally Smith, the youngest daughter of Harry and Maggie Blake. Thank you."

All the reporters began shouting questions, but Sally moved quickly to her car and off to meet her father and husband at the grocery store.

Chapter 5

In the grocery store parking lot, Harry called Clay and told him what happened at the funeral home. They discussed the possibility of what could be happening at Harry's house. After considering the options, Clay agreed to send a deputy to screen visitors to the house. Plus, Clay decided to draft a statement that he would release to the press. They would talk when Harry returned home.

After purchasing a massive amount of groceries, Harry, Sally, and Troy returned to the house, where they were met by several news trucks and other cars on both sides of the road. A sheriff's sawhorse barricade blocked the driveway, so no one could enter. Immediately the press vacated their vehicles and headed for the driveway. As the two cars started down the long steep driveway, they saw two pickups and a utility trailer. In the doorway was Ed Tuttle and two helpers installing a new front door. Harry pulled his car into the garage. Sally and Troy pulled in close to the garage door opening. When they got out, Ed came walking over to Sally and Troy, "My name is Ed Tuttle, and I can look at you and know for sure you belong to Mrs. Maggie."

At the sound of her mother's name, Sally began to tear up.

"Oh, I'm so sorry, I didn't mean to upset you."

Sally waved her hand in front of her face and choked out, "It's okay, it's okay." Harry walked out of the garage to join the group and Ed with tears in his eyes, took off his sweaty NRA cap revealing his thinning gray hair plastered against his head. He grabbed Harry and began to cry, "Mr. Harry, I am so, so, so sorry. You know I loved Mrs. Maggie." He immediately thought he had made a mistake. "I mean, I really liked her a lot. I shouldn't of said love. I'm sorry."

"Ed, it's alright, you said nothing wrong; she loved you too."

"Mr. Harry, what in the world happened?"

"I'll tell you all about it later, but first, how's the work coming?"

Sally now composed said, "Dad, you go on with Mr. Tuttle and Troy and I will unload everything."

"It's Ed, ma'am. I ain't no mister," he said with a sheepish grin as he replaced his hat. Harry and Ed walked to the front door and Harry could see they were almost finished.

"It's different than what you had, but it was the nicest one I could find."

"It's beautiful, Ed; Maggie would have loved it."

"You think? Well, it ought to be, it cost enough. Let's go see how the others are doing." They went through the great room to the porch and the doorway to the master suite. There were two more men who were finishing their work.

"Ed, where did you get all the help on such short notice?"

"Ol' Ed can still make it happen, Mr. Harry. We'll be out of here in about ten more minutes, and you can be alone with your family. Your daughter is beautiful like Mrs. Maggie."

"Thank you, Ed, now let's settle up."

"Mr. Harry I'm just charging you for materials, the labor is my gift to Mrs. Maggie."

"No way, Ed. Maggie would have my head if I did that."

Ed stared across the edge of the guest room through the porch and out across the lake. After a minute he said, "I would really like to do it."

"Ed, Maggie would never have it."

Ed finally reached in the back pocket of his jeans and pulled out his little notebook and a wooden pencil. He put the dull lead point in his mouth, scribbled several things on the page tore it out and handed it to Harry.

"I'll be right back, Ed." Harry went to his desk to write the check. He made it out for triple. Who else could have done all this in this short amount of time?

"Mr. Harry, you can't do this. I can't take this."

"Ed, this is for Maggie, this is from Maggie."

Ed started tearing up, and he turned and walked away.

As he left, Troy appeared in the great room with a bucket of soapy water and rags. Before Harry could speak Troy said, "Harry, why don't you help Sally with the groceries. There's a couple of things I think I should do." Harry then became fully aware of the blood stains on the glass table and the floor and hearth at the fireplace. Without responding, Harry went to join Sally in the kitchen.

"How's the work coming?"

"It's done. New doors, frames plus other minor repairs. Amazing."

"He must really like y'all, especially Mom."

"Your mother had him charmed. He would have done anything for her."

"Dad, it must have been awful last night. How did you survive?"

"The grace of God, only by His grace that I was down the hallway when they broke in. After that, it was all instinct, no time to think. They were evil. They could have broken in, held a gun on us, and I would have given them the coins. They had ski masks on; they could have gotten away free and clean. Why He saved me, I don't know."

Sally stared at her dad, walked across the room and held him.

"I love you so much, Dad."

"I love you too, honey."

Chapter 6

There was a vacation rental home down the street from the Blake's house, and luckily it was available. Sally had made the arrangements for the rental for the family. Maggie had insisted when they had moved to the lake that they have five guest bedrooms, one for each of their children. Grandchildren, spouses and great-grandchildren would be just down the street. It was a difficult three days. The evening of the third day turned out to be much better. Everyone had gone back to their lives except for the children.

The evening turned into a night of sharing Maggie stories. Each person had multiple experiences that were all pure Maggie. She could be the most generous, loving, forgiving person on the planet. But she could also be the hardest, coldest, nastiest person. The one thing that was for sure, Maggie was loved by her children. They all laughed and cried and knew one thing on which they could all agree; Maggie Blake was in a better place; she was with the good Lord.

The next morning, everyone left except Millie and Sallie. They were concerned for their father's wellbeing. Maggie had always done all the housekeeping except for heavy cleaning. They wanted to go over every detail to make sure their father could do or find someone to do all things required.

After all, he had never washed clothes, ironed, changed sheets, or run the dishwasher. They weren't worried about food preparation, he was as competent as Maggie in the kitchen, maybe more so. Also, both girls had agreed they would try to talk Harry into moving in with them or at least moving into the same town. They both knew the odds were slim to none that Harry would agree to leave the lake.

With everyone gone, the two girls sat Harry down, and each one made their pitch for their father's relocation.

Harry listened attentively and nodded and smiled and thanked each one and gave each the same answer. He would think about it. They pushed for a time frame for an answer. He responded with, "Let me think about it." At the end of the conversation, they knew their father would not leave until he was forced to do so. By the time they were ready to go, they felt they had made enough arrangements to take care of their father.

The two Mexican cleaning ladies who came every two weeks to help Maggie would come every week with expanded duties including washing, ironing, changing bed linens, etc. They wanted their father not to have to deal with the things Maggie did for him. They also had a private deal with the girls to call them if Harry's behavior changed in any way. Ruth, the lead person, seemed responsible and promised the girls she would make sure their father was well taken care of.

Chapter 7

It had been two weeks since his girls had left and the arrangements they made with Ruth were working better than he had ever expected. Not only was the house spotless, but his bed linens were changed every week plus he had fresh towels always available. His laundry was done with clothes folded or ironed and carefully placed in the proper drawer or closet. It had doubled his cost but truly worth every penny. Ruth had gone out of her way to make sure everything was the way he wanted it. Besides, with Maggie gone, his monthly expense reduction would more than cover the additional expense. All in all, this was a suitable arrangement for him now that Maggie was gone.

Even though two weeks had passed, he could barely get over the fact that Maggie and Belle weren't there. He missed them. He was lonely.

With so much time alone, his mind produced thoughts at a rapid pace. He could not stop thinking about the two intruders who needn't have fired a shot to achieve their objective. What kind of people shoot an innocent woman and dog without a word? He knew he was not supposed to hate, but he couldn't help himself. He hated them both and hoped they were burning in hell. He knew he shouldn't wish that, but he did. And it surprised him that he often thought about Belle. She was the little princess of the house. She was his as long as Maggie was out or too busy for her undivided attention. But when Maggie was home and settled, Belle was her baby. He knew it would be a real comfort if Belle were still around.

Then there were his thoughts about Maggie. What a life they'd had together. When they had met those many years before, it was terrific. Forty-seven years ago, she was divorced with two children, and he was going through a nasty divorce with Paula. He had two children also. They worked in different parts of the same company. She was very attractive, pleasant and very outgoing, so he always made time to talk to her. She always seemed like she was glad to see him. She was such a change from what his life at home was like.

Then, as would happen, the company opened a new facility on the north side of town, and she was transferred there as the secretary to the boss. And as fate sometimes works, he was asked to take over and manage the new facility. It only took a short while of working together for them to bond as co-workers. It was not just bonding; he was just relaxed and happy around her. Harry remembered, even though it was so many years ago, how much more comfortable he was at work than at home.

He was trying to live in his house while they were sorting through their divorce. They had agreed this would be better for their two small boys. It was one of the few things on which they could agree. He had the guest bedroom and worked late almost every night for obvious reasons. That finally became unlivable, and the arguing was having an impact on the boys, so he left permanently and moved back in with his parents. He remembered thinking moving out might be a way to expedite the divorce.

After a month of going to his parents' house each night, he knew he needed to have some time for himself. He stayed at his office and buried himself in his work. On a Saturday morning when he had asked for her to work, they were the only two people in the office. She needed the over-time trying to raise her two kids with an ex who rarely paid his child support on time. Harry remembered that morning like it was yesterday. He had asked her to come into his office. Harry could tell that she was apprehensive probably because his tone was different than usual. He was so nervous; he had been thinking about her so much that he had finally overcome the fear of approaching her not only about his feelings but the consideration of a co-worker. It didn't matter; he would not rest until he went forward.

"Have I done something?"

"No, no, Maggie, I just wanted to ask you if you were happy with your job? I know I get in the heat of the battle and I am maybe not as polite as I should be."

He could see her whole body relax.

"No, Mr. Blake, I love it here, and I think you're great. I mean I don't think you are rude or anything. You are the best boss I've ever had." Then she blushed.

"Thank you, Maggie, that means a lot to me, and by the way, I think you're great also."

She sat there continuing to blush.

"I don't have anything else; I just wanted to be sure you were happy working here. I have one other thing, but I want to walk you to your car and say it outside the office."

Now she was apprehensive again. She could not imagine what her boss wanted to say outside the building.

When they were at her car, he opened her door. "Maggie, I'm sure you know from some of my conversations, I am in the process of getting a divorce," he paused, and she fell silent. "Anyway, I wondered if you would consider going out with me even though the divorce is not final. I have moved out. I also know I shouldn't do this as your boss, but, Maggie, I have to admit I am very attracted to you. If you say no, I understand. It's a complicated situation with all these issues, but I…"

"You don't have to say anything else. Yes, the answer is yes, yes, I would be more than happy to go out with you." She smiled the most mischievous smile and left.

Harry was sitting on his porch looking at the lake when he remembered that Saturday so many years ago; smiling now just like he was then.

Then he remembered their first date. He had asked Maggie to dinner, but she had promised a neighbor she would babysit at 7:45 pm which would not work. Harry then suggested they meet for a drink at 6:00pm and that would enable her to keep her commitment. She agreed and recommended a place near where she lived the opposite side of town from the office and where Harry lived. This was good since he did not need to be seen with a woman until his divorce was final, and especially by a coworker.

They both arrived in the parking lot at the same time. He remembered telling her how strange it felt since he had not had a date in over seven years. She asked him if he was sorry that he asked her.

"Absolutely not! Ever since I first met you, I thought about what it would be like to be with you. I mean, you know, on a date." He could not admit that was not exactly what he meant. Over drinks, he said, "I am really surprised you were available. Why hasn't somebody snatched you up."

She told him she had dated some men, but none of the relationships worked out. Not everyone wanted to be involved with a working woman with two kids. Most of their conversation centered on kids and divorce.

At 7:00 pm, he said he did not want her to be late and they should probably leave. They went out to the large foyer which was now empty, and he had said he needed to catch the men's room since he had a 40-minute drive across town. He told her he had a great time and for her to drive carefully. As he turned to go to the men's room, Maggie had grabbed his arm, and he turned back to her, and she was against him and gave him the warmest, sweetest kiss he thought he had ever had. It seemed to last forever, and she finally said, "I had a good time, and you drive carefully," then she was gone.

He went to the door and watched her walk to her car and watched as she disappeared from the parking lot. He remembered thinking what did that kiss mean. He had never even thought about a kiss. Well, that wasn't exactly true. He had thought about a kiss and more but not on their first date. What a ride over 46 years of the highest of highs and also the lowest of lows. Maybe that was the way marriage was supposed to be. He had wished it had not been. There were too many times that she had been dead wrong and unfortunately there were just as many times that he also had been dead wrong.

Chapter 8

Two more weeks passed, the only thing Harry had left the house to do was to buy food and booze and go to church. He had taken the boat out a couple of times, but it just wasn't as much fun without Maggie. Harry decided to invite Sheriff Hardaway for dinner. Hardaway was by himself also, and maybe he would enjoy the company and a good home-cooked meal.

Harry extended the invitation, but Clay insisted that Harry come to his place. Harry agreed and the time and day were set. Harry had insisted he bring the wine which in his mind also included a bottle of Michter's bourbon. He had a few vintage bottles of wine, and he selected a bottle of 1993 Silver Oak Cabernet.

Clay Hardaway lived on five acres of woods about eight miles north of Harry. It was a beautiful piece of property with 500 feet of lakefront, a double covered dock that housed one aluminum fishing boat and one big high-powered speedboat. His house was almost 100 yards off the road with a gate that could be activated from his home. The outside of his house looked like a roughly built log cabin. The inside looked like a hunting lodge with all the modern conveniences.

When he walked in the front door, he was taken back at the charm and beauty of the place.

"Clay, this is extraordinary. This is beautiful."

"Thank you, Harry. I wish I could take credit for it, this is pretty much all Louise. You and Maggie would have liked her. She liked to fish and hunt more than I do. She always said she wanted her house to make her feel like she was on vacation."

"Well, she did a great job."

Harry handed the two bottles he brought to Clay.

"Silver Oak 93! Harry, you have outdone yourself. I hope the steaks are going to be worthy. And Michter, I've seen it but never had it. Leave your jacket on, we are going to sit on the porch. I have a fire going, and we can test the bourbon."

As they entered the kitchen, Harry was again impressed. All of the appliances were gourmet. He was especially impressed with the eight-burner Wolfe stove with double ovens.

"Very impressive, Clay, do you cook?"

"Oh, I won't ever go hungry but again, this was Louise, she liked to cook as much as she liked hunting and fishing."

"Wow, I'm really sorry that Maggie and I never got to meet her."

Clay didn't respond, he had finished pouring the drinks and led Harry to the back porch. It was huge, running the entire length of the house. At one end, there was a massive fireplace where a fire was crackling and providing heat for the cool evening air. The light was just enough to reveal the magnificent view of Pine Lake. There was a ceiling-mounted big screen TV that was on a national news channel with the sound muted. They sat down in front of the fire to enjoy their drinks. When they had settled in, the President of the United States appeared on the screen, and Clay asked Harry if he minded if he brought up the sound to hear his speech. The President was speaking about the latest terrorist attack attempt.

They listened as the President explained for the umpteenth time that the previous administration's lack of enforcement of immigration laws had created so much jeopardy for U.S. citizens. He said that it wasn't just Hispanics who had penetrated our borders but those same borders had allowed others including Muslims with undetermined backgrounds that could easily set up terror cells in our country. He continued saying that investigations of the recent attacks and attempts indicate the leaders were illegals who came into our country during the previous administration. When the President concluded his remarks, Clay powered off the TV and refreshed their drinks.

Harry said, "I guess we are pretty safe here at Pine Lake," expecting Clay to confirm his comment.

"I wish I could agree, Harry, but I can't. We have seen these times coming after eight years of abandoning our laws and enforcement. That group glorified the criminals and admonished law officers. It was frankly disgraceful, but I am sure I am prejudiced. But at least our leaders here in the county and town have allowed me to hire a team of former military young folks who are highly qualified for anything. And Al, who you met, is like a godfather to everybody. I am blessed to have a team like them."

"Clay, tell me what kind of risks we have here."

"Well, the most numerous threats are the gangs. There are two decent sized black gangs here. You got a taste of that group. The Mexicans have two gangs, one that is big. We also have a Guatemalan gang. And we have a group of Skinheads who think the law does not apply to them. And finally, we even have a Muslim community. They own and/or operate a lot of our convenience and liquor stores. Mostly they live in one community, and they have been outspoken about us leaving them alone and letting them enforce Sharia law for themselves. I don't trust them, and we are not going to have two sets of laws in this county."

"Clay, I never dreamed there was all that in our county."

"Most folks aren't aware either, and let's hope it stays that way. For now, these gangs have acted more like social clubs than gangs, but what happened at your house is the thing we have worried about. How 'bout I cook some meat. Come on in the kitchen, and I'll show you how Louise prepared our steaks. She said it was an old family recipe."

In the kitchen, Clay opened the double doors to the Sub-Zero and removed two salad plates with sliced tomatoes covered with chunks of bleu cheese. There was a pan with a lump of dough that he placed in one of the ovens to join to two potatoes that were well on their way to being done. Then he took the foil off two of the prettiest T-bones Harry had ever seen.

"Okay Harry, watch me apply Louise's prep to the meat."

Clay took fresh garlic and rubbed it on one side of each of the steaks. Then he used garlic salt and black pepper generously to the same side of each steak. He finished the sides with a drizzle of garlic olive oil. He turned the steaks and repeated the process. "Now just a little fire and we are ready to go."

Harry said, "Let me get the wine ready to breathe a little."

Clay seared the steaks on both sides, and they sat down to eat.

The meal and the wine were fantastic. They went back to the porch and fireplace for coffee.

"Harry, I feel like I have talked way too much tonight. Tell me how you are doing. What's it been, about a month?"

"About that, I felt like I had something in common with you and I wanted to spend some time and talk to you. I'm lonely, Clay. I miss Maggie so much, Belle too. Maggie and I had less than an ideal marriage, but we both loved each other. With 46+ years on the books, there had to be a lot of good things. How long does it take to get over being lonely? From missing her? Do you ever get over it? Do you ever stop loving them?"

"I don't know if my answer to those questions would fit your situation. I know I will always love Louise. I've had several very attractive women come on to me, but Louise was so perfect for me. Don't get me wrong, I like to get laid occasionally but never more than that. Luckily there are some attractive women our age, and that's all they want too. It works. As far as the lonely goes, I had my work. I just buried myself in it. I worked double shifts so when I got home, I just crashed and burned. I still miss her and I will always love her, but it is what it is, Harry, you need to find something to do. How about another book?"

"Clay, you're right. I'm editing the screenwriter's version of my two books, but that is a slow process. I want to write a prequel to the other books, but I haven't started because of the amount of research I am going to need to do. I just haven't been able to get my mind right to work. Oh, by the way, I took your advice and had my alarm system upgraded. It's about 1000% better than before."

"Good, you needed to do that, and Harry, you just need time, give it more time, it will get better. And by the way, you being sort of a celebrity as an author and a movie being made when you're ready, you can have all the companionship you want." Clay said smiling and laughing.

"All I want now is to head home, and put this old body in bed."

"Are you okay to drive, I've plenty of room here, no shame in that."

"It's okay, Officer. I'm in good shape."

Before Harry had cranked his car, Clay had called his dispatch and had them patch him through to Will Jackson who was patrolling the area between his house and Harry's. He told Will to make sure Harry made it home safely without being obvious. Clay was uncomfortable with the attack at the Blakes. How many shootouts could a 72-year-old survive?

Chapter 9

"Clay, Will here, Harry Blake is home safe and sound."

"Thanks, Will. Harry's a good guy."

"One other thing, Clay. When you called, I was very close to his home, and I swung by there before I ran him down. The place was pitch black, no lights at all. I had stopped at the end of his driveway and suddenly the headlights came on from down the street and what appeared to be one of those lowriders hot-footed it by me and out of the neighborhood. As you know, that's not a lowrider neighborhood. I just thought you would want to know."

"Thanks again, Will. Do one other thing for me. Before you check out, how 'bout making one more pass by his home."

"Will do, Boss."

The next morning Clay stopped by Harry's on his way to his office.

Clay rang the doorbell and Harry greeted him in shorts and a flannel shirt.

"Come in, did I leave something at your place or you just couldn't get enough of my charming personality."

Clay smiling, "No, neither, serious subject, plus I could use some coffee."

"I thought we covered all the serious subjects last night. How about breakfast."

"Just coffee, I had leftover steak earlier, and it was still good."

Harry poured the coffee and took Clay to the porch.

"What's up?"

"Harry, one of my deputies happened by your house last night and said your place was black as pitch. Did you mean to leave the lights off?"

"No, Maggie was always in charge of lights. I didn't even think about it until I got home. That's not that serious, is it?"

"Not by itself, but, while he was here, a lowrider had been parked lights off in your cul-de-sac. When they saw the cruiser, they made a hasty exit from the neighborhood. It's much better security if the lights are on at night. And Harry, I see you still got those gold coins in the same spot on the table. Why don't you get a safe or a safety deposit box?"

"You are right about the lights, my error. However, I will not move my coins. I am sorry to hear about the possibility of what could be one of your Mexican gangs hanging around here. I guess after hearing about all those potential gang problems, maybe whoever steals the coins becomes the baddest of the bad. But

Clay, it pisses me off. They are the same kind of thugs who killed Maggie and Belle. They may be thinking baddest of the bad, but I promise you I'm thinking deadest of the dead."

"Don't say that, Harry. You are 72 years old, and you don't need to be in any more shootouts. You don't hurt for money. Relax, enjoy your golden years."

"What about you, Clay?"

"It's my job, Harry! I like that we have become friends and I would like to think we could share a lot more evenings like last night, so don't be foolish."

"I do appreciate your concern, Clay; honestly I do. But if they come here, I will kill them." Harry smiled, stood up, looked out at the lake for about a minute, turned back to Clay, and said with a sad smile, "Since you are concerned, you come here next Friday night and don't bring anything. I have plenty of good wine and bourbon, and without Maggie spending my money, I have plenty of that too."

With that Clay stood. "As I get to know you better, Harry, I'm beginning to think you might be a hard head. I got to get to work." Clay turned halfway to the front door, "See you Friday, Harry."

The next week was somewhat easier for Harry. He stayed busy. He sold Maggie's car, canceled her insurance, and received her life insurance check minus the portion that went for the funeral. After everything, he ended up with about $50,000. He and Maggie both loved Samaritan's Purse, so Harry sent a substantial check to them in Maggie's name.

Harry then decided to find Clay's cabin by boat. He went north and after about 45 minutes, found the big cove and Clay's dock. He saw a big pine down in the water in the back of the inlet. It appeared to have been down for a while. He anchored the Lowe pontoon boat and began to work a green jig around the edges of the pine. No luck – he tried yellow, no luck again. Then when he was about to give up, he put on a white doll fly and bingo, the crappie wanted white. He boated and saved four hand-sized fish. He couldn't wait for dinner and to tell Clay about the 'honey hole' he had found in sight of his dock.

When he was home and had cleaned and prepared the fish for grilling, he poured a Knob Creek and sat down on his porch. He became sad thinking about Maggie. She would have been thrilled with the crappie. She had a special touch frying fish. How many times had he caught catfish off their dock and Maggie would make his favorite breakfast of fried catfish, scrambled eggs, and biscuits. He would grill these fish; he just didn't want the mess of frying without her. Grilled fish, yellow rice and sliced tomatoes and onions with a nice bottle of chardonnay. No white for Maggie or at least very rarely. She always preferred reds. God, he missed her. When his grief began to peak, he had to remind himself that she was in a far better place than him.

The week had gone faster than any since the 'incident.' Clay was right, he had to stay busy, and it had been a busy week. Speaking of Clay, the doorbell rang and the big man was at the door with a package in his hand.

Harry opened the door. "Clay, welcome but I told you not to bring anything."

"I know, but I brought you some of the best homemade pork sausage in the south. It comes from Earls. Have you met Earl Brown? Earl's Meats? His place is in East Union, and you are missing an opportunity if you haven't been there."

"I can't wait to try it. Come on in, and tonight we are drinking Baker's."

Harry poured the bourbons, and they headed for the porch.

"You didn't have to buy me sausage. Can I pay you for it?"

"Lord no, I didn't pay for it. I'll have to tell you the story behind the sausage sometime."

Harry held up his glass, "The night is young, don't you know writers love stories."

"Okay, this goes back to when Louise was still alive. She was pretty sick taking big doses of nasty stuff, and her appetite had not been good. She called me at the office about 6:30 one night and said she was hungry for a change and wanted one of Earl's big filets and we had none in the freezer. She wanted me to swing by and pick some up for our dinner. This was Saturday, and I knew I would need to hurry because Earl closed at 7:00 pm. Sometimes it's just hard to leave in a hurry. By the time I got to East Union, it was already ten after. I was just hoping I could catch Earl before he had gone. You will see when you go, Earl's sits off the road on a massive lot with nothing else really close by. When I pulled off the road, I was relieved to see lights on, and a car was parked beside the building. The curtain was down on the glass front door indicating he had already closed. But why would the car be parked beside the store and not out front close to the door? With my job you get a suspicious nature, so I killed my lights and eased to the back of the store to see if I could see Earl's pick-up. It was the only vehicle there. All the other employees' vehicles were gone.

"I parked next to the pickup and took a chance that the last man out had not locked the back door. I was lucky the door was unlocked. I eased through the rear work area until I was close to Earl's office and the front sales area. I looked inside the office and saw Earl lying on the floor tied up, gagged with a big cut on his head and bleeding. I pulled my weapon and moved next to the doorway and peered around the corner.

"There were two men with ski masks on, and they were filling up boxes with meat. Next to them were plastic bags that appeared to be brimming with cash. There was a lot of cash because it was Saturday. Friday and Saturday are his two biggest sale days and no bank open. The two men were laughing and talking about how well they had done, all that plus enough prime meat for a month. Beside one of the cash bags, there was a shotgun. I stepped in quickly and told them to hold their hands high. Both men were in a crouched position at the back of a big display cooler. I scared one of them so bad he actually fell over. They recovered and both stood, but only one held up his hands. I repeated my demand for hands up. The one on the right with his hands up repeated my demand and told his partner to put his hands up. The one on the left of them went hard for a pistol in his jacket pocket. I had no choice, I shot him, and he was dead by the time he hit the floor. The man on the right was now hysterical. He jerked his mask off and fell on his partner. He yanked his partner's mask off revealing a much younger version of him. The man started screaming, 'He's my son, my son.'

"I told him I warned him twice. The older man was sobbing, 'I know, I know, he don't listen to nobody. Oh Lord, his mama's gonna kill me.' I got him handcuffed, freed up Earl and called for backup and emergency medical.

"Now finally the answer to the sausage. Earl knows Louise and her condition, so when I told him she wanted one of his filets, he ran to the cooler and got a whole tenderloin. Then he says, 'I made sausage today,' and he goes and gets a box with at least 25 pounds of fresh sausage. I told him I don't need that much of either and he says, 'That one, the young one, he was going to kill me. You not only saved my money but you saved my life.'

"Harry, he was hysterical, so I pulled out my wallet, and he started yelling, 'Hell no, hell no, don't even think about it.' I told him my job wouldn't let me take those things. He said, 'Clay, you dumb ass, this is not for you, it's for Louise,' and he puts them in my car. So now I have 25 pounds of great sausage that I've been eating on for over a year, and I still have plenty, so enjoy."

"What a story. It sounds like you may have saved Earl's life. And by the way, do you mind if I use the story in my next book?"

"Are you kidding me?"

"No, Clay, it's a great story, so can I use it?"

"Harry, you are crazy, but if you're serious, okay."

"Thanks. Why don't you refresh our drinks and I'll show you how I make grilled salmon."

In the kitchen, Harry took two salmon fillets and basted them with a mixture of dry white wine, lemon infused olive oil, and lemon juice. With the basting completed, he put salt, pepper, and chopped fresh dill on the filets.

"Now we let them sit a bit and then to the grill. Now back to the porch and I want to know about your family."

They settled back in on the porch and Clay began.

"Well you know about Louise, and you know we had no kids. My folks are both dead. Our family has been in Polk County for probably a hundred years. I have one sibling, Andy. Andy's spouse died 20 years ago and never remarried."

Harry interrupted, "Runs in the family, I guess. How old is Andy?"

"Andy is 60 and lives on our family's home place. Our family has had the property since our ancestors came here. My dad was a horse trainer and so is Andy. We have 50 acres at the tip of the lake. It's beautiful; part woods, part pasture. Dad had built a big horse barn and a covered structure, I guess you would describe it as a place to work horses. Andy called it the equestrian center. The old home place was torn down years ago and Andy rebuilt a modern place. Andy owns four horses and usually boards four or five and trains them. The money is pretty good. I think you will like Andy. I'll take you up for a meet and a meal soon."

They finally sat down to eat. Harry had opened a bottle of Tavel Rosé.

"Excuse me, Harry, would you think it rude if I asked for say a dry chardonnay. I don't want a sweet pink with this wonderful-looking meal."

"I'll be happy to, but only if you try the Tavel first."

"Fair enough."

Harry poured, and Clay sipped. Then he sipped again and again.

"I'll be damned. Boy, was I wrong. Thank you, Harry, you taught me something. I'm sorry."

"No need to apologize, just enjoy."

The meal was grilled salmon with an accompanying sauce made of sour cream, horseradish, lemon juice, and capers. The salmon was served with a mushroom and spinach risotto and a caprese salad. It was a treat.

"Clay, don't feel bad about the rosé; I bet I've converted more than 20 people over the years."

"Harry, I know you don't want to hear this, but I think you need to be careful when you are here alone at night. I can't get that lowrider off my mind. I get the sense this might be some kind of gang challenge. 'Who can get Harry's gold?' You know like some stupid macho thing."

"Clay, the alarm system has been so juiced up, if somebody comes in, I'll have enough notice to be ready. I'll be as armed and dangerous as they say."

"I worry you are too cavalier about this, Harry. Loaded weapons are serious business."

"I know, listen, they have this system set so I can hit one button and it calls your folks and says come help the old fart and fast."

"I'll shut up, but be careful, Harry."

"Oh, Clay, I almost forgot. One thing before you go. I went to find your place by boat, and I found one of your little 'honey holes.'"

"What are you talking about, Harry?"

"I eased the boat down to the back of your cove to where a big pine is half-way in the water."

Harry took out his cell phone and pulled up a photo of four big hand size crappies.

"I was in and out with my meal in a half hour. I don't know how many I could have caught if I had stayed. What a spot. You of course already knew that, right?"

"Heck no, I'm embarrassed, and in my own backyard. Harry, you are something! Will you tell me what you used?"

"White doll fly."

Clay left shaking his head.

Chapter 10

Hector Wente was a 22-year-old Guatemalan who lived in the south end of Lakeview. The south end was where most of the Hispanics lived. There were families from Guatemala and EL Salvador mixed with the other families in the community who were mostly from Mexico. He had been in the U.S. for four years and hated being in such a rural area. Being at Pine Lake meant nothing to him. The only reason he stayed was that his family needed his paycheck to survive.

Hector wanted to be in New York and specifically Long Island so he could join the MS-13 gang. Since that was not going to happen in the near future, he along with four of his Guatemalan buddies had formed a gang which they called MS-5. MS after the gang he admired and 5 for their number.

Hector was ambitious and reasonably smart. He knew the leaders of the two Mexican gangs. He didn't like them and they didn't like him. So far they tolerated each other. He knew a little about the black gangs. He thought they were stupid changas. They had let an old white man not only stop them from stealing the gold coins but they got themselves killed. They truly were stupid. They all tolerated each other at least for the time being.

Hector had decided they could raise their status if they could do what the blacks had failed to do. Part of his plan had been to secretly put together a lowrider that would appear to belong to the Mexicans. They had scouted out the house and the neighborhood and he had developed a plan. He just had to decide when to go through with it.

Chapter 11

The day had come when Clay was taking Harry to his family's home place and meeting Andy. It was about a 45-minute drive to the horse farm and it was a beautiful ride. Lots of hardwoods, whose leaves were beginning to be in full color, framed the drive. Like Clay's place, the house, barn, and equestrian center were over a hundred yards from the road. As Clay's Tahoe came to a stop by the house, his phone rang. He told Harry he had to take the call and that he should take a look around. Harry got out of the Tahoe and could see a big fenced pasture off to the right. Oaks, maples, and pines surrounded the house.

There was a path from the drive going around the house which Harry decided to follow. The path wound its way through the trees and, as he could see, toward the barn. As he reached the barn, a most beautiful woman emerged. She was in jeans, boots, a green plaid shirt. She wore a cowboy hat, and red hair showed between the hat and her shoulders. She was tall, at least equal to him. Her face exhibited an outdoor lifestyle with loads of freckles and bright green eyes. As she looked at him walking toward her, a big smile came across her face. She was stunning. For a moment he didn't know what to say.

"My name is Harry Blake, and I am here with Andy's brother Clay Hardaway. He's on a call and told me to look around."

"Oh he did, did he?"

"Yes, ma'am. Are you a customer?"

"No."

"A friend of Andy's?"

"You could say that," she said smiling.

"And your name is?"

"Andrea Wilson."

"Nice to meet you, Andrea. Is Andy out here or at the house? I didn't try there I just started walking around. I hope he doesn't think I'm rude. Clay said to take a look around."

"You are the writer, aren't you?"

"Why yes, I am. I am always surprised when somebody recognizes my name."

"I read the papers, and I actually read your books."

"Really?"

40

She took off her hat revealing the rest of her red hair thus showing streaks of grey.

"Let me take you back to the house, and you can have a drink with Andy," she said, trying to control a laugh. "You know Andy is trying to become much more feminine, don't you?"

Harry was stunned, "Uh, well no, I've never met Andy before."

What the hell is going on? Clay should have said something.

"Are you shocked, Mr. Blake?"

"Shocked about what?" As soon as he said he knew it sounded stupid.

"What do you think about people enhancing their feminine side?"

"Can I be honest?"

"Please do."

"I think, if you will excuse my language, it's a bunch of horseshit."

"Harry, there is a lot of people that don't agree with you."

"Andrea, there's a lot of people that don't agree with me on a lot of things. It doesn't make me wrong." Harry thought, *Another liberal, but a damn pretty one.*

They reached the steps to the home and waved to Clay who was still on the phone in the car. She led him into the foyer and down the hall to the kitchen. The house had been rebuilt but that was 25 years ago but obviously the kitchen more recently since it was up to date in every way.

There was a granite island in the middle with six barstools where she seated him. She walked out of the room, and the smell from the stove started to get his attention. It had to be lamb and something. He immediately was hungry. As he slowly scoped out the room and focused on a picture of a younger Clay and Andrea.

She was back with a bottle of Buffalo Trace and three glasses of ice.

"How did you know?"

"Clay of course."

"How long have you known the family? I saw your picture with Clay from a few years ago."

"Oh, I've known the family my entire life."

Harry sat silently and then looked again at the picture.

"Damn, you have been pulling my chain."

"Why, Harry, what are you talking about?" she said laughing out loud.

"I'm talking about Andrea or Andy, whichever you prefer."

She was now laughing and talking at the same time, "Clay said he wasn't sure but thought you might have assumed I was his brother. I just couldn't resist when you came down that path looking for Clay's 'brother.' You should have seen your face when I started the feminine dialogue. You looked like you were ready to run for the car." She was still laughing.

Harry thought, *She's not a lefty, she's a loony.* He was beginning to be pissed. She walked to the stove, raised the lid on the pot, and stirred the contents.

"I hope you like lamb."

"One of my favorites, but you can look at my figure and see I have lots of favorites."

"Clay says you are quite the chef. Would you be my taste tester?"

She didn't wait for him to answer, she brought the big wooden spoon to him. He blew the contents lightly and tasted. She had included a small piece of the meat. It was succulent.

"It's delicious."

"How about seasoning? Does it need something?"

He thought for a minute and said, "No I don't think I would do a thing."

As he watched as she walked back to the stove, he thought her body looked mighty good for sixty.

"Harry, you were talking about your body, how old are you?"

"What do you think?"

"Oh no, I won't fall into that trap."

"Seventy-two."

"Right, now you are, what did you say, pulling my chain."

"No, seventy-two, that's the truth."

"I should have guessed you would have liked my answer."

Now Harry's vanity kicked in, and he wanted to hear her say it.

"Tell me what you thought."

She laughed and smiled and said, "Oh, not a day over 70," and she laughed out loud again.

He liked the sound of her laugh but not when it was at him.

Clay walked into the kitchen apologizing for being on the call so long. He described it as a minor departmental crisis and would say no more.

"I see you two are properly introduced." He looked at Andy and said, "Was I right?"

She smiled, "Oh yes, and I think I might have overdone it. I think Harry may be ticked at me for carrying the ruse so far."

Before Harry could speak, Clay jumped in, "I don't know how this happened the way it did, but you provided some real grins for us."

Harry tried to dismiss the whole thing, but their talk wasn't that funny to Harry.

"It's time to move on, Clay. Harry, would you be offended if I didn't change for dinner? I don't want to be rude, but I would like to enjoy my drink and get to know you better."

"You are fine. I think Clay knows me well enough, I'm really just a down-to-earth kind of guy." He didn't say, but he thought she looked fantastic the way she was though she was a little looney and may even be a lefty. Feminine side.

"Harry, Clay filled me in on the tragedy, and I want to tell you how sorry I am for your loss. I was only married for ten years, and it was not easy when he passed. Thank goodness as we did, y'all had your faith to get you through it. Clay had told me that you and your wife were firm in your faith."

"Thank you, but by the way, what do I call you? Andrea, Andy, hey you," and he laughed trying to make up for the earlier awkward moment.

"Forevermore, Andy, unless you are going to be really serious," and she laughed and winked at him.

The lamb stew and the 93 Silver Oak Cab were perfect as was the rest of the evening. Before they left, she invited Harry back for a daytime visit to see the horses and the rest of the property. She asked him if he rode, he said no but had always wanted to try but time just passed him by. She told him maybe not. She hugged them both before they left. Harry knew he liked her looks but was unsure if he liked her personality.

Chapter 12

It had now had been over four months since the 'incident.' The daily calls from his girls had now changed to weekly check-ins. The weekly calls from his boys had now been reduced to every two, three or four weeks depending on which son. That was fine, how many times can you ask "how are you doing and you say fine."

It had been over a month since any of his family had visited and that was alright. The big family issue was about who would host Thanksgiving and Christmas. To their dismay he had said, in no uncertain terms, he fully intended to have both holidays at his house on the lake as they had done in the past. Their big concern was that it would be an upsetting reminder of Maggie. His response was if he could live there every day, they could handle a few days – grow up and move on like he was trying to do.

He was staying busy. He and Clay continued to host each other for dinners every week to ten days and had become good friends. He also was looking forward to a second visit with Andy. Harry had even started a new book about a small rural county sheriff and Clay agreed to allow Harry to use him and his department for research. He was still working with the screenwriters as they worked on the script for making a mini-series of his first two books. With his church activities and household duties, he was about as busy as he wanted to be.

Some days he never thought about Maggie until the day's end and sat out on the porch to look at the lake and have his evening cocktail. He thought about their early days and the heat and passion that had been unlike any he had ever felt. He remembered the conversations about a child. At first, Maggie had been very cynical about the subject. She was 28, and he was 26, and she did not want to be pregnant in her 30s. That was all he needed to hear. It opened the door for him to make a deal to give it a year and let the good Lord decide. Thank goodness they did because that brought Sally into the world. And she probably was the tie that bound. He thought about their time of separation and truly believed that they were done. It would have been easy to say you take yours and go and I'll take mine and go.

But there was Sally…so much more than Sally. He remembered it well when they married, they committed to each other from day one there would never be hers or his or yours or mine. They all would be ours. It was the right thing to do, and it worked. The separation was unfortunate, and he didn't want to think about it. But hardly any thought of Maggie brought reminders of the gang issues. Thank goodness it appeared Clay had been overly concerned about Polk County gangs.

Chapter 13

Hector Wente was small in stature at 5'5" and 135 pounds. What he lacked in size was more than compensated in ego and drive. Hector considered himself a good man and a good leader. He tried to set a good example for the others in MS5 by going to mass reasonably often with his family. But even though his mother pushed him hard, he refused to go to confession.

Hector had big goals for his life. The main one was to go to New York and join up with MS13 in Long Island. He had convinced the others in MS5 that this should be their common goal and, they had all agreed. He had explained to them it was not just making the trip as a bunch of ignorant Guatemalan immigrants wanting to join. No, they had to go showing they had earned respect. To do that, they had to do something big; he already had the plan laid out in his mind.

The idea had come to him when two blacks botched the job of stealing the gold coins from the old man. Not only had they screwed up this job but they got themselves killed. He always knew the blacks were not very smart. But one thing he was sure of, he was not stupid.

His plan started with the low rider. They had stolen everything they needed to make the old car pass as a low rider. And to bring home his point, the sheriff's department had spent all their time trying to prove the Mexicans stole the parts. It was just more proof for his crew that he was smarter, not only than other gangs but also the law.

He paid attention to detail. The MS5s had determined that Harry Blake's neighbor's house on the right was a vacation home. They only came on weekends in the summer and an occasional holiday. The neighbor on the left only lived there from May until November. They spent their winters in south Florida. The Blake house and the two neighbors were on steep lots tilting toward the lake. From the street, you could only see the housetops. The Blake's house was concealed on both sides by large thick magnolias and evergreens. It afforded great privacy for all.

He had told his crew why the blacks had failed. First of all, they went too early; the couple was still up. Secondly based on the newspaper account they had pulled their van right up to the front door. They could have easily been blocked in by cops rushing in for the silent alarm. Lastly, they let a seventy-something-year-old man outgun them. Stupid.

He laid out his plan for them. First, they would go between three and four a.m. The old man should be in a deep sleep by then. Secondly, they would come down the street with lights out in the low rider. Then they would park in the neighbors on the right side of the driveway. Going in through the thick trees, making four separate but simultaneous entries, they would give the old man a chance to surrender and be tied up, but, if he resisted in the least, they would send him on to join his wife. They would take the gold coins and go. If he were correct, they would be back in town before breakfast.

As with the last attempt, he was sure there would be lots of publicity. This brazen act would be their ticket into MS13. There would be enough money to ensure his family didn't need his paycheck to survive and surely MS13 would welcome him into a leadership position. The only thing left to do was pick the time.

Chapter 14

Harry was now staying busy. He was as active as he had been since his retirement. Harry had become so busy that lately, he would go several days at a time without missing Maggie. He would think about her and felt guilty that a few days had come and gone with no thought of her. He called Ray Andrews, his pastor, and set up lunch. Harry and Ray had become good friends soon after they met. They were of similar age, similar likes, and both from the same state.

They met at a large lakefront restaurant that was big enough that they could find a quiet table out of the way. After welcoming hugs, Ray started, "Harry, forgive me for not setting this time up. We see each other a couple of times a week, but we never get to talk one on one. How are you holding up?"

"No apologies necessary. That's why I wanted to talk. I have gotten so busy; I have gone days at a time without the first thought of Maggie. I feel guilty as the devil. What's wrong with me, Ray?"

Ray looked at Harry, turned his head and looked out at the lake, squinted, and finally spoke, "You know, Harry, the Bible tells us there is a time and a season for everything. It doesn't give us the length of time or season. Everybody is different."

"Yeah, but is there some minimum time to be proper?"

"What are you expecting to accomplish, Harry? You want the folks at church or around town to say poor Harry, he just can't seem to get over losing Maggie?"

"No, I don't want any sympathy, I just don't want to feel guilty."

"For what it's worth, I believe it's necessary and God wants us to grieve. Having said that, even Jesus said in so many words you got to move on man. The living need to be with the living. Here's another thing I think, you are leading a blessed life. You have grieved for months, and it sounds like your season has passed. I personally think it's a blessing. At our age, only the good Lord knows how many years we have left. Make the most of your time."

Harry sat silently pondering what Ray just said.

Ray leaned forward and smiled a most mischievous smile, "Hey old man, you starting to think about women?"

Harry sat up straight; acted as if he was shocked at the question. "I haven't been around any women socially, so no. I take that back, I have been around one, but I think she might be a left wing looney."

"Oh yeah. Can I ask who?"

"Sure, Clay Hardaway and I have become good friends, and he took me up to meet his sister and have dinner."

"Unmarried?"

"Ten years a widow."

"How old?"

"Sixty."

"Attractive?"

"Unfortunately yes, very."

"Why, unfortunately?"

"I think she's looney and a lefty. Ray, I'm not looking for a woman. I'm too busy."

"Tell me what you are doing to stay so busy."

Harry told him about the research, the new book, the miniseries, and the other odds and ends in his life. Ray blessed their food, and they ate with the conversation focusing on activities at the church. At the conclusion of their meal, Ray said he had one final thing, he wanted to say before they left.

"My good friend, count your blessings. If the good Lord wants you to think about Maggie and grieve more, he will make sure it happens. If he gives you peace to move on, then for His sake, move on and enjoy life. And for sure don't worry about what some old hens think about your grieving time."

Harry thanked Ray and vowed to do his best not to feel guilty.

When he got home, there was a message on his phone. "Hello Harry, I hope you are well. This is Andy, I was wondering if you might be interested in speaking to a women's group that I belong to. Please give me a call and I'll fill you in on the details. Also, we need to set up a time for you to have a proper tour of the farm."

Harry's first thought was some sort of feminist group. *Why would they want me of all people to speak? Lord, what must she be thinking? Lefties don't always think,* he thought.

Chapter 15

It was 3:00 am on a moonless Thursday night when the lowrider eased out of town headed for the lake. When they reached Harry's street, the lights were shut off, and they reduced their speed. At this time of the morning, the only lights to be seen were the street lights which were more than adequate to get them to their destination, Harry's neighbor's driveway. Everyone knew what they were to do. Two men around the house and two downstairs, each would take a door. One man would take the stairs on the rear side of the house and use that entrance. The fourth man, Hector, next in charge, Felipe, he was assigned the front door. After everyone was in place, Hector would use a bell on his phone as the signal to go. Hector was to wait outside until the first assault and then he would come in the front door as back up.

Hector lined the men up in single file with Felipe in the lead position. He would go first and make sure the others went in the proper direction. When Felipe cleared the tree line and was on his second step in the clearing between the trees and the house, an array of floodlights came on and made the area brighter than the midday sun. Felipe froze for an instant and then dove back into the trees. The four scrambled for the car, but Hector held his ground and waited. There were no alarms and so far no opening doors. His men were pleading with him to get in the car so they could leave. Hector waited patiently by the tree line until he heard the information he needed. He looked through the trees and spoke aloud to himself, "You live another day, old man, but we will be back."

The light on the alarm panel by Harry's lit up bright red but not enough to wake him from a deep sleep. The installer wanted to have a buzzer go off, but Harry said absolutely no way. He didn't want to be jarred awake every time a deer came onto his property.

When Harry woke up the next morning, he saw the red light. The alarm system was pretty neat. He could see the time of the incident in this case 3:42 am and the location over by the garage. He congratulated himself on the no buzzer decision.

Chapter 16

He had not returned Andy's call yesterday. He had put it off. Lord, he did not want to be involved in any sort of women's movement. But he knew he had to call her.

"Andy, Harry Blake."

"Thank you for calling me back Harry. How are you?"

"I'm well and you?"

"I'm great, Harry. Let me tell you about our women's group."

Before she could go further, he interrupted, "Look here, Andy, I haven't done any public speaking in years, and quite frankly, I have no interest in being involved with some sort of movement."

Andy covered the phone so that her laughter could not be heard.

"Harry, let me explain. Based on our first meeting I thought you would be perfect for us. I mean you were a successful business executive. You are a famous author. You would bring a totally different insight to our group. I thought you might make some opening remarks about our group and then take questions. The whole thing would be certainly less than an hour, and then we will feed you while we wrap up. It will be a memorable event, I'm sure of it."

Harry's chin had dropped to his chest, his eyes were closed and his head was turning back and forth. How could someone so attractive be so...so...so... whatever.

"Oh, I'm in charge of setting the date so I decided I would make it fit around your schedule." Under his breath he said, "Oh shit."

"What did you say, I'm sorry I didn't hear you."

"Nothing, not a thing."

"Please Harry, think about it, check your calendar, and let me know as soon as you can."

Harry hesitated and finally said, "Okay."

"Now second subject; I was going to invite you for the farm tour on Saturday afternoon, but Clay tells me you don't do anything on Saturdays during college football season. So, how about after church on Sunday afternoon. I froze the leftover lamb stew and unless you, how did you say it, unless you were 'pulling my chain,' you did like it."

"No, no, I was serious, the stew was great, and Sunday will be fine. I probably won't be able to get there until one o'clock or so. Is that too late?"

"Perfect, I'll see you then. One last thing, please try to have a date for me on Sunday."

Harry didn't answer the request.

"I'll see you then." He wondered what he had gotten himself into with this woman.

Chapter 17

Hector knew before they reached the end of the blackened street what his new plan would be. His four men were all talking at the same time about how impossible it would be with all the perimeter lighting and motion sensors. Hector finally shouted, "Quiet! I have the plan ready for our next assault." The four men sat quietly waiting for Hector to explain.

The next night at the same time they pulled the lowrider into the same spot in Harry's neighbor's driveway as the previous night. Hector put his men two by two and sent them through the trees into the opening and quietly under the house's eaves. He followed before the perimeter lights went out. Hector believed that since there were no alarms, no inside lights that came on, and doors opened that nothing happened inside that would alert the old man.

He then sent them to their assigned locations staying close to the house not breaking the eaves and resetting off the outside lights. Two men at different doors on the back and downstairs, one up the side stairs and Felipe at the front door. Hector would be behind Felipe and would only enter if there was trouble or after they completed their mission. After a time he was sure everyone was in place, he blew one quick burst of a whistle. All four men broke the glass on their doors at the same time.

The loud buzzer went off beside Harry's bed. He was awake instantly, rolling out of bed to look at the screen on the alarm panel. He was taken aback – four doors breached at the same time. He first thought there might be a glitch in the system, but then he could hear noises in his house. He could hear the alarm loudly pulsating and see lights flashing down the hallway to the master suite.

In addition to upgrading his alarm system, Harry had mounted his shotgun on his beds sideboard, plus he had two additional shells mounted on each side of the stock of the double barrel shotgun. He had also mounted the .38 Ruger beside the shotgun. Harry decided maybe the porch was his best option. He stepped into his bedroom slippers but did not bother with his pants and eased out the door from the bedroom to the porch. Two steps onto the porch he could see into his great room and further into the dining area and ultimately his kitchen. The scene was eerie with the strobe lights flashing and the alarm blaring. He could see masked men moving toward the dining area and the location of his gold coins. He decided to go further down the porch to the entrance to the dining area. Halfway there the alarm stopped, but the strobe lights kept flashing.

He remembered he had forgotten to press the button on the alarm panel to have the automatic call to the sheriff's department. But he also remembered the call would be made automatically if the alarm had not been manually turned off. Thank goodness, but he had lost four or five minutes which could mean his life. He crouched behind a big plant on the porch and saw four men standing by his gold coins all holding weapons.

The assault had gone just as Hector had planned. The man on the side and Felipe reached the edge of the great room and dining room at the same time. The man from the side had already spotted the coins. The two men from downstairs came up together minutes later, and now they were together at the table displaying the coins. The men were tense and looking in all directions expecting to see the old man at any time.

Harry now realized he had made a mistake. The porch was definitely the wrong place for him to be. If they saw him, it would only be a matter of time before they got him. He was afraid they would see him if he tried to return to the bedroom. He needed a distraction. He could think of only one thing. He eased the shotgun through the leaves and against the glass in the direction of the four men. He turned his head and fired both barrels. The explosion was deafening. Harry could not afford to stay and see the results. He headed for the bedroom trying to remain crouched as he went. He heard four or five gunshots exploding behind him.

As he passed the great room, he looked toward the front door and saw a man entering and moving toward the other men. Harry made it to the bedroom; he eased in and quietly closed the door. He realized he was shivering and he slipped his pants on and reloaded the shotgun. Harry was not comfortable waiting for them to come for him there. He eased down the hallway toward the bathroom. He had to cross the hall out to the great room and rest of the house. From the entrance to the bathroom, he could see straight back to the bedroom in case they came in from the porch. To his right, he could see the rest of the house and all the way to where the four intruders had been standing. He could only see the back of one man who was now near the table containing the coins. The strobe lights were still flashing, and the whole scene was frightening.

Harry could hear the man talking but could not understand the language. From different positions, the other four men slowly appeared and stood in front of the last man. The man was obviously in charge and giving instructions. Then two men picked up the box of coins and started moving toward Harry's office and the side entrance.

The four men had been standing next to the coins trying to decide their next move since they had not encountered the old man nor had they heard from Hector. Then the room exploded with glass and buckshot spraying everywhere but doing no real harm. The four ducked for cover and fired at the door where the blast originated. They waited for return fire, but there was none. Then Hector showed up. Everyone started talking at once, and Hector held one finger to his closed lips to quiet them.

Then Felipe spoke, "Are we going to go get the old bastard?"

"No, you are going out the side entrance and to the car. Quickly, I will join you in a minute," stated Hector.

The four left with the coins out the side entrance and to the car. Hector watched and made sure they were all out the door. His first instinct was to find the old man and kill him but the more he thought about it he had a better idea. If this was only stolen property, the efforts of the law would be much less intense. Murder would cause a lot more excitement. He knew he was right about this. That's why he was the leader.

Harry had watched the four men disappear and watched the other man watch them. Then the lone man started walking toward Harry. Harry took the safety off the shotgun. The man stopped, pointed his pistol in Harry's direction, and said, "Bang, bang," turned left and headed out the front door.

Harry's heart was pounding. Was it over? He moved cautiously down the hall to the great room. He could see the man was gone and the front door was closed. He went down to his office and saw the entrance to the outside closed. He looked out of the glass and could see no sign of the man, but he knew they must be parked in the neighbor's drive. Then the thought hit him, he might try to block them or at least follow them. He made a mad dash to the garage for his car.

Chapter 18

Harry roared out of his garage and up his driveway. As he turned left onto the street, he saw the lowrider also turn left onto the road with lights off. Harry's lights had come on automatically. He hadn't even thought of that. Too late, now they knew he was behind them. One hundred yards ahead the street dropped steeply down into a wooded valley: about twenty yards of flat road and then straight back up a high hill. The left side of the road fell steeply down toward the lake, and the right side was straight up a hill into a wooded area with no homes. As the lowrider and Harry's car started down the hill, they could both see the flashing lights of a squad car coming down the other hill towards them. It was Morris Canady who had been on patrol when the call came in from dispatch. The dispatcher had told Canady that it was an automatic call and they had not been able to get a response from Harry. Everyone in the department now knew Harry because of the time he spent interviewing and talking with them as he gathered details for his latest book. Everyone in the department really liked Harry.

Morris Canady saw the lowrider with lights off and he was pretty sure that was Harry's car behind it. The question was, had they stolen Harry's car or was Harry in pursuit? He wasn't sure which was the best thought. He decided he was not going to let them pass. As he approached the bottom of the hill he swerved left as far as he dared and then turned hard right and slammed on the brakes. He was now blocking the road. With the steep banks on both sides of the road, there was no way a car could pass. The only problem was he was exposed big time in the driver's seat. He immediately slid to the passenger seat and grabbed his shotgun. He was out the passenger door. He leaned in, got the mike to his radio and switched to broadcast. By now the low rider had stopped and so had Harry's car. At this point, Morris was giving thanks for how bright the street lights were.

Inside the low rider Hector, in the passenger seat, turned to Felipe, who was driving, and once again pressed his finger to his lips to indicate he did not want him to speak. The three men in the back were all talking at the same time about what were they going to do. Hector quieted them and explained it was five against one; Harry didn't count. If Harry were a threat, there would have been action in the house. Hector said the old man is afraid and not to worry about him; he explained the plan and told them to go. The doors to the low rider opened and the three men in the back got out with their hands raised but not dropping their guns.

They spread out with one on each side of the road and one in the middle. Meanwhile, Hector and Felipe stood behind their respective doors.

Harry waited to see what would happen. He watched as the three walked at a very slow pace toward Morris Canady. Canady was yelling into the mike for the men to drop their weapons. When the three men were about 20 yards from Canady, Hector and Felipe each fired one round at Canady. Neither shot found its mark, but it caused Canady to duck down behind his car. When he ducked, the three men started running and shooting towards Canady. Then Hector and Felipe turned and started running up the bank into the woods.

When Harry saw this, he jumped out of his car and headed past the low rider. He decided on the man on the left was his first target. The man's back was to Harry. Harry was trying to run, but at 72 it wasn't much of a run. But he was moving toward the man, and he fired his first barrel without stopping. It got the man's attention. He turned to shoot, but Harry dropped to one knee and the last few steps he had taken made the difference. When the second barrel from Harry's shotgun exploded, so did the man's chest.

Meanwhile, Canady was taking care of his business. He slipped to his right around the front of the windshield and fired the 12-gauge and almost decapitated the middle man. Seeing this, the man on the right froze momentarily in shock. By this time Canady and Harry both had him covered, and he offered no further resistance. Canady cuffed him and locked him down in the back seat of the cruiser.

Clay Hardaway's big black Tahoe, lights flashing screeched to a stop behind the squad car, to be followed quickly by a second squad car driven by Will Jackson. Clay sprinted around Canady's car, 12-gauge in hand followed by Will Jackson who had gone around the other side service weapon in hand.

"Relax, it's over, well almost. There's two more who went up the bank and into the woods." Canady paused turned to Harry and said, "You crazy old man you could have gotten killed."

Canady handed his shotgun to Will Jackson turned walked over to Harry and gave him a huge bear hug, "But you no doubt saved my life."

Hardaway was surveying the scene, two bodies obviously dead; one man locked up in the squad car and a line of neighbors at the top of the hill behind Harry's car. Hardaway was shaking his head trying to figure out what to say. Will Jackson finally spoke. "Hey, Harry we are going to rename your street the OK Corral." Everybody grinned but Harry who was now down on one knee and trembling.

Chapter 19

After a few minutes, Harry recovered enough to walk up the hill and assure his neighbors he was okay, and everyone could go back home. Harry walked past his car, retrieved the keys from the low rider's ignition, and opened the trunk to find his box of gold coins intact and unharmed.

Hardaway sent Will Jackson to patrol the road on the other side of the woods where Hector and Felipe had fled. He also called dispatch for reinforcements to help Will Jackson. Hardaway and Canady questioned the man who was locked down in the back of the squad car. They were surprised to find out he was Guatemalan and not from one of the Mexican gangs. They had all assumed, because of the low rider, it was some of the Mexicans. After seeing Hector and Felipe abandon him and his two companions, he was quick to give up both Felipe and Hector. MS5 and the dream of New York and MS13 now out of the question. Canady left for town with the man who was now begging for help for his cooperation regarding Felipe and Hector.

Hardaway called Al Johnson for a tow truck, an ambulance, and the coroner. He then followed Harry back to his house to get the details on the home invasion. At the house, they decided to make coffee before doing anything while they waited for Al. Previously they had removed the coins from the low rider, and now they were back in their proper place on Harry's table.

"Harry, you have got to get these coins out of here. This is crazy."

"No way, José." Harry fired back.

"Dammit Clay, this is America. This is my home. You don't tell people with expensive artwork they can't display it. I will not be intimidated by a bunch of punk gang members. Screw them all; we'll get every damn one of them." Harry was now pissed, and he began to reflect on the earlier happenings.

They were in the kitchen with Harry sitting on a bar stool at the kitchen island. Clay had been there so often, he walked to the cabinet, took out three coffee cups, and poured two full. He served Harry and sat down two stools away to wait for Al.

A short time later, Al Johnson arrived and filled the 3rd cup with coffee. He looked at Clay and spoke, "The tow truck has gone with the car, and Jesse is doing his thing with the bodies and the EMTs are there waiting on Jesse."

Hardaway nodded and wanted the three of them to walk through the house and then sit down to put on paper the events of the evening.

After examining the lake house's damage, both Hardaway and Johnson were impressed with the planning and execution of the assault.

"Harry, it's a good thing you had that alarm system upgraded. Also, dispatch said the call they received was the automatic one and not the one initiated by you. Why would that be, Harry?" Hardaway asked.

"I forgot, too busy getting my guns and trying to figure out what to do: four entries at one time. At first, I thought it was a glitch, but then I could hear the bastards."

"But what about the perimeter lights and alarm that sounded giving you extra time before they started breaking the glass?"

Harry looked away from the two men and sheepishly said: "I keep that buzzer turned off so that when deer come on the property in the middle of the night, it won't wake me."

Al grinned but didn't speak. Hardaway smiled, closed his eyes, and shook his head. Hardaway then said, "Harry, you damn fool, you're going to get yourself killed. And speaking of getting yourself killed, what were you doing in a firefight in the street with these thugs and Morris?"

"Well, he looked like he could use some help."

"Canady said you charged the hill like it was Iwo Jima."

"Not much of a charge. I don't run so well anymore," Harry said smiling.

Al Johnson who had spent a fair amount of time with Harry while he was doing his new book research looked at Hardaway with his most serious face and said, "Clay I think you're going to have to consider deputizing Harry."

Hardaway reaction was incredulous and said, "No, the only thing I am going to consider is retiring you. I think you are both turning senile."

Then all three men laughed out loud.

Chapter 20

Harry was finally alone. Clay had finished up the initial paperwork and was gone. A few neighbors had dropped by to find out what had happened. A couple of them weren't happy that Harry was attracting such violence to their once quiet street.

He had called Ed Tuttle to get him started on the extensive repairs on his house. Broken glass at the four entry points of the gang, plus where he had fired his shotgun on the porch. Then there was their revolver fire that had damaged the door facing and sheetrock damage. It was a widespread mess. Thank goodness he had somebody like Ed who would know exactly what to do.

Harry showered but didn't dress. It was 8:15 am and he lay down across his bed and went immediately to sleep. He was dreaming about Maggie and Belle when his ringing phone woke him. It was Clay wanting to know if he had forgotten to come by and verify the statement they had put together and sign it. Harry said of course not, why what's the time? When Clay told him it was 2:30 pm, Harry couldn't believe how long he had slept.

An hour later Harry arrived at Clay's office, "Did y'all get the other two?"

"Not yet, disappeared like ghosts."

Clay, Al, and Harry went carefully over the write-up. When they finished, Clay said, "I need to tell you something, Harry."

"And I need to ask you something," Harry replied.

Clay nodded at Al, and he excused himself. "You first Harry."

"I've gotten myself in somewhat a predicament Clay. I am going to meet Andy at the farm Sunday after church, and she is pressing me pretty hard to speak at some women's group. Can you tell me what kind of group she's involved with?"

"Not really, we don't get involved with each other's day to day lives. I really can't say Harry, but what's your concern?"

"I'm afraid it's some kind of women's movement, something political and I am the wrong person for that. I know she's your sister, but I'm not sure that she's maybe a little more left-leaning."

Clay grinned, "Well I'm sure it will be fine, but that's all I can offer." Clay was trying to contain his grin thinking Andy had got ole Harry again.

"I don't know," Harry said and added, "What subject did you want to discuss with me?"

Clay closed the door to his office. "Harry, I had a visitor this morning. Roscoe Abernathy, who is a black attorney and head of the NAACP in our county, came here and blew my mind. He asked me if I would call you in and question you about Maggie's murder. He said he is representing the families of the two boys you killed. He said when he heard about the shots to their faces, he was disturbed. He said they believe maybe you hired the two boys to kill your wife and then murdered them to keep them from talking."

"Clay, that's pure bullshit!"

"I know, but listen, there's more to this story. Roscoe has decided he may run for the US Senate. He tells me this kind of story could be good for my re-election and would be a terrific way for him to kick off his campaign."

"That son of a bitch!"

"I refused him of course and did my best to discourage him, but he is probably going to call you and ask you to meet him and discuss his theory."

"Meet with him, yeah I'll meet with him and my double barrel."

"Harry, Harry, don't do anything foolish."

"Oh, I won't but the gall of that jerk."

"Consider the source and circumstances, Harry; maybe it could be an idea for a book."

"No thanks, that's a little close to home."

"Be careful how you handle yourself; he can get a lot of attention, and he is one slick dude."

"Thanks, Clay I'll try to control myself."

As Harry was leaving, Clay said, "I hope you and Andy have a good time, and Harry, Remember she's just a harmless female."

"There's no such thing," Harry said as he left.

When Harry walked into his kitchen on his return home, his phone was ringing. Harry answered.

"Mr. Blake my name is Roscoe Abernathy. I'm sure you have probably heard of me."

Harry thought, *What arrogance.*

"No, I don't believe we have met nor do I remember ever hearing of you. Listen, if you're selling something, I don't buy over the phone."

"Mr. Blake I am not a salesman. I am an attorney, plus I am in charge of the NAACP in Polk County."

"Look Roscoe, whatever your name is, I don't make contributions over the phone either."

"Mr. Blake, please. I am not calling for a contribution. I'm calling because I represent the families of the two boys you recently murdered."

Before he could continue, Harry interrupted, "Hold on Roscoe, are you talking about the two assholes that broke into my house and killed my wife and dog? Are those the two jackasses whose family you represent? It's too late for a call to apologize. I am sure there could be no other reason for this call."

"You are a vulgar man, Mr. Blake. There is a theory that you might have paid these boys to do what they did and then killed them to keep them quiet. I want you to come into my office and discuss this matter. And by the way, I am about to announce my candidacy for the US Senate, and I will most certainly be in the spotlight. I think it would be in your best interest to come in and speak with me. We might even work out something for you to join my team as a supporter, which is if you can convince me that this allegation against you is untrue. What do you say?"

Harry sat silently for a moment and then responded in the kindest softest voice he could muster, "Roscoe, I want you to listen carefully. I will never under any circumstances meet with you. As far as publicity is concerned, a mini-series of my first two books is about to be released, and I too will be getting a lot of publicity, but I suspect you already know that. I'll make you a promise; if you pursue this, I will oppose you on every front. I have reasonable resources, and I will use them to support your opposition. I will go on the trail with your opponent and speak against you. I will inform every news outlet that will listen about your offer to me. I hope you have heard what I said. Roscoe, you do not want me as your enemy. Do you understand?"

"Mr. Blake, that sounds like a threat."

"Take it as you will and act according to your conscience if you have one. And, never contact me again."

Harry hung up hoping it was the last he would ever hear from Roscoe Abernathy. Instead of concern, he was now looking forward to an afternoon with Andy.

Chapter 21

It was Sunday morning, and Harry slept later than usual. He just didn't snap back the way he used to. He slept well and long, but he was still tired. He decided he would skip church, watch his favorite TV preacher, and hope the good Lord would understand this morning.

At noon he grabbed a bottle of Tavel, not for the lamb stew, but maybe to introduce Andy to good rosé if she was like her brother. The ride up the lake was beautiful, but it didn't stop Harry from worrying about this women's group and how he was going to avoid a problem with Andy gracefully. In spite of that, he found himself a little apprehensive about spending time with such a lovely woman. He had to tell himself to stop being so nervous. This afternoon should be fun.

When Harry arrived, the wooden front door was open, and only the screen door separated Harry from the inside. He knocked and called out to Andy at the same time.

"Harry, you are early, come on in, I'm in the kitchen."

Harry looked at his watch and realized he was indeed 15 minutes early. He let himself in and went to the kitchen. She was at the stove stirring a big pot that obviously by the aroma, was the leftover lamb. When Harry saw her, he stopped and just stared. Again she was in well-fitting jeans, boots and a blue satin western style blouse. When she turned and smiled at him, he saw the first three buttons of her blouse unbuttoned, revealing her golden-freckled chest. His first thought was, *Oh, to be sixty again.*

"Don't just stand there Harry, come on in. Come over here and check out the stew."

He walked toward her, and she turned to face him, held out her arms and embraced him. He stood motionless for a moment and then returned the embrace. His heart rate jumped a notch when she turned and kissed him on the cheek.

"I'm so glad to see you, Harry. Thank you for coming."

"My pleasure, I'm looking forward to the lamb and the tour."

"Well, I'm looking forward to spending time with you and getting to know you better."

He wasn't sure how to respond, but he wished he had said that to her.

"Me too, and I brought a bottle of rosé. I introduced this to Clay a while back. He thought all pink wines were sweet and for little old ladies."

"He told me about that. I can't wait to taste it. Can we open it?"

"It's yours now; you can do anything you want."

"Let me get the corkscrew, here, you stir the lamb."

She opened the bottle and poured two glasses while Harry stopped his stirring and put a lid on the bubbling pot.

She handed Harry a glass, and she made a toast, "To a long friendship, Harry."

"I couldn't have said it better," he said wishing he could have thought of something better to add. For some reason, he was having a hard time expressing himself with Andy. Maybe it was those green eyes or the tan face with dark freckles or…what the hell was wrong with him.

"What are you thinking about Harry, I can see your wheels turning?"

"Me, oh, nothing, uh, I think the lamb is ready, and I'm starving."

She smiled a gotcha smile and said, "Okay, let's eat."

Harry turned away from her and took two steps toward the kitchen window, "Beautiful day."

Dadgum that woman, she's starting to read me. Lord, she looks good.

They made small talk while they ate and as they were finishing, she said, "Harry, can we talk about my women's group now?"

Harry picked up his wine glass and was savoring the final sip trying to decide how to respond.

"How about the tour first and we talk about that later. I've been looking forward to seeing all you have."

She looked at him with a crooked little smile and said, "Okay, let's go, and I'll show you what I have."

Harry realized there might have been a further meaning to what he said and hoped she had not taken it the wrong way. He smiled, and she led him out of the house toward the barn where they had met for the first time.

When they entered the barn, Harry was immediately impressed. It was neat, organized and everything smelled of fresh hay and animals. There was an office on the left and a tack room on the right. There were five stalls on the left and four on the right. There was a storage area on the other end on the right. He noticed ladders on each end going to a second floor.

There were two horses in stalls on the left side and four on the right. Andy explained that the two on the left were not hers but both belonged to a man who had hired her to get them ready for his two daughters.

She led him down the right side and introduced Harry to the four horses as if they were family. The two horses in the end stall were both saddled and ready to go. The horse in the end stall was gray and introduced as Callie the Old Gray Mare.

"She's my oldest and most gentle. I thought she would be perfect for you to start out on."

"The old gray mare for the old gray man," Harry said smiling at her.

"Oh, Harry, you know what I mean; she is great with riders with little experience."

"How about no experience," he added wryly.

"Harry, I was thinking we would take a nice slow walk around the property, probably about an hour's ride. It should be a nice, easy way for you to start."

"I think that's a good plan but I'm going to ask you for a rain check. I'm just not sure I'm up for it. I don't recover like I used to and I still haven't reenergized."

"I'm sorry Harry, I've missed something. What are you talking about?"

"Andy, I apologize. I assumed you had probably heard from Clay or seen it in the newspaper."

"Oh, I've got three days of unread papers in my den and Clay did call, but I haven't taken the time to call him back. Harry, please tell me what happened."

Harry gave her a blow by blow description of what happened not only at his house but also in the street. He ended by telling her, "I'm thinking I may be getting too old for all this excitement."

She stood there for a moment shaking her head with the saddest look on her face that Harry thought he had ever seen. She then took a step toward him and embraced him. She whispered in his ear, "Harry, I am so, so sorry."

He gently separated himself from her and said, "Andy it's okay. I'm fine, just tired. I'll bounce back; I just need a little more time."

"Of course, you will. We have plenty of time to ride together."

About that time a Hispanic man in his early fifties came into the barn.

"Harry, I want you to meet Juan. He makes everything work here."

The two men shook hands and she spoke again, "We have decided not to ride today so you can unsaddle the horses and that's all for today. Enjoy the rest of your day."

She led Harry to the equestrian center and then back to the house and they decided to sit on the front porch.

"Harry, can I get you something?"

"No, no, Andy I'm fine. I just need a little more time to recover. It's no fun getting old."

"Harry, can I get personal with you?"

"Sure."

"How are you dealing with being alone? You were married a long time."

"It's interesting that you asked. The first three or four months were difficult, but lately, I find myself sometimes going days without any thought of my life with Maggie. I started feeling guilty. I called Ray Andrews, my pastor, and had a long talk with him about my guilt. Ray gave me a lot of peace. He said the Bible says there is a season for grieving, but it doesn't say how long the season is. He told me it appeared to him my season was over. He told me to move on, we don't know how many days we have, and I should not waste one of them."

They both were silent for a few minutes, then she spoke: "How do you feel about that advice?"

"I've been thinking about it for a while and you know I think he's probably right. You know it's kinda like being over 70. How are you supposed to feel, how are you supposed to act? You have no experience; you've never been there or here before. It's weird."

"So does that mean you might make a pass at me?" she said this without a trace of a smile.

"If I were ten years younger, there would be no doubt," he said this without thinking, and he regretted it.

"Do I take that as a no?" she said again without smiling.

Now he was puzzled. He knew what he wanted to say, but there were so many things he didn't know about her. Is she a lefty? As bad, is she a loon? He finally said, "Are you making a pass at me?" He thought this was a good response.

"Do you want it to be?" Again she made the response without any sign of emotion.

Harry thought I can never get ahead of this woman. He stood up walked to the rail of the porch and stared at the pasture and woods bordering the open area.

Before he could speak, she said, "Harry I'm sorry. I can see I'm stressing you. I apologize."

Harry turned and faced her, "No Andy, no, you haven't stressed me, but you have forced me to see if I am really where I think I am. In a way, it's like being a teenager trying to figure out girls for the first time. Quite frankly Andy, part of my confusion is because I don't understand why you might be interested in me in this way."

"What do you mean Harry?"

"Andy, one, you are much younger. Two, you are one of the most beautiful women I've ever met and I'm not in the best shape, my hair is disappearing, and at my age, I could die at any time. Other than that, I'm probably perfect for you."

She finally smiled, "Harry I didn't want us to call a wedding planner. I just thought it might be a good idea if we got to know each other better. I've been by myself for ten years. Oh, I've had some dates none of which turned out suitably from my standpoint. Most of the men I've been around are either so self-centered, or they just want to get in my bed. I need someone who I can respect. I need someone to talk with and who will not only listen but hear what I have to say. I don't know if I ever want another husband, but I do want a good friend and companion. I thought, with time, it might be you. Lordy, I've said way too much. I'm sorry, you must think I'm crazy."

Harry was still standing by the porch rail, but now he was smiling, "Do you mind standing?"

"No, but why?" she said standing.

Harry stepped toward her, "Because I want to hold you and thank you."

They embraced, and she said, "Thank me for what, Harry?"

"For saying what I needed to say, or hear, or both. I can't think of anything I'd rather do than get to know you better." As soon as he said it, he thought about her women's group and knew he had to face that conversation probably sooner than later.

"Harry, I think I would like another glass of your rosé."

"Sure." They separated from their embrace and headed back to the kitchen.

They emptied the bottle and sat down at the kitchen table. "How about a date for our women's group. Have you got one for me?"

"Tell me again about this group and its purpose."

"Our group, the WBO of Polk County is a group of strong women that want to demonstrate there are many things women can do as well as men, maybe better."

Harry's thoughts immediately turned to the women's liberation movement.

"Tell me what WBO stands for." *Might as well have this out with her and get it over with, this whole deal may be over before it gets started.*

She answered in a soft voice, so soft Harry could not understand her.

"Women's Business Owners of Polk County."

"I couldn't understand you, say again but louder."

"Do you wear a hearing aid Harry?" she said smiling but turning away so her smile could not be seen.

"No, I don't wear a hearing aid. My hearing is just fine, thank you. So in a normal voice say again."

"Okay, okay, Women's Business Owners of Polk County."

Harry looked up at the ceiling as to invoke divine relief, and said laughingly, "What a scoundrel, you've been," but before he could finish, she cut him off. "Pulling your chain I think you once told me," she was laughing out loud and he was shaking his head and smiling.

Harry stared at her and thought, *She is beautiful and she is funny.* The two worked out the details of the event and agreed she would visit Harry for dinner soon. Harry drove home with a smile on his face, thinking he was the most blessed man on the planet.

Chapter 22

It was Monday mid-morning, and Harry was in his office and enjoying the memories of yesterday's visit to Andy's. He was working on his notes from his first round of interviews from the Polk County Sheriff's department when his phone rang. It was Clay.

"Harry, I have some maybe not so good news. Roscoe Abernathy just left here with everything he legally could take out of here involving the shooting of the two black men at your house. He says he is probably going to file a civil suit against you for wrongful death. He says the two shots to the face prove you had to make sure they were dead so they could not testify against you. He also said it would show the world what a cruel, heartless bastard you were. I'm sorry to have to tell you this."

Harry was quiet for a moment and then spoke, "Not your fault, Clay. This is all about publicity and votes. I am sorry he has decided to go this route. But I may have an answer for him. Maybe, just maybe, I can turn the tables on Mr. Abernathy. Clay, you have any thoughts about how I might get a third party to pass some information to Roscoe?"

"Let me think about that. Do you know what the message is going to be?"

"I do."

"Do you mind sharing?"

"Well, I am going to speak at Andy's Women Business Owners groups. I think we could encourage a lot of press coverage for the event. I think I can structure my talk to include political corruption and what these politicians do that is unsavory. It would be pretty easy to give a first-hand account of threats and blackmail, and everyone would know exactly who I would be talking about. If someone whispered in ole Roscoe's ear, he might want to reconsider his civil suit."

"That might just work. I'll get back to you. Oh, how did the farm tour go? Andy take care of you?"

"Better than I could have hoped. She's great. She's coming to dinner soon."

"Really? Hmm, I'll get back with you."

Clay hung up thinking about his sister but telling dispatch he needed to see Morris Canady.

Chapter 23

Hector and Felipe had hidden in the woods all day and night after the failed effort to capture the gold coins. They were so close. They had the coins and a matter of minutes separated them from success and failure. Now they were in a mess. Two of their five were dead and another in jail. The one in jail had given them up. They had their cell phones and had talked to their families. They knew the law had been to their homes looking for them. The sheriff's department knew exactly who they were. They obviously had lost their jobs, so no more income to help the families with expenses, as modest as it was.

Their families were also impacted. The little Guatemalan community was in turmoil. Two families were grieving over the loss of their sons. Two families were angry that one of their community had ratted out their sons, making it impossible for them to return to their community. And all the families would suffer because of the income contribution from the five men. To make matters worse, there was a reward available for Hector and Felipe.

At least they had gotten away with their cell phones and weapons. Because of the reward, they could only trust their own families. They had been picked up in the middle of the night and hidden at Hector's house. Felipe was almost continually pressing Hector for an escape plan. Hector kept telling him he had to be patient. Hector had replayed the incident at the Blakes over and over in his head. He was sure he and Felipe could get the coins without any help. The old man had not been a threat. When they had escaped, they had not realized the old man had shot one of their gang. He had fired his shotgun in the house but was never a threat. They simply needed a better escape plan. The more he thought it through, he knew it was their only hope for getting to New York and MS-13.

Chapter 24

Morris Canady listened as Clay explained what had gone on with Roscoe Abernathy and Harry. After hearing the proposed plan, Canady said, "I owe Harry, he probably saved my life. Besides I can't stand that blowhard. I've always thought he hurt black causes more than he helped. He does what he does for himself and no one else. I'll be happy to do it."

An hour later, Morris entered Roscoe's office. Roscoe kept him waiting 20 minutes, but he finally was allowed into Roscoe's big office. It was luxurious. Big, oversized mahogany desk, cherry cabinets, and bookcases filled the room along with pictures of Roscoe and Barack Obama and two other Democratic presidents.

"Morris Canady, Mr. Abernathy," he said as he entered and extended his right hand.

"Oh, I know who you are. You are our only representative at the sheriff's department. That, by the way, will be one of my upcoming projects. Too much white power by Clay Hardaway, don't you think?"

"Clay's been a good boss," Canady said without emotion.

"That's good to hear. What can I do for you, deputy?"

"Nothing, but I think I can do something for you."

"Well, that's not usually the way it is when people come to see me. What can you do for me?" Roscoe was skeptical but curious.

"I thought you might want to know about a conversation I overheard between Sheriff Hardaway and Harry Blake today." Morris paused, waiting for a response.

"You heard this today?" Morris shook his head affirmatively. "Go ahead."

"Harry Blake is going to be the speaker at a Women Business Owners meeting. They are going to make a big deal out of this with lots of publicity. TV, newspaper, everybody they can round up. He's going to talk up his new mini-series. He also said he was going to talk about political corruption and blackmail and when he got through, everyone would know he was talking about you. He said he was going to volunteer for private interviews on the subject. He said you have declared war on the wrong guy."

Roscoe leaned back in his big leather chair and momentarily stared out his office window.

"Let me ask you, deputy, what do you think of the theory that's going around?"

"What theory?"

"You haven't heard that Harry Blake hired those two boys to kill his wife. He then killed them to make sure they didn't talk. He viciously shot them in the face."

Morris shook his head negatively and stared at the floor.

"I don't understand why your department didn't pursue this. Do you agree?"

"Actually, I don't. I was one of the first on the scene. The crime scene told us the exact opposite of what you just said. Nobody who has the facts could ever possibly think that's what happened."

"What about the shots to their faces? He was making sure they were dead." Roscoe was now becoming frustrated.

"It was rage. I assure you the intruders were already dead. If you don't believe me, check with the coroner, Jesse will tell you. No, I believe what Harry told us. When it was over, he sat down and saw the shotgun blasts had violated his wife and dog and he was pissed. Rage, it was all about rage."

Roscoe paused, looked out the window again, and said, "Deputy Canady, is there anything I could do to keep you from expressing your views in a court case. You know, if you were helping the families?"

"I think I understand what you are saying."

"Good, I'm sure a man of Blake's standing has a liability policy, and it wouldn't cost him anything out of his pocket."

Morris stood up and leaned over Roscoe's big desk, "You know that is exactly why some people don't trust us, because we are black. They think when it comes to white vs black, we can't be trusted. You can find somebody else to do your dirty work. I came here to help you and you try to make me out a liar."

"NO, NO, I didn't mean to," Roscoe didn't finish his sentence because Morris Canady was gone.

Chapter 25

Judge Felton Henry had spent the last 20 minutes doing what he knew he shouldn't have nor what he wanted to do. He had spent the time on an off the record meeting with Roscoe Abernathy. Every time he had ever met with the man, he felt like he needed a bath. The fact that Roscoe was black had nothing to do with the feeling. Twenty-eight years on the bench had proven that his court, and his rulings were colorblind.

No, it was Roscoe, he was always wheeling and dealing around the edges of the law. Roscoe had run the local NAACP the same way. He had stretched facts, redefined words, and defined situations always into racial discrimination. Hardly a month passed without Roscoe being involved in a news story. Now it appeared he was going to make a run for the Senate and he was looking for a way to have a big campaign kick-off.

Judge Henry had to give Roscoe credit, a civil suit, wrongful death against Harry Blake would involve all the news outlets. And, it did not matter one bit whether the case had any legal merit. Harry Blake might not be a celebrity, but he was a famous author, won the big award and supposedly had a mini-series in the works. He had now been involved in two break-ins at his home and had lost his wife in one of them.

With all that in mind, Roscoe could end up with all he probably wanted in the first place. He would get the publicity, and he would portray himself as the defender of the families who lost sons to a wealthy white man who possibly set them up. There would be no proof, and it would probably be thrown out. If Roscoe was lucky, he might get a trial, create some divides in the community which also gets him more time in front of the cameras. Unbelievable! Roscoe was a slimy black snake.

Judge Henry's curiosity had been tweaked and he decided to continue in the off record mode. He picked up his phone.

"Clay, Felton Henry here. I got an off the record question for you. You aware Roscoe Abernathy may bring a wrongful death against Harry Blake with the insinuation Blake hired the black boys to kill his wife?"

Clay paused, "Yeah, Roscoe's been here, got all the information he was entitled to get, and told me what a poor job we did for not having a major investigation of Harry."

"Any doubts in your mind after your interrogation of Harry?"

"No sir, Roscoe cares not for justice, he only cares about his rise up the ladder."

"I shouldn't say this, but Clay, I think Mr. Blake should hire Mack Peters."

"Thanks, Judge." And he hung up.

Clay did not put his phone down. He immediately called Harry. "Harry, do you have a good local lawyer?"

"No, why, do I need one?"

"It looks like it. I think Roscoe is going forward with his suit."

"That son of a bitch! He has no case."

"Harry, he knows that. It's not about winning; it's about the publicity. It's about making him the hero, the defender of the downtrodden."

Harry was silent.

"Well, do you?"

"Do I what?"

"Have a good local lawyer?"

"Of course not, no reason to. Could you recommend one?"

"Of course."

"Mack Peters, probably the meanest SOB in a courtroom in Polk County and he hates Roscoe."

"Do you know him well enough to call him for me, Clay?"

"Yeah, I'll call him. I'll fill him in and tell him you will call. Don't call him until at least tomorrow, he's a busy guy."

"Thanks, Clay."

Harry started to worry now. He didn't need this in his life especially as they made progress on the mini-series. That no good SOB.

Chapter 26

McKenzie 'Mack' Peters was the most known personality in the Polk County legal system. His reputation extended all the way to the state capital. The Republican Party had done everything in their power to recruit him as a national candidate. Everyone in the courthouse loved Mack. He was a friend to everyone from the janitors to the judges. As good a friend as he was to those he liked, he was the foremost SOB if you opposed him.

Mack hated those who tried to twist the truth and to finagle the law to their advantage. He had proven that he was colorblind in how he chose and handled clients. He had taken many pro bono cases where he felt someone was being prosecuted wrongly. This included blacks and whites equally. Mack was an outstanding trial lawyer. It was said when Mack stepped in front of a jury, there was no evangelist alive who could match him. In his arsenal, he carried a full range of emotions that he never failed to display.

Mack despised Roscoe Abernathy. Mack had said on many occasions, "Ol' Roscoe would walk a mile to tell you something totally untrue versus standing right here and telling the truth."

He and Roscoe were exact opposites. Roscoe was a big man who dressed in expensive suits, tailored shirts, silk ties and alligator shoes. As much as Mack was loved around the courthouse Roscoe was hated. He was arrogant and talked down to everyone.

Mack, on the other hand, was short, overweight, had red curly hair that always looked like he had been in a windstorm. His suits came from Belk and always needed pressing. It wasn't as if he couldn't afford better clothes; Mack charged significant fees to his clients who could afford to pay. He had a beautiful estate on the lake with a wine cellar that supposedly was better stocked than any of the finest restaurants in the state. He was just Mack being Mack. Mack and Roscoe had been on opposite sides numerous times, and Mack had never lost. When asked by a reporter recently about his thoughts on never losing to Roscoe, he commented, "We can all take heart when good overcomes evil."

Mack was looking forward to meeting Harry Blake today.

Harry arrived at the appointed time at Mack's office in an old downtown building. He introduced himself to the pretty young girl who was the receptionist.

She immediately took him to Mack's office and opened the door to allow Harry to enter. Mack was at his desk and on the phone.

Mack spoke, "Hold on a minute darlin', don't bring folks in here when I'm on the phone. Lordy."

Harry started to back into the hallway.

"No, No, come on in."

The two visitors' chairs and the desk were littered with stacks of files. "Darlin', move those files so the man can sit."

Mack pointed at one of the chairs and turned back to the phone. "I'm back, I'll have to call you later, but you need to consider my request. There's just no merit here for a trial. I see, well, you have a good day.

"I'm so sorry, the girl is as dumb as a gourd, but she's my niece and couldn't find a job. I truly didn't think being a receptionist would tax her so. Enough of that. McKenzie Peters, you can call me Mack. Mister Harry Blake, it's an honor to make your acquaintance. We have so few celebrities in our upstate county."

"Please, I don't feel like a celebrity."

"Believe me, can I call you Harry? Believe me, Harry; you are a celebrity in the sight of ol' Roscoe. Celebrity means money, and when he's close to it, he's like an ol' hound in heat." Mack said this with his best poker face. "Our mutual friend Clay allowed me to interrogate him when he called about your situation. It's good to have a friend like Clay."

"Does that mean you are going to take my case?"

"Let's talk some more before we talk about that. I want to ask you some questions, and I want you to give me honest direct answers. These will be part of attorney-client private communication, so tell me the complete truth."

"Even though we don't have a deal yet?"

"Yes."

"Okay."

"Had you ever met or seen the two black men before they broke into your home?"

"Never."

"Have you ever had a conversation with anyone about killing or harming your wife?"

"Never, ever."

"Why did you leave the room when they pulled into your driveway?"

"I didn't, I was already in the hallway to our bedroom."

"Why were you there and not sitting with your wife and dog?"

"Damn, Clay told you everything."

"Our friend is almost as thorough as yours truly."

"I was going for a sweater. I was cold, Maggie keeps, I mean kept the house so cold."

"So you are saying, you were just lucky."

"No, blessed by the grace of God is what I call it."

"Well said Harry, well said. Why did you finish killing these men by shooting them in the face?"

"I didn't."

"Are you telling me you didn't shoot both men at close range in the face?"

"No, I did, but they were already dead when I shot them in the face."

"If that's true, why shoot them again?"

"They violated my wife, and I wanted to violate them. In retrospect, I wish I had reloaded the shotgun and blown their heads off. I was in a rage."

"How do you know for sure they were dead?"

"I knew, I could see. You can look at the coroner's reports if you don't believe me."

"Clay says you're a stubborn man who seems to have a propensity for getting into fights and gunfights at that. What do you have to say about that?"

Harry sat still and quiet for a couple of minutes. He stared at Mack and Mack back at him.

Harry finally spoke, "You know Mack I'm 72 years old. I hadn't been involved in hardly any physical fighting. But as I have aged, I have come to despise evil. I just can't tolerate it, and by the way, I doubt Clay called me stubborn. Hard head, yes hard head, is what he would say."

For the first time in their meeting Mack smiled and half laughed, "Harry, the questions I asked are the kinds that snake Roscoe will ask, only he will greatly embellish the way he asks them. He will do his best to piss you off. I normally tell my clients that they should show no emotion, but in your case, I say if he insults you, let him know it. The judge will admonish you, but that's okay."

"Does that mean you are now my attorney?"

"Yes, sir, absolutely."

"When do you think we will go to court?"

"I don't know, I'm trying to get it thrown out. There's just not enough there."

"You sound like you already started."

"Off the record I have. I talked off the record to Judge Henry today."

"Is that normal?"

"Harry, ain't nothin' normal in the Polk County Court System," he said smiling.

"Oh, Harry, I read your books. Good stories. By the way, do you have your checkbook with you?"

"I do, you need some money?"

"Leave 5K with my sweet, but dumb, little niece on your way out."

Harry started to speak, but Mack already had his phone in hand and had his back to Harry. Harry left thinking 5K!

Chapter 27

Harry left Mack's office and went straight home. It was almost 4:30 pm and he realized he was just flat, wore out. Most of the time he didn't feel his age, but now he felt like a really old man. He thought about a drink but instead went straight to his big recliner. The last few days had taken their toll. All his life he had the ability to focus on whatever situation was at hand. He could keep his feelings hidden until the work was complete. But it wasn't that he didn't have feelings. He did. Now they were catching up with him.

More than the physical strain, it was the mental stress that seemed to take the most out of him. In his whole life, he had never hunted or killed anything. He never wanted to hunt except maybe birds. He had thought he would like to have hunted quail and pheasant. He just never found the time.

But now he had been in two shootouts and had killed three men. He had never dreamed this is what his retirement would become. If he had to do it over, he would not change a thing. No, he had thought long and hard, and he believed he had done the right thing. Evil needed to be confronted and God had given him the ability and grace to do it and survive. That was the last thought until his phone rang and woke him. It was 7:30 p.m. It was Andy.

"Harry, I hope I'm not disturbing your supper."

"No, not at all. As a matter of fact, I was sound asleep in my recliner. I think these last few days have pretty well done me in."

"Oh Harry, I was calling to see what I could bring tomorrow but maybe we need to postpone our dinner until another day when you are more rested. Clay told me some of what happened and I just can't believe it happened again."

Harry was quiet for a moment and then spoke, "Andy, it's kind of you to offer, but I think I'd like to have some company, your company. I had planned an elaborate display to impress you but how would you handle a steak and baked potato, salad and a great bottle of wine."

"Harry are you sure? You know I could pick up a pizza."

"Lord no, I can handle the meal."

"I'll bring dessert, Harry. I need to bring something."

"Okay, but the dress is casual, I'm wearing jeans."

Chapter 28

Harry slept in the next day and didn't even shower and shave until after lunch. He had gone to Earl's Meats to pick up filets and then to the grocery to get the rest of the items he needed for his dinner with Andy. When he returned home, he found himself settling into his recliner for another nap.

When he awoke, he could hardly believe it was 4:30 pm. He went to his office to straighten up his usual mess. Harry was a stacker. To the outsider, it looked totally disorganized, but Harry knew the contents of each stack. He smiled thinking how it used to drive Maggie crazy. Maggie, my...my, what would she think, a single woman coming to dinner.

As Harry finished, he started to the refrigerator to take the steaks out? The doorbell rang, Harry looked at his watch, 5:05 pm he could not imagine who would be at the door, maybe UPS. He walked to the front door and found Andy standing there. He was surprised he had not expected her until 6:00 or 6:30. She was holding a big bag and her smile so inviting, he was sure it could make time stand still. Then it hit him he was barefoot and in old jeans and a sweatshirt. He could only see her from the waist up and she was wearing a gold embroidered western style shirt. He just could hardly believe how beautiful she looked. Harry was just standing there staring when she cocked her head and shrugged wondering why she was not invited to enter.

Harry finally opened the door, "Andy, I'm sorry. I just didn't expect you until later."

She stepped in, and Harry took the bag from her.

"I'm sorry Harry, but I had an idea, and I felt if I told you in advance, you would say no. Can we go to the kitchen, there's gelato in the bag that needs to go in the freezer?"

Harry led her to the kitchen.

"Your house is beautiful and what a view of the lake."

"Thanks, it was Maggie's choice, I really didn't want this house. But I have to admit it's worked out better than I could have imagined. Now, what's this secret plan?"

"Harry, I came early to get here before you had started preparing anything. I want you to sit have a drink and let me do everything. But I want you to tell me to do it the way you would. I talked to Clay again and when he told me again what you have been through, and Harry I think it is frankly amazing you are not in bed right now! I appreciate your wanting to do this for me but…it's you Harry that needs to be waited on, and I want to do this for you. Please let me do this, Harry."

Harry started to choke up. He was fighting to control his emotions; this was stupid to react this way. He knew it was fatigue and he was struggling.

She could see him fighting to control himself and she wanted to go over and hold him, but she decided it might be better to go another route.

"Harry I am assuming a non-response means yes, but before we begin, I'm hoping you will give me a tour of your home."

Harry had turned away from her while he tried to regain his composure. "Okay, but we need to fix a drink to take on the tour."

"Harry, you sit and direct me."

He sat at the kitchen island and directed her to the bar where she poured them both a Knob Creek on the rocks. Harry then gave her the complete tour. Afterward, she said, "I can see why your wife liked this place so much. It's lovely but is also practical. It's pretty much perfect for a family your size."

They came back to the kitchen, and she made him sit at the island but refused to do anything unless Harry directed her. She wouldn't even allow him to refresh their drinks. When the potatoes were in the oven, the salads made, she sat down beside him.

"Andy, I think I should at least change my clothes before we eat."

"Nonsense, relax. You said casual, and you were going to wear jeans, and you are and so am I."

Harry looked at her and thought, *Perfectly fitting black jeans, loafers and that fancy gold blouse, she is something.* And he felt like a slob in his sweatshirt.

"Andy, question and I hope you will answer honestly."

She didn't reply but shifted in her seat, so she was looking directly at him.

"When I told Clay you were coming for dinner, he seemed surprised. I wonder if I hurt his feelings because I did not include him? Or, does he not like the idea of his sister seeing an old man like me? What do you think?"

She took a moment, stared at her drink, and then spoke, "Harry, Clay considers you a good, close friend. He respects you. He has said to me on several occasions that he hopes he can do what you do when he's your age. That said, I think he is surprised I have not remarried, and I think he thinks I still will. I know he wishes I would choose someone closer to my age. My only marriage was to a man two years younger than me and look what that accomplished. He's been dead for ten years. I respect Clay, but he lives his life, and I live mine. We are both self-sufficient adults."

Harry sat there absorbing what Andy had said. He was trying to think of how to respond when she spoke again, "I hope that answers your question about Clay.

Now, different subject. What's your opinion of how long to season steaks before grilling?"

Harry hesitated; he didn't want to leave that subject but was unsure how to respond.

"Well, out of the cooler, at least two hours before grilling, seasoning should go on when they are out of the cooler. The salt in the seasoning needs a couple of hours to do its thing."

"Where did you learn this and all the other cooking skills you have? Clay says you have a real talent in the kitchen."

"Well, I don't know how much talent I have, but it is one of my pleasures in life. The answer to your question is cooking shows. When Maggie and I moved up north, about all I could do was grill a little. Let me say I don't like cold weather activities. Never wanted to skate or ski, I never liked to watch hockey, and I think the NBA is a joke. So, when college football season ended, I started watching cooking shows because I like to eat. I got hooked. I was fascinated to the point that I told Maggie I wanted to try cooking. She was thrilled, and it turned out I was reasonably good at it. Even today, I enjoy watching certain people, there's just so much to learn."

"Harry, that's a great story. You are a complex and interesting man, Harry Blake."

They finished their meal, and she cleaned the kitchen and put everything back in its place even though Harry pleaded with her to leave it for him tomorrow. When she had finished, he led her to the great room. With his iPad and Bose speakers, they listened to Smokey Robinson on Harry's favorite app, Pandora. He lit the fireplace, and they sat finishing the last of the dinner wine.

She seated herself in the middle of the big leather sectional sofa and set her wine on the big glass coffee table. Harry without thinking sat in his big recliner at the end of the couch. He looked at her and realized she was sitting exactly where Maggie had always sat. He also realized he should have joined her on the couch. Dumb ass!

He started to move, but before he could get out of the recliner, she stood up picked up her wine and said, "Do you mind if I move closer, so we don't have to talk so loud?"

Now he was embarrassed, "No of course not, I'm sorry I should not have sat here, old habit."

"It's okay, Harry."

Harry stood up, "No it's not, it was rude and as if I didn't want to sit beside you. As I told you earlier, I'm not quite back to normalcy. Why would I not want to sit next to a beautiful woman like you, please forgive me."

"Harry, honestly it's okay, I can see the fatigue in your face especially your eyes. I probably should go and let you get to bed."

"No, please, it's way too early for bed. Let's enjoy the fire, the wine and get to know each other better."

They were now sitting side by side on the sofa. Harry turned and looked at her and asked, "Andy, you've been alone for ten years. Have you lived with anybody? If I'm getting too personal, just tell me."

"No, I think I told you before, I've dated a few men, but nothing I felt was serious even though one, in particular, was pretty upset when I told him I wouldn't see him anymore. He was very persistent to a fault. He said he wanted to marry me. He said he had told his family and friends he was going to marry me. He was insistent I give in to him. The conversation got heated, and we both got very ugly with each other. It was obvious we did not need to be with each other. Harry, my standards have changed as I have aged. My list of requirements has changed and grown. Plus, after ten years I know I don't have to be married."

Harry had listened intently; he had already eliminated one of his significant doubts about her. She was definitely not a looney.

"Andy, do you ever get lonely?"

She smiled paused and said, "Yeah, I do, but it's not a constant or all the time kind of thing. I do my best to stay busy. I like to read, watch movies, and of course I have my work and my horses. There's always work around the farm. It's the nights sometimes. Especially as I have gotten older when I come back to the house tired, and I would like a man to make me a drink, give me a hug, maybe hold me for just a minute or two and maybe even wash my back. Oh, listen to me; I sound so selfish. It would be nice to have someone you care enough about to do things for, somebody to make happy."

She blushed, "Goodness, enough about me. I want to talk about you. I know the last time we were together, you told me about your guilt and meeting with your pastor. Are the guilt feelings getting better?"

Harry gazed at the fireplace, "You know one of the nicer things about cooler weather is having a good fire. I love a good fire." Harry paused to get his thoughts together, "I'm not avoiding your question, by the way, just trying to give an answer that's coherent. I have always been a bottom line kind of guy, maybe that's why I was pretty good in business. So, bottom line, I have no guilt about seeing you or being with you. The only fly in the ointment is that I know, my children, deep down, will not be happy. Now having said that, how important is that? And quite frankly who knows what's best for me? Is it them or is it me?"

"How do you know that for sure Harry?" she had now turned toward him with a hand on his shoulder. "Maybe they would surprise you?"

"It would be a heck of a surprise. No, I think the three boys, yes, the two girls, no."

"So, how are you going to handle it?"

"I'm not, until I have to. If somebody asks, I won't back away, I will be as honest as I can be. Until then, keep moving forward, no harm, no foul."

"I know you said you did not think about her constantly now, but how about being alone. Are you feeling lonely?"

"Yeah, sometimes. It's kind of like what you said. You have a tiring day, and you would like someone to pamper you a little bit. I too would like a long hug, a kiss, someone to make my drink. I don't know why I think that because that was not her thing. She just didn't do that. She was kind of a 'Hey, suck it up, it'll be better tomorrow.' I guess it was just my fantasy to have someone care about me that much."

"Harry, that doesn't sound good."

"Well I think she loved me, but over the years we just evolved into a certain lifestyle. Listen, we all have our faults. I'm probably not easy to live with. The older we get, it's probably harder to change your ways and habits."

"It sounds like you are on your way to spending the rest of your life alone."

"I don't know, maybe. Maybe just try to have some good friends to spend time with."

"How about intimacy, Harry? Are you beyond needing that? And Harry, I'm not necessarily talking about sex."

"Andy, to be frank, I haven't had a lot of intimacy in recent years. As I said, we had a different lifestyle. Having said that, no I'm not beyond wanting or needing it. I feel like I am entering a new world and I'm not sure how I should navigate it."

Harry decided to plunge ahead, "You know when I was young, I had so much confidence around women. I felt like I knew what they liked. But, older women, I know for sure I don't know what they like, what they want or what they think. And, I'm not even sure I should be concerned about it."

Andy smiled at him and said, "Well Harry, if you need any help, you feel free to let me know."

Harry thought to himself, *Now what does that mean?*

Their talk turned to Harry's upcoming appearance at the women's group. Either the subject or his fatigue caused Harry to begin to yawn.

"Okay, Harry, you are going to bed, and I am going home."

"Are you okay to drive that far tonight. You know 45 minutes is a long drive. And of course, you're welcome to stay. I have plenty of bedrooms, and I'm so tired I promise I won't be a threat," he said smiling.

"Thanks for the offer but actually I am staying at baby brothers, so I don't have to make the long drive. But if offered, I might consider a rain check."

Harry raised his eyebrows, smiled and said, "I'll have a stack of them printed."

Harry opened the front door for her, and she turned, gave him a quick kiss on the lips, and left.

Chapter 29

Freddy Lopez was a 52-year-old Mexican who had been in the U.S. eighteen years and fifteen of those in Polk County. He was a quiet, plain, almost unnoticeable man. He ran a manpower company that provided day laborers; some skilled, some not. His men were reliable; if Freddy said four men at a particular place at a specific time, they would be there and probably early. His rates were fair, and Freddy was well-off.

He also ran a respected and successful cleaning business. If you needed a crew for a big, one time clean or permanent weekly or bi-weekly house cleaners, he had them available. In this case, his rates were on the high side, but his ladies were very good at their jobs.

Everyone knew there were two Mexican gangs in the county, but everyone was wrong. There was one gang with two arms. Freddy always said to be successful, a man must have two arms.

Freddy Lopez was a successful businessman and a crook. Freddy was the godfather to the men and women of these gangs. Freddy had read about the mafia of the '40s and '50s and used what he learned as his model. He had maintained a state of complete secrecy of his involvement with gangs or anything illegal.

It did not for an instant mean that Freddy was not a strong leader. The story goes, that a few years earlier a strong, young man challenged Freddy for the leader's job. The day after the challenge, the young man had never been seen or heard from again. When asked, Freddy said the young man must have changed his mind.

Freddy had followed the two attempts on Harry Blake's gold coins closely. Freddy's sister, Ruth, was the lead cleaning lady taking care of Harry Blake.

Chapter 30

Judge Henry's office called Roscoe and Mack to say that they had a number of settlements and withdrawals, and the court calendar would allow the trial to begin next week if the two attorneys could adapt to this change. Roscoe complained but reluctantly accepted. Mack's response had been, "Hell, yeah!"

The publicity had been as big as it gets in Polk County. Roscoe had gained more than he had hoped for, he was in full bloom.

The Trial

Roscoe was resplendent in a $1500 Brooks Brothers black suit, white French-cuffed shirt and a neon red tie with matching suspenders. His dress was capped off by perfectly shined black alligator shoes.

Mack was attired in a Belk's best funeral blue suit that appeared as if it should have been at the dry cleaners instead of a courtroom. He wore a short-sleeved white shirt with a tartan bow tie that was not tied square to the collar. His shoes were old and brown and needed a shine. He was his version of 'court ready.'

Opening Remarks

ROSCOE: "Ladies and gentlemen, I know Judge Henry has told you this is not a criminal case, it's a civil case. What that really means is you and I have a chance to do something good and right and fair. Harry Blake is a well-off celebrity – he has income, assets, and resources. He is about to become more famous when his books' mini-series is released. Listen, all we have to do is open a newspaper, turn on our TVs, and we see famous people are many times, not good people. They do bad things.

"Now let's back up just a bit. I'm not attempting to try to prove any criminal liability here to get Mr. Blake put in jail. Our good sheriff, by the way, a good friend of Mr. Blake's has already determined there would be no charges against his friend, Mr. Blake. That's okay. They have to live with that, but we don't have to go away from here without some justice. That's what you and I are going to do here. Thank you."

MACK: "My, my, counselor Abernathy is so eloquent. Makes you wonder why we are needed. Condemning the sheriffs' department and Mista Blake in one quick sentence and being a celebrity himself, I am sure he knows well about the foibles of celebrities.

"Now folks, why do you think there were no criminal charges or a trial? Is it because Sheriff Hardaway is a friend? Of course not. It's called a lack of, or in this case, no evidence whatsoever of wrongdoing by Harry Blake. Is it wrong for a man to defend himself? No, I don't think so, nor do I think you are foolish enough to do so. I'm through your honor; let's get this travesty completed."

The judge told Roscoe to call his witnesses. His first witness was Sheriff Hardaway. After some preliminary meaningless questions, Roscoe got to the heart of his subjects.

"Sheriff, who looked at the evidence in this horrible crime besides you?"

"Assistant Sheriff, Al Johnson and Deputy, Morris Canady. We all concluded the same thing. Also as per procedure in cases like this, we run it by the D.A. and he agreed."

Roscoe, in his accusatory tone continued, "It was hard for him to disagree based on the way you presented it, right? After all, you can make these things go the way you want them to, isn't that true?"

Mack stood up, slammed his pencil down, "I object, your honor. I believe that is a terrible disrespect to our honorable District Attorney. I believe him to be quite competent and not a man that could be pushed around."

The judge stared at the jury and spoke, "Mr. Peters your objection is sustained. The jury will ignore Mr. Abernathy's speculations and Mr. Abernathy you know better. Continue."

"Sheriff, did you or your deputies interview the families of the two murdered young men?"

Mack was up again, "Objection the term 'murdered' is very offensive here, your honor."

Before he could reply Roscoe erupted, "Those young men were brutally shot, that is murder, and you are right; the way they were murdered was offensive."

The judge never spoke, he merely motioned Mack to his seat and nodded for Roscoe to continue.

"Answer the question, Sheriff."

"We did have conversations with both families and found no reason to pursue anything further."

"Did you specifically ask if they knew if their precious boys had been hired for a job?"

"Not specifically."

"I thought not. That's all I have for the sheriff."

Mack and Roscoe passed each other, changing places without any eye contact.

"Sheriff, did y'all ask the families of the two murders if they had seen their boys with a white man, or did they know Mr. Harry Blake and if you did, how did they respond?"

"We did in both cases and in both cases the answer was no."

"I'm through with Mr. Hardaway, your honor," Mack said walking back to his table.

Roscoe called Mrs. Daisy Watson to the stand.

"Mrs. Watson, first, we are all so sorry for your loss. It's a terrible thing to lose a child."

"Get on with it Mr. Abernathy," judge Henry snapped.

"Mrs. Watson, I know you loved your boy, did he confide in you?"

"Yessir, he did."

"Did he tell you he was going to have some big money soon?"

"Yessir, he did."

"Did he say someone had hired him?"

"He say he had a big job coming up."

"So he intimated he had been hired for a big job."

Judge Henry half rose just as Mack shouted, "Objection!"

Judge Henry looked at Mrs. Watson and said, "Mrs. Watson, do not answer that."

She nodded affirmatively and said, "Yessir."

"Mrs. Watson do you think it was right for someone to shoot your boy in the face at point-blank range while he was lying in the floor dying."

"Objection!" Mack screamed.

"Sustained!" Judge Henry's voice was loud. "I want the jury to strike that from your minds and memories." Without lowering his voice, Judge Henry said, "Mr. Abernathy, my bucket is full of your antics. Do you understand?"

Roscoe stared at the judge but did not respond.

Mack came to the stand to talk with Mrs. Watson.

"Mrs. Watson, did your son ever say to you I've been hired by so and so to do a job or some work?"

"Hmm, yessir."

"And when was that?"

"'Bout a month for he got kilt. He say a man at the Walmart needed some help cleaning the parking lot, all his help had the flu."

"I see, any other time?"

"Not in a long time."

"Do you know or have you ever seen that man at the table over there?" pointing at Harry.

"No, sir."

"Why did you and your friend think you deserved to take money from Mr. Blake for defending himself from someone trying to kill him who had already killed his wife and dog."

"Objection!" Roscoe was livid.

"Sustained."

"Did Mr. Abernathy tell you he would get some money for y'all for coming to court?"

Roscoe shrieked, "Objection!" again, but poor Mrs. Watson was already shaking her head affirmatively.

"Sustained."

"I'm through your honor."

After that, he decided to skip the other mother and went to Harry Blake.

"Mr. Blake, you are a very famous and successful person, right."

"Objection."

"Overruled."

"Thank you, your honor. Mr. Blake, a man like you must carry a fair amount of personal liability insurance, right?"

"Objection."

Judge Henry spoke, "When did you develop a hearing problem, Mr. Abernathy?"

"Sir?"

"I told you my bucket was full. No more warnings, only contempt."

"Mr. Blake why weren't you in the room with your wife and dog when your house was supposedly broken into?"

"Objection!"

"Your honor, I would like to pursue a theory."

"Go ahead."

Mack jumped up, "I want my formal objection for the record."

Judge Henry smiled, "So noted, continue."

"I left the room to get a sweater, I was cold."

"Didn't you see the vehicle lights coming down your driveway?"

"The lights were out."

"So you were just a lucky man?"

"I would call it blessed."

"So according to your story, the two men killed your wife and dog and while they did this, you armed yourself with a shotgun and .38 caliber revolver? How old are you, Mr. Blake? Never mind my notes say you are 72, right?"

"Yes, on both counts, I armed myself, and I am 72."

"So you would have us believe that a 72-year-old could and did win a shootout with two armed twenty-somethings who were equally armed?"

"By the grace of God."

"Well, Mr. Blake, I think that's just too far-fetched for me, but I have an idea that makes much more sense. Here's what may have happened; you hired the boys to kill your wife. Your marriage was stale, there was a new lady in your life. You could afford to make it happen. It wasn't hard to make a deal with a pair of gang members then double cross them to make sure they never talked. Am I close, Mr. Blake?"

"You sir, are a lunatic."

"That's uncalled for, just yes or no. I suspect I'm getting close to home."

"Objection, your honor. How long do we endure Mr. Abernathy's fantasy?"

"I'm going to let him finish."

"Again, your honor, I want my objection on the record."

"Granted. Continue, Mr. Abernathy."

"Thank you, your honor. This was not a difficult plan for you, was it, Mr. Blake, based on your past military history? You served three years in a very secret special ops unit. That's where you plan and execute detailed plans to murder and destroy. Tell us about that, Mr. Blake."

Harry was caught off guard. He never wanted to talk about that time again. He never wanted to think about those days again. He had joined at 18 to keep from getting drafted. Somehow he had been assigned to a select group and got training that equipped him to do things he didn't want to remember. Harry spent most of his time in Vietnam in country. He also spent some time in the Middle East.

"Mr. Blake, please answer my question."

"It was a long time ago, and I can't talk about secret ops."

"But you did plan and murder people, did you not?"

"I cannot answer."

"I think the correct word is won't, not can't. How many people have you killed in your lifetime?"

"My military service is top secret."

"How many people have you killed since you moved to Polk County? Wait, I'll answer for you. According to public record, three, that's all we know about."

"Objection, your honor, this is out of bounds."

"Mr. Peters, I don't need your help managing my courtroom."

"It's okay your honor, I'm through with Mr. Blake."

Mack walked to the stand, he had taken his coat off, and his shirttail was hanging over his backside.

"Mr. Blake, I apologize that you had to endure an off-the-wall conspiracy theory. Just a few questions to set the record straight. During your time here in Polk County before your wife was murdered, have you had a female companion, love interest or interests?"

"Absolutely not."

"How long ago were you in the military?"

"A little over 50 years."

"Wow 50 years ago, amazing. Had you ever seen the boys represented here before they invaded your home and viciously murdered your wife and dog?"

"Never."

"Mr. Abernathy never asked you about your shooting the boys in the face after they were dead. I suspect that's his big ending so let you and I see if we can't take all the wind from his sails. Did you, after the two men were dead, go back and shoot them again in the face."

"I did."

"Why would you do that? They were dead."

Harry dropped his head and stared at his shoes then looked up and stared at the jury, "The whole thing finally had ended. I looked at my little dog; a mass of hair, blood, and guts. I looked at my wife who had been blown onto her back on top of our glass coffee table. Her blouse was basically gone and her chest had been opened up, exposing bone and blood. She had been totally violated. Mack, I sat there thinking if they had just held us at gunpoint, I would've given them anything they wanted. All they had to do was ask. But no, they acted like animals, and so I was in a rage, and I wanted to violate them as they violated my wife and dog, and so I did."

"Harry if you had to do it over, would you do it the same?"

"No, I would do it differently."

"How different, Harry?"

Long pause, finally Harry said, "I wouldn't have used my pistol, I would have reloaded my shotgun and blown their heads off."

Everyone in the courtroom groaned and shouted. The judge had to call order.

Mack smiled and said, "I believe I'm finished, your honor."

Roscoe felt the whole thing slipping away.

Summation

Roscoe: "Ladies and gentlemen, you have heard a lot of things here today. Let me see if I can sort out the bottom line for you. We have Harry Blake, a man of privilege, a celebrity, a man of wealth and substance. His background is that of an elite military killer, planner.

"On the other side, we have two families who struggle to get by. They have both lost not only their precious sons but also an income stream that helps them to survive on a daily basis. Now, I'm not foolish enough to say what the boys did was not wrong. However, did they really do this on their own or could they have been hired? Could they have been done in by a 72-year-old if they maybe had not let their guard down because they thought they were safe?

"Then there is the brutality of gunshots to the face. I can't imagine how their two mamas felt when they saw their precious boys. And finally remorse, there was none whatsoever. No, no…no remorse only a vicious desire to have a chance to do it again and take a shotgun and blow their heads off. Can you imagine how their poor mamas could have handled that? Lord help them.

"Ladies and gentlemen, the boys will never be back in their mamas' lives but I want you to consider helping these two dear ladies with compensation for their loss and not only their loss but the brutal way it was inflicted upon their precious boys.

"Harry Blake is wealthy. Harry Blake has a substantial personal liability insurance policy. Anything you agree to pay these mamas will go unnoticed by Harry Blake. The compensation you grant will be your choice knowing full well the only impact of this compensation will be on these poor mamas. I know full well you will do the right thing."

Mack took his wrinkled jacket from the back of his chair and stepped behind Harry and put a hand on each of Harry's shoulders and stared at the ceiling for a moment. He then slowly walked toward the jury box.

Mack: "Folks, pardon me if I seem distracted. I thought after hearing what I just heard I had been transported somehow into another courtroom and another case. But as I refocus, I see you are the same folks who have been here today, Judge Henry is still there. No, this is the same place, and I now realize my opponent must have picked up the notes of another case. He is such a good lawyer; how could he forget what happened to the Blake family on that horrific night?

"I want you to put yourself there. You and your wife and your little dog have settled in to enjoy some TV. Now you're 72 years old, and you find yourself getting chilled more often as you get older. Not to mention your wife is always warm and keeps your house extra cool. I'd say that probably happens in more than the Blake house, wouldn't you?" A number of jurors nod in agreement. Mack unbuttons his jacket and smiles, "I thought so. So Harry gets out of his easy chair and heads for their bedroom to get a sweater. As he enters the hallway to their bedroom, he hears an explosion of a shotgun blast and sounds of glass and wood shattering in his foyer. He steps back and sees two masked men, armed, trying to get through his shattered front door.

"Now, I want to pause for a moment to make a critical point. Pay attention now. A big deal was made about Harry Blake being a trained killer. Even though it was 50 years ago, Mr. Abernathy's made a big deal out of it. Now he is a smart man, and he was right. Yes, he was right but for the wrong reason. His training and instincts from his past kicked in, and that, folks, is why Harry Blake is here with us today. Even though I don't see any 72-year-olds on the jury, could you have survived a shootout with two armed 20-somethings? I know my answer is – my background has not prepared me for anything like that. So let's you and I agree that Harry Blake's military experience is not a detriment but as Harry so eloquently said God's grace had Harry prepared to survive the savage attack.

"Now let's clear up another point about Harry Blake hiring these boys to kill his wife. Harry and Maggie Blake had been married 46 years, five children, ten grandchildren and four great-grandchildren. I don't think so. But let's look at another fallacy in this thinking. If they were hired by Harry, do you think one man would have stood still while Harry killed his partner? Remember one man was shot with a shotgun and another with a revolver. What about the blood trail, one man in the hallway and the other in the bedroom? I don't think they posed for their deaths, do you?"

Mack walked back to his table and removed his jacket and hung it on the back of his chair. He then walked to one end of the jury box and walked slowly to the other end and back to the center.

"I want to apologize to y'all cause I'm gonna have to get ugly to make my point. Now, I know children are precious to their mamas, but when those two men turned the lights off in their van and came down the Blake's driveway, they were pure savages. They were animals. They blew the front door open and didn't warn or instruct the Blakes in any way, shape, or form. No, they murdered Maggie Blake in cold blood. They blew the blouse off her body, opening up her chest, revealing blood and bone. There was nothing precious about these savages. And then they came after Harry to do the same to him. But we all know exactly what happened after that."

Tears were flowing from Mack's face. He turned to Harry, "I'm sorry, Harry, that you have had to relive this horrible night." Mack turned back to the jury removed his handkerchief, dried his eyes, and blew his nose.

"My humble apologies to the jury. But things like this upset me. I get mad as hell! The audacity that Harry Blake should compensate savages and animals, for crying out loud. Harry Blake should be compensated for his loss.

"You folks are part of our Polk County family, and we are good people for the most part in this county. I know full well you will not, I say again, will not add insult to injury to Harry Blake by having him pay one red cent for the deeds of savages. Folks I trust you to do the right thing."

Roscoe watched Mack walk back to his table and wink at Harry. Roscoe knew in his heart he had been done in again by the little redhead.

The jury was out for two hours and the verdict was no compensation. One juror said that they needed only 20 minutes to reach a verdict, but they stayed only for appearance sake.

When the trial was over, Roscoe actually made the first move and came over to Mack, offered his hand, and congratulations. Roscoe turned to Harry, extended his hand, and said, "No hard feelings. I only did it to get a little cash for the mamas. I was correct, it would not hurt you."

Harry did not offer his hand; he looked Roscoe in the eyes, "Get away from me, you are truly one pathetic person."

Roscoe started to respond, but Mack stepped in and said, "Best be on your way Roscoe, nothing to be gained here. Go lick your wounds." Roscoe turned and silently left the court.

The courtroom was now empty except for four people. Harry and Mack still at their table and Clay and Andy making their way to congratulate them. Andy walked straight to Harry embraced him, kissed him on the cheek, and put her arm in his.

"Congrats gents, Mack you were great again and old Harry was pretty damn good support," Clay said looking at his sister holding on to Harry.

"Thanks, Clay and you are correct, Harry was superb," Mack said also looking at Harry and Andy.

Harry said, "Thank y'all, I'm glad it's over. Let's go celebrate. I have some very expensive bubbly already chilled in my office."

Chapter 31

The four left through the private back entrance to the court to avoid the press who were being held captive by Roscoe. Roscoe was explaining he knew he would probably lose but he felt an obligation to try to help these poor women. He had made sure they knew he had done the work pro bono and he had hinted about expanding his role as a public servant.

The four drove separately to Mack's office, and since it was now almost 6:00 pm the office had closed, and Mack took out his keys to unlock the door only to find out it was not locked. Mack stood there momentarily shaking his head. Clay's mind went law enforcement way and immediately thought foul play. Mack turned to the others and said, "My sweet niece didn't lock up when she left. God bless her, she's clueless."

Clay said, "Maybe she's still here waiting on you."

"I wish, but no car out here," Mack said opening the door and turning on lights which were all off. "Let's go into the conference room, my office is a mess."

He directed them down a hallway to a big, plush conference room. He went to the other side of the room through a door to a fully equipped kitchen. He removed a bottle of champagne and got four crystal champagne flutes from a cabinet. Mack poured four glasses, and Clay insisted he make two toasts. "First, to Mack Peters, for keeping his streak alive by taking old Roscoe apart again. May the streak never end. And then to my friend, Harry Blake, until today I always wondered how a guy from a three-piece suit background could have done what you have, but now I understand. To my friend, the former special ops guy."

They all added their cheers and Harry spoke, "Come on Clay, that was 50 years ago. I don't ever like to think about those days."

"Some things, Harry, are like learning to ride a bicycle. Once you learn, you never forget," Mack added.

"Well, my thought is you were both terrific today," Andy said, and she placed her hand on Harry's arm which did not go unnoticed by Clay and Mack.

"Andy, I didn't realize you were acquainted with Harry," Mack said.

"Oh yes, Clay introduced us, and we are becoming good friends," she answered.

"I can see that," Mack looked at Harry and finished. "You are a fortunate man Harry Blake to have such good friends as Clay and Andy."

"As usual, you are right, sir," Harry replied and tipped his glass toward Mack.

They emptied the bottle of bubbly and Harry suggested they go to The Lighthouse for dinner and finish the celebration.

Clay said, "I wish I could, but I have to go fill in for one of my men who has a family issue to deal with, but y'all go ahead."

Mack said, "I, too, am committed to a client dinner at my home tonight. Sorry, I know I would have more fun with y'all."

"Well, Harry, I guess you are stuck with me," Andy said with a mischievous smile.

Mack grinned, "Poor ol' Harry, stuck with Andy."

Clay didn't smile, just turned and said, "I gotta go. See y'all later."

The other three sets of eyes exchanged glances, but nobody spoke except to say goodbye.

Harry and Andy were standing at the hostess desk of The Lighthouse waiting to be seated when who should walk straight to them as they were leaving, Pastor Ray Andrews and his wife, Pam.

"Harry, we already heard the good news, congratulations," Pam said while Ray could not or did not take his eyes off Andy.

"Thanks, Pam and let me introduce y'all. Ray and Pam Andrews this is Andrea Wilson. She is Clay Hardaway's sister."

Andy spoke next, "Harry, nobody calls me Andrea, Andy please."

Ray spoke next, "Well, it's easy to see who got all the looks in the family and you sure were right, Harry."

Pam gave Ray the 'look' and he was silenced. The ladies exchanged words, and Ray just stood silently smiling at Harry. Ray invited Harry to bring Andy to church with him, and the two couples parted company.

When Harry and Andy were seated, she said, "What was that about, Harry?"

"Oh, as a pastor, Ray is always inviting folks to church."

"No, no, you know what I mean. The 'you were right' comment."

"Oh, that," he said.

"Yes, Harry, that," she said.

"Well, I told you I talked to Ray about my grieving or the end of it. In the course of that conversation, he asked me if I had met someone and I said yes. Then he asked if she was attractive. And I said more than attractive, she's gorgeous."

Andy blushed and said, "Do all writers exaggerate?"

"Actually Andy, good writers have a keen eye for the truth," Harry said this with a straight face.

"Harry, you are terrible, but you know that already, don't you?"

They finished dinner, and Harry walked her to her car where she promptly embraced him and kissed him on the lips. Not a long kiss but a kiss on the mouth nonetheless. Harry drove home thinking dating when you're older was much more comfortable than he thought it was going to be.

Chapter 32

Harry was a happy man driving home, a great day in court and a genuine sense of progress in his relationship with Andy. As he turned into his driveway, it was lit like daylight which would make Clay and his team happy. Then he stopped in the middle of his driveway. There was a black two-seater Mercedes parked, and then he noticed a suitcase on his front porch.

None of his kids drove Mercedes; he couldn't imagine who would be here without notice. He saw the front door of the Mercedes open, and someone exited the car. When the light revealed their identity, his heart sank to his groin. *Oh no,* he thought. *What in the world is she doing here?*

Zelda Mintz was a friend and neighbor of him and Maggie where they had moved from on the coast. Her husband Jim had been a good friend of Harry's and had died of cancer three years earlier. Zelda had visited him and Maggie about a year ago. Zelda and others from the old neighborhood had come to Maggie's funeral. She had called a couple of times to check on him and the last call, which was a few weeks ago, she said she would like to come by for a visit when she went to the mountains to see her sister. He thought she meant for lunch or a cup of coffee or something. Goodness, her suitcase was on his front steps. What was he supposed to do?

She was standing behind her car waving and waiting for him to finish coming down the driveway. Harry was frozen, how the hell he was going to handle this. He needed time to think. Then Harry had an idea. He grabbed his cell phone, put it to his ear, and eased the car down next to her, stopped, and got out. He spoke into the phone, "Hold on just a minute; Zelda what a surprise. You'll have to excuse me, I'm on a conference call with the west coast. They are still working out there."

She was already putting her arms around him. He half-heartedly hugged her back and gently pushed her back saying, "Let me open the front door for you. Make yourself at home, I'll try not to be too long." He opened the door trying not to notice her suitcase. He eased her in and immediately went back out to his car and pulled into his garage.

He called Andy, and she was halfway to the farm. "Andy, it's Harry, I'm in trouble, and I need your help."

Andy swerved off the road and to a complete stop. She could sense the desperation in his voice, "Harry what's happened, it's not another attack is it?"

Harry realized he had probably just scared her badly, "Andy no, I'm so sorry; I didn't mean to sound so desperate. But I do need your help, I'm in a mess."

She breathed a sigh of relief and said, "Okay Harry, what's happened, my goodness, have you had a wreck?"

"No, no, nothing like that, but I got home, turned into my driveway, and there was a car parked there and a suitcase on my front porch. It was a Mercedes, so I knew it was not one of my kids. Then out steps one of our old neighbors from when we lived on the coast. She and her husband were good friends. We played golf and spent time together."

"Harry, was her husband not with her?" Andy inquired.

"No, no, Jim died over three years ago. She's called since Maggie was killed and said she was going to come by and see me. She has a sister who lives in the mountains which she visits, and I thought she meant to stop by for lunch or coffee but my gracious, her suitcase is on my front porch."

"Harry, it probably got late, and she got tired and decided to see you and get a free overnight. She'll probably be out by mid-morning, relax."

"Andy, you don't know Zelda. She's very aggressive and she's made it quite clear that she wants a husband. I don't ever want a conversation about that."

"Is she ugly, Harry?"

"Well, no, but that's not the point."

"Harry, I think you are taking a lot for granted. Don't you think you could just be imagining this?"

"Well, maybe but I know Zelda, and I think I'm probably correct."

"Where are you and where is she?"

"I'm in my car in the garage, and she's in the house. I told her I was on a conference call with the west coast on the mini-series."

"Harry, I think you need to go in, have a conversation with her, and let her spend the night and move on. My goodness, Harry, you fight off armed gunmen and don't flinch, and you sound frightened to death of a 60 something harmless female."

"Andy, there is no such thing, and I have said that before."

Andy laughed, "And Harry how in the world was I supposed to help you with this situation?"

Now what Harry had thought in his mind seemed much harder to put into words, "Um, well I, I thought that maybe you could come to my house and pretend you were late in coming to spend the night with me. This would then let her know, you know, send the message I'm not available, and I'm committed, you know. I mean Andy, I could sleep in the bathroom or on the floor, she would never know, and I swear you would not be compromised. I know it's a lot to ask and I know I have panicked a bit and I am sorry, but I am desperate."

"Harry, I don't know whether I should be mad or sad. I can't imagine my first time we would spend the night together would be under such devious circumstances."

Harry realized he had screwed up. He didn't know what to say, so he said, "Oh Andy, I'm sorry, I tried to drag you into my problem. I hope you will forgive me. Drive carefully." Harry hung up without waiting for a reply.

Harry left the garage and entered through the kitchen hoping maybe Andy was correct. Maybe his imagination had run amuck.

"Harry, I'm starting to feel like you are not happy to see me. And I didn't think you would mind; I opened us some wine. So, Harry, are you not happy to see me?"

"No, no, Zelda it's these calls on the mini-series. Remember it's still early in L.A. No, Zelda, you really caught me by surprise, you should have called to let me know you were coming."

"Harry, have some of your wine and sit next to me. We need to talk."

Harry's antenna went up, and he tried to put this off as long as possible. First, he washed his hands, then he suggested some cheese and crackers with the wine. Zelda passed, but Harry said he wanted to fix a few, so he stepped into the pantry for crackers. He loitered there until she called.

"Harry, what's taking so long, are you alright?"

"I'm fine, just trying to decide what kind of crackers for the cheese."

He came back, selected the cheese and slowly began to cut slices and match them with the crackers. He made it a tedious process. Running out of things to do, he sat down next to her.

"Harry, are you through with everything because I have some things to say and I don't want to be interrupted."

Harry groaned inside and said, "No, I'm fine. Zelda, I hope you are not going to be too serious." He smiled and tipped his wine glass toward her.

"Well, I am going to be serious, very serious."

Harry felt his stomach turn. "Ever since we talked a few months ago and you said you were no longer in mourning and moving on, I was so happy for you. And, I just couldn't stop thinking about you. Now, this part is very important. I know how religious you are, and I realized it was God sending me a message. He wanted you and me to be together."

"Zelda."

"Don't interrupt Harry, let me finish. You were happy, I was happy for you, and we were both happy together. Then I knew Jim and Maggie were in heaven together and everybody is happy in heaven right. So, when I thought about it, I knew they would want you and me to be happy and together."

Harry was starting to feel light headed. "I was so sure of this. Listen, Harry, I have been looking for a man for well over a year, and there are no good prospects. But Harry, in your case, I already know you very well. I mean we both know each other well. And I like you. You are kind, considerate, charming, good looking, and to tell the truth, I can't wait to have sex with you. Hey, I'm sorry, it's the truth. If we are going to be together, we should have no secrets, right?"

Harry stood up, "Zelda, please!"

"Well, Harry, I wanted you to know how I feel."

"Zelda, you can't just come in here and drop a bomb like this!"

"Harry, neither of us is getting any younger. We don't need to waste time, we already know each other, we just need to start enjoying each other, and I say let's start tonight."

"Zelda, please!"

"Harry don't plead, I'm ready. Harry, please let me lead. You just follow, and I'll make you happy. Okay, here's what we are going to do. First, we take a shower, together, of course, you wash me, I'll wash you, and we go to bed and have sex. And if you don't like it, I'll go home in the morning. I can make you happy, Harry."

"Zelda, you have got to stop this!"

"Harry, do you think I'm ugly?"

"No, of course not."

"So, what's the problem."

"Zelda, I have a life here at the lake."

"Harry, I know that. We will live here. I'll sell my place. Harry, Jim left me so much money, you and I will never spend it all. We can travel first class anywhere we want to go."

Harry had to stop this, but good Lord, she was so determined. So he decided on a different approach.

"Zelda, I can't tell you how flattered I am that you would consider me with such regard. It's just overwhelming. I think we should go to bed and talk again in the morning."

"Sounds good, I'm ready."

"Zelda, I mean separately. You can have the room you had last time you were here, if that's okay."

"Harry, don't you think tomorrow morning would be easier if we shared your bed?"

"No, Zelda, I need time to think, okay?"

Harry finally got Zelda settled in one of the downstairs bedrooms and was back upstairs. He was now exhausted. A full day in court and now this, but he couldn't imagine sleeping. Good Lord, the woman had the rest of his life planned. Plus sex; is this the way older single people acted? He decided he needed a drink. He poured one and went to his office to check emails and try to compose himself and find a way to handle this without hurting her feelings. Maybe she would have a less aggressive attitude in the morning.

Then there was Andy. He wished he could take back the call to her, knowing he must have sounded like a fool. But damn, he was right. Women. Maybe he should just write, cook, fish, and stay the hell away from them all. The fact was perhaps he was not very good with them. But he really was attracted to Andy.

Harry heard a noise and stepped out of his office looked at the other side of the house. He had closed the door to the hallway to the master suite, and there was Zelda wearing hardly anything knocking on the door. She just would not give up.

Harry started toward her determined to send her immediately back downstairs to her bedroom. As he reached the foyer, the doorbell rang, scaring him half to death. He turned to see Andy standing, smiling at his front door. Shit! What should he do now? Zelda had turned; surprised by the bell and the fact that Harry was behind her.

Zelda came out of the hallway and headed as fast as she could back down the stairs but not unseen by Andy. Andy's view was a half-dressed woman running from the direction of Harry's bedroom.

Harry rushed to and opened the front door as Andy was starting back to her car.

"Sorry, so sorry, Harry, I thought you might have been right, and you might need help. Boy, was I stupid and wrong! Have a good night, which it appears you already are."

"Dammit, Andy, stop!"

She stopped, she had never heard that tone from him.

"Andy, you were right. I was right I mean, you were right to come, I needed help big time. I was right about her intentions."

"Harry, she just left your bedroom wearing basically nothing."

"No, no you are wrong, Andy."

"I just saw her, Harry. Hey, Harry, it's okay, you owe me no explanation."

"Will you please let me explain?"

"I told you, not necessary."

"Dammit, woman hear me out."

She stood still staring toward the stairs.

"Andy, listen carefully. You saw her leaving the hallway to my bedroom not leaving my bedroom."

"Right."

"Listen! When did you see me? You saw me coming from my office when I heard her. She had supposedly gone to bed, and after the night I have had, I went to my office for a drink and to try to figure out what the hell to do."

Her expression softened a bit.

"Andy, you were right to come. No, that's wrong. You were an angel to come. I should have never asked. I was wrong. Andy, please don't misread this. Andy, I care about you. I am so thankful for you. I promise you nothing has happened here between Zelda and me. I thought I had finally gotten her to go downstairs on the promise that we would have a serious discussion in the morning."

She turned and started to kiss Harry and then pulled away. "She's at the door, Harry."

Harry turned, and there was Zelda dressed in a robe staring at them. He led Andy inside, and the three of them sat in the great room and talked for over an hour. It was a very unpleasant conversation. Zelda was pissed, trying to ignore Andy as if she were not there. She badgered Harry because he had not told her about 'this woman' before she had emptied her heart and her plan for them, which she still insisted would be the best for Harry. Harry was bolstered by Andy's presence and firmly told her that she was a friend and always would be. He told her he felt he owed her to hear her out, but then it got out of hand when she proposed a new arrangement. He admitted it scared him and he panicked. He apologized for not speaking of Andy and not telling her Andy was coming. He and Andy both knew he could not tell her what he didn't know.

Zelda finally ran out of things to say and went downstairs to bed. They watched her disappear downstairs, and Harry said, "My Lord in heaven, what a day. It seems like it has lasted a week. I'm exhausted."

Andy cocked her head, grinned and said, "Harry, how could you possibly resist her. She is certainly not unattractive with or without clothes. She says she has more money than she can ever spend, and, Harry, just think you would never have to make decisions again."

"Unfortunately, everything you said is absolutely true. I doubt I could make it 24 hours."

"But she obviously cares about you, Harry."

"You know ever since she got over Jim's passing, she has kind of gone man crazy. She's been all about finding a man. She has, of course, been unsuccessful so far. Zelda knows me, and I became a convenient choice. When you think about it, you have to feel a bit sorry for her."

"You are too nice, Harry Blake."

Chapter 33

The next morning, Andy put on her robe and walked from Harry's bedroom to the kitchen and started a pot of coffee. She could hear the sound of light snoring coming from Harry's office. She walked to the door and found Harry asleep on his office couch. He had told her he was going to the upstairs bedroom when he left her the previous night. Harry had insisted he wanted her in his bedroom in case there was more contact with Zelda. She had made it very clear he was welcome to stay, but he had felt it was not the right time after the previous night's events and Zelda still in the house.

Zelda was gone. Andy had not heard her leave. Zelda had left a note on the kitchen island. It was brief.

"Harry, I forgive you and I understand about the other woman. I still believe Jim and Maggie would want you and me to be together. When you come to your senses, you know how to find me."

Love Z.

"Andy, you are a lucky lady."

Andy read the note twice and poured her a cup of the freshly brewed coffee. She thought about the events of the previous evening. She wondered what would have happened if she had not come to Harry's aid. But she didn't dwell on that. He had called her for help. She knew that it was his first instinct to call her. There was something different between them. Every other man she had gone out with more than once, all wanted to bed her. Harry had never tried. She was somehow drawn to him, and she knew even though there had not been a lot of physical things, Harry was drawn to her. Their relationship had grown not like a lightning strike but more like butter melting on warm bread. As time allowed the butter to cover the bread, the two together were far better than either by themselves.

She was thinking more and more that maybe Harry didn't have the physical desire or needs that he did when he was younger. She had already decided if that were true, she had lived for ten years without sex and all the other parts of their relationship were more important. She didn't understand how they had connected the way they did, but she knew for sure they were connected.

Then she was startled; she felt his hands on her shoulders, and he bent and put his face in her hair and kissed her head.

"Harry, I didn't hear you. I thought you were going to the upstairs bedroom." She turned to face him, and he just smiled and kissed her on the lips.

"Good morning, this is such a treat to see you looking beautiful as always in my kitchen at this hour."

"Oh, Harry, I have no makeup, and I know what I look like, I am an old woman."

"An older beautiful woman. Sweetheart, you don't need makeup."

"Stop it, Harry, I know better."

"Have you seen Zelda this morning?"

"She's gone. She left this," handing Harry the note.

He read it put it down and said, "She doesn't give up easily, does she?"

"On the 'other woman' I agree."

Harry laughed, "Did you ever think you would be the other woman?"

"Please Harry, don't go there."

******

Meanwhile, next door Hector and Felipe had settled into a routine that seemed to be working for them. They were using the house on the opposite side of the Blake house than the one they had used on their failed attempt to get the coins. The driveway was like most of the others on the street, steep so you could only see the house's roof from the road. This one even had a sharp left turn at the bottom so they could park their car almost in a line of magnolias.

The lot on the opposite side of this house was wooded and undeveloped. It was perfect. The back had a big deck and screened porch that could be seen from the Blake house. It was the ideal place for them to camp. They left every Wednesday because that was the day the landscapers came. They went in and out only late at night or just before daylight to avoid detections by the neighbors.

Hector had carefully developed a plan he was sure would allow him and Felipe to be able to steal the coins.

Chapter 34

It had been five days since the incident with Zelda, and now Andy had come back to his house and saved him. Harry had talked to Andy twice to tell her what she had done for him had meant so much. He had also called Clay twice but had not made contact. Harry was beginning to think Clay was avoiding him. He wanted to have a serious conversation with Clay about his relationship with Andy. Harry felt he and Andy were about to take their relationship to the next level and he wanted to make sure it would not impact their friendship. Even though Clay had said that he and Andy did not get involved with each other's personal lives, Harry was not so sure that was indeed the case. Maybe Clay was psychic and knew why Harry was calling.

The other sort of interesting thing that had happened was a call from Dan Walker, his neighbor who lived three doors away. Dan and his wife, Myra, ran the HOA for their neighborhood. Dan had called to tell him that there had been a bear sighting within a mile of their community. Dan told Harry most of the people were already gone to their winter homes and only six families were remaining. Dan was suggesting that the men who had handguns should keep them with them when they went out in the mornings to get newspapers or mail. It was not to use the weapons on a bear but to fire a shot to hopefully scare the bear away and secondly alert the other neighbors that there was a bear in the area.

Harry had agreed to participate and began to think about what he would do if the bear didn't run. Surely a handgun would not be much defense against a bear. He wanted Clay's advice on this. Harry was thinking about his long uphill driveway that he walked daily to get to his mailbox and his morning paper. He was absolutely sure he could not outrun a bear. As a matter of fact, Harry didn't think he could outrun anything or anybody.

Hector and Felipe had settled into a comfortable routine on the back porch of Harry's neighbor. Felipe was not entirely satisfied with Hector's plan. He did not want to wait after they stole the coins; he wanted to run as fast as they could. Hector was adamant that was the wrong way to go. However, he had not executed the plan because he was not totally comfortable with their escape plan. He was afraid the law would discover the car and ultimately them. It had been bugging him for weeks. He finally came up with a solution. There was an old logging road less than two miles away. After the neighborhood was fast asleep, they would drive their car down the logging road and hide it. They would walk back in and wait. Then they would make the heist, wait, then walk to the car in the middle of the night and head for Long Island and their new life.

Chapter 35

It was the second morning after the bear sighting, and Harry had his .38 in his jacket pocket as he walked up his long driveway to get his newspaper. He had always considered himself a fairly observant person, but now, since the warning of the bear sighting, he watched and listened carefully to everything around him. Harry had always noticed the rustling of leaves under the giant azaleas that lined his driveway, but now he slowed his walk enough to know if it came from chipmunks or brown thrashers. When he reached the top of his driveway, he scanned not only both ways of his street but the wooded lots of his neighbors' homes.

As soon as Harry started to disappear over the top of his driveway, Hector and Felipe dashed across Harry's driveway and up his front steps. Felipe was first, and as soon as he leaned on the door, it opened. It was not latched and Felipe thought nothing of it, Hector entered and closed the door until it latched. They reached for their prize and began stuffing the box of coins into backpack which would be carried by Felipe.

Harry stepped up on his front porch thinking maybe this bear thing and carrying a handgun to your mailbox was overblown. He pushed on his front door as he always did but the door did not open, it was latched. Now Harry had a quirk with his front door. He never closed the door until it latched when he went for the paper or mail. He closed it just enough to say it was closed. Why, no reason, it was a quirk.

Now, Harry's antenna went up on alert. Maybe it was all the commotion about bears. But no bear latched his door. He opened the door, stepped in, and stood still listening for sounds that might be coming. Sure enough the sound of footsteps on the wooden stairs from Harry's office to the bottom level of the house. Harry rushed toward his office but hesitated as he passed the now empty table where the box of golden coins was displayed. Harry pulled his .38 and sped toward his office. He opened the outside door looked down the stairwell which was now empty. He immediately looked to his right which is the way the intruders had come the last time. Nothing, no sign of anything. He went down the stairs as fast as his aging legs would allow. When he reached the bottom, the patio on the back of his home was empty, but as he looked toward his neighbor's yard on the other side of his house, he saw a man's back supporting a backpack disappear into the magnolias, his first instinct was to fire the .38 at the area. Then he thought better of it. Too far, too late. And, as he thought about it, maybe it was better if they didn't know he knew the way they had gone.

He needed to get to the street to see if he could stop them or at least identify the car. The problem was he didn't have his cell phone; it was on the charger in his office. He was torn should he take the time to get his phone which he needed to call for help or not take a chance on seeing the getaway car.

He opted for heading for the street. He crossed into the neighbor's driveway that he'd used before and went as fast as he could to the road. He looked left and could see the long hill that led out of the neighborhood and the street was empty, so he focused on the right where they would be coming. Nothing, he waited ten minutes and there had been no activity. He walked down the street to his driveway. Everything was quiet. Walking far enough down the driveway, he could see there were no vehicles there. Damn, he immediately assumed they had gotten away. Maybe someone was waiting in a vehicle, and that's how they moved so fast. Normally he would have cut through the magnolias to get to his driveway, but instead, he walked back up his neighbor's driveway and over to his. He needed to get to his phone. That's when he noticed a neighbor Claire Turner walking her dog.

He started down the street toward her, and he saw her begin to cower expressing fear. Then he realized he still had his .38 in his hands.

"Claire, I'm sorry," he said as he put the weapon in his jacket pocket. "The bear thing," he said trying to calm her.

"Dan Walker is an alarmist. We've never had a bear in this community," she said now looking more settled.

"How long have you been out with your dog?"

"Oh, about a half hour, we walked up to the main road and came back," she said curiously as to why he asked.

"Have you seen any car coming or going?"

"Oh no, you know how quiet our little street is unless of course, the sheriffs' cars are invading," she said with a wry smile.

"Thanks, Claire, have a great day," he said turning and heading as fast as he could toward his house.

Harry dialed Clay's direct line, and for the third time in five days, the phone switched to voicemail. Clay was avoiding him. He then dialed 911 and identified himself and the problem and asked to be put through to Clay.

Clay finally answered, and Harry gave him a brief summary of the events of the morning. Deputy Will Jackson was already out and was directed to Harry's. Clay and Al Johnson in separate vehicles headed that way. By phone, Clay directed Will who would arrive first to block the neighbor's driveway that was thought to be the last place the intruder had been seen. Clay and Al using their flashing lights made it to Harry's street in a hurry. Killing their lights as they turned onto Harry's street, they eased along and into Harry's driveway where they found Harry standing on his front porch.

Clay, Harry, and Al huddled, and Clay led the conversation, "Based on what your neighbor said, it appears the man you saw or men you didn't see may still be here close by."

Harry chimed in, "But Clay, there is no vehicle, how do they escape?"

Al added, "Maybe by boat?"

Clay's eyebrows raised and he said, "Al get around back and check out the shoreline and docks. Harry show me where you saw the guy with the backpack go into the trees. Al be careful in the neighbor's yard, we don't know if they are there or not and they may be waiting for us."

Harry said to Clay, "You keep talking like there is more than one but I only saw one."

"It's a hunch, but I think it could be our two missing Guats. Harry, let me go through the trees first and make sure it's safe." Clay eased through the trees and waited a few minutes before he allowed Harry to come through.

"Tell me about the house, where are the entry points."

Harry said, "Let me see, okay front door, of course, side door there that you saw, and of course, the two rear doors you can see. On the other side of the house are stairs that lead to that back deck you can see which lead to that screened porch you can also see."

Clay called Will Jackson and had him come down the driveway and check the front door. In just a few minutes, Will called back and said all looked normal and the door was locked. Clay ordered Harry to stay by the tree line. Clay walked to the side door, checked it, and then did the same thing to the two back downstairs doors. Clay then called Al Johnson and told him to come up from the lake using the tree line for cover and join him and Harry who he had signaled to come to him under the portico of the house.

Clay spoke, "Well, we have checked all the entries to the house except through the big screened porch above us. The big fireplace and shape make it nearly impossible to see if anybody might be hiding there. Harry, Al and I are going up and check it out. Harry, you stay down at the bottom of the stairs. If anybody but me or Al come down those stairs, you stop them."

"You mean you want me to shoot them?"

"Harry, I trust your judgment."

They were ready to go when Clay stopped and sent Al to get three vests.

Hector and Felipe lay on their bellies peeping over the bottom frame of the screen porch. Each time Clay and his team moved, Felipe whispered, "What are we going to do?"

"We are going to stay quiet and still, we know we cannot be seen from the screen door if we stay close to the side of the fireplace. They will look in and not see us and then they will move on."

Felipe wasn't convinced, "Maybe we should just kill the three of them and drive out of here in the sheriff's vehicle."

"Felipe, think man, too much noise. The whole community would be out and about. Relax, be cool man."

Al returned and the three men put on their vests. Clay and Al walked slowly and carefully up the stairs to the deck. They then carefully crossed the deck to the screen door. They looked in and around. Clay put his fingers to his lips to let Al know he wanted no dialogue. Clay pointed to a wicker chair and then pointed down. It was a beer bottle cap sitting against a chair leg. The screen door was locked.

Clay said, "Well, it looks like it is secure." Clay seemed ready to walk away when Al touched Clay's arm and pointed to a place where the screen had been cut at the corner of the door frame. Whoever cut it had done a good job of putting it back the way it was, but it definitely had been cut.

Clay unholstered his weapon and Al followed suit. "Okay men, it's over. We know you are on the porch, and we have you surrounded."

Hector grabbed Felipe's arm as he reached for his pistol. He put his hand on his mouth to signal quiet.

Clay used the barrel of his weapon to push open the cut part of the screen enough to stick a big thick finger on the latch and flick it open. Hector and Felipe new the sound meant they were ready to enter the porch.

"Last warning come out with hands above your head, or we come in and we will not hesitate to shoot you. You have 'til a count of three. One, two,"

"Okay, okay," Hector was on his feet with hands over his head. Felipe reluctantly did the same. Hector had decided jail was a better option than death.

Chapter 36

Everything had been wrapped up by Clay and his team. The coins were back where they belonged, and only Harry and Clay were in Harry's kitchen.

"Damn, Clay, I haven't even had a cup of coffee this morning. What a start to a day. How about a cup?"

"Naw, I got a lot to do, better get going."

"Clay Hardaway, you're avoiding me. Why? We need to talk. Now sit down, have a cup of coffee and talk to me." Harry was showing his frustration.

Clay grimaced as Harry poured two cups of coffee. They both sat at opposite ends of the granite kitchen island.

"Clay, have I done something to offend you?"

"No, not exactly."

"Clay, you and I need to talk about Andy."

He saw Clay's expression, and he knew that was the problem.

"Well, at least I know where our issue lays. Clay, Andy and I have really grown to enjoy each other's company, and I believe we are approaching moving our relationship up another level, but I have sensed this could be an issue with you. Clay, I hope you know I consider you one of my best friends and I would never want to do anything to jeopardize our relationship. And I know having your sister involved could make the situation more sensitive. So please tell me what's going on with you. Please don't hold back. I need to know the truth."

Clay sipped his coffee and stared at the granite top, "You are right, Harry, I need to tell you what's on my mind. I guess with age comes wisdom." Clay said this with a half smirk, half smile.

"Harry, I too consider you my good friend. I guess that's why I have avoided this conversation. I don't have to tell you how I feel about my older sister. She and I are all that's left of our family. Look, at first, I thought this was a good idea. Remember I introduced you to her. I see now how naive I was. Three friends sharing dinners, drinks whatever together. Frankly, because of her age, I would like to see Andy find the right guy to look after her and spend the rest of their lives together. I think Andy deserves that. I would like her to have that. Harry, I wish she could find a guy like you but not one who is 72 years old. I don't think it's right. I don't think it's fair. Hey, if you were 60 and she was 50, I wouldn't even mind. The odds would be in your favor to have a lot of years together. But that's not the case and therein lies my problem.

"Let me just be blunt. If you two get together and just have a few years together and you have a heart attack and die, I'm okay with that. As long as you die. What I don't want to see is you have a stroke or some other long-term debilitating disease where she is left to spend the rest of her life taking care of you and basically getting nothing in return. I'm sorry, I know that's hard and blunt but those are my thoughts, Harry. You are a friend, and I value that, but she is my only family."

Clay finally looked up and looked at Harry.

Harry cocked his head and thought carefully on how to respond.

"Thank you, Clay, for being honest, I truly understand everything you have said and how you feel. But Clay, I think you have jumped way too far ahead. We are not talking about hiring a wedding planner. Thus far our relationship has been very casual and informal. I think we are both ready to spend more quality time together."

"Harry, Harry, Andy just spent the night at your house, that's pretty serious in my book."

"Clay, Andy saved my ass. This woman Zelda put me in a huge bind, and Andy bailed me out. She slept in my bedroom, and I slept on the couch in my office. It was all very innocent, I swear."

Clay shook his head, "So you say."

Harry was now offended, "Are you questioning what I say is untrue? Be careful Clay, she and I are both adults and don't need your permission to do anything." Harry was now standing and very defensive.

Clay now standing said, "I've told you how I feel, I don't think there is more for me to say."

"Clay, Clay, listen to me. I think Andy and I have reached a point where we would like to get to know each other better. Once that happens, who knows maybe she won't allow it to go further or maybe I won't. I'm asking you to withhold your position until we at least get past that point?"

"Harry, that won't be necessary if it doesn't go there."

"Clay, I think that's an unfair position." Harry's tone was now calm and his body language no longer tense.

Clay, still standing was no longer defiant, but simply again staring at the granite top. "I'll think about it, but you think about what I said. Now I've got to go."

"Clay, are you not going to thank me before you go?"

"I'm sorry, Harry, but thank you for what?" Clay said tersely.

"For helping you round up two more bad guys. My coins and I are going to make you man of the year in Polk County." Harry was smiling.

Clay just shook his head, doing his best to hide the smile on his face as he left.

Harry poured himself more coffee and thought about what Clay had said. Maybe he, Harry, had been selfish. He had never allowed himself to think those kind of thoughts. He already cared too much for her not to consider Clay's words.

Chapter 37

Harry spent the entire rest of the day thinking about Andy. Thinking about what Clay had said and all the what-ifs that might happen. The first few hours he tried to convince himself that walking away from a deeper relationship with Andy was the noble and right thing to do. He knew Clay was right about the possible health issues he could have. He now had to figure out the best way to handle this with Andy. Should he talk about the conversation with Clay, probably not? Maybe just say he had moved too fast and he needed more time to get over Maggie. That made more sense, and there was some logic to it.

The weather had turned cold. Winter was arriving. Harry put on his coat and hat and walked down to his dock. The wind had come up, and a few white caps had begun to appear. He sat in one of the wrought iron chairs on the dock and stared across the vast expanse of choppy gray water. The sun that had been bright earlier had now given way to a mass of white, gray, and even some black billowy clouds. Rain was coming for sure. He was beginning to feel sorry for himself. He had been enjoying himself having someone in his life again. He tried to think of some scripture that would apply. The only one he could think of was the one Ray Andrews used about a season for mourning. Maybe his season for having someone special had ended with Maggie. Yes, this was turning into a good pity party.

The cold air and wind were urging Harry to go back to the warmth of his house. Then there was a voice in his head as clear as any he ever heard, "Hey, Harry, now that you know where you are going, why don't you call Dobbins and take care of your funeral arrangements. You can save your kids from the trouble." There was a chuckle from the voice, "Yessir, now that you are throwing in the towel, might as well, Harry."

"No, damn you," Harry said this out loud. "No damn way!" he shouted as he walked up the hill to his house. Screw Clay Hardaway. Clay was his friend, but he was wrong, and Harry intended to set him straight. Harry got into his car and drove straight to Clay's office. After all the research he had done there, he was comfortable going straight to Clay's office without being announced or escorted.

Clay was at his desk doing some sort of paperwork when Harry walked in and closed the door behind him.

"We need to talk," Harry said this in an apparent agitated tone. Clay didn't speak, he just pointed at the chairs in front of his desk.

"Clay, you were dead wrong in our earlier conversation regarding Andy and yours truly. Every point you made might happen, but it might happen to your sister. Once we all pass 50, all kinds of things can happen. How 'bout Andy's first husband? How old was he when he passed, 47, 48. People our age know these things can happen. Hell, Clay, in your line of work, how many people younger than us are crippled or killed in all sorts of accidents. I refuse to live my life being afraid to live and love. You told me you and Andy stay out of each other's lives, and I believed you when you said it. I think you have made a mistake and I'm here to tell you I'm moving forward. Who knows, it may go nowhere but right now, I hope it does. Finally, as far as I'm concerned, our conversations are off the record as far as Andy's concerned. I don't think it would do much for your relationship with her. Clay, you are my friend, and I don't want to lose that. I hope our relationship won't change." Harry found himself leaning forward on the edge of his chair, so he slid back and sat silent.

Clay stared at Harry with a blank expression on his face. After a period of silence, he finally spoke. "Are you through?"

Harry just nodded.

"I have always heard, the older we get, the more wisdom we have. I guess it's true because, Harry, you are a truly old fart." Clay said this as he finally grinned.

"Harry, I hate to say this, but I was wrong. I don't need to be in Andy's business nor yours for that matter. You are correct, only the good Lord knows what is in store for us in the future. We all just have to keep on keeping on and do the best we can. We are friends and this won't change a thing. And by the way, thanks for keeping this away from Andy. If she knew, she'd probably kill me."

Chapter 38

Harry couldn't wait to get back home and call Andy. What had started out as a disastrous day had ended as good as he could have ever hoped. His friendship with Clay was an important part of his life, and he felt that was as secure as ever. He was excited about the next step with Andy.

When he got home, it was almost 6:00 pm and the rains had begun. Andy should be through for the day, so he called while pouring a celebratory drink. He got her voicemail and left a message. The wind picked up with the rain and Harry decided a fire would be in order. He fixed leftovers for dinner and now at almost 8:00 pm he had not heard from Andy. He called again and once again got her voicemail. At 10:00 pm he was ready for bed but had still not heard from Andy. He tried again, but this time he left no message.

At 8:30 am the next morning he was in his kitchen working on his second cup of coffee and reading the Kindle version of the Atlanta newspaper when his doorbell rang.

His first thought was that Clay was stopping by as he sometimes did. He walked to the front door and was surprised but pleasantly so, to see Andy. He opened the door to see her in black slacks, yellow silk blouse and high heels, gorgeous. He was prepared for a big hug and kiss, but all he got was a quick smile as she walked past him toward the kitchen.

"Harry, I hope you have coffee," she said walking into the kitchen and not looking at him.

"Of course I do. And what's up with you dressed up like a million dollars."

"Harry, we need to talk or rather I need to talk to you." She poured her own coffee and sat down on the stool next to Harry's coffee and Kindle.

Harry looked puzzled, "This must be important for such an early visit and especially the attire."

"Harry, it is. I'm going away."

"Oh yeah, where are you going."

"I'm going to Ocala, Florida and a 700-acre world-class horse farm and training facility."

"Great, do you have a new customer?"

"No, Harry it's an existing customer. Let me explain. Do you remember the two client horses I had when you toured my barn? I don't know if you remember, but I told you the horses were there to be trained for two girls in the family that owned them. Well, there is a lot more to this story. Do you know the name, John Winstone?"

"Yes, I think I do, oil, natural gas multi, multi rich. That one?"

"That's correct. His son Jack and my husband did some business together and we got to know each other as a result. Jack had married a beautiful model and had two girls in the first two years they were married. Shortly afterward, she died of cancer. Jack has raised the two girls and never remarried. The girls got older and got interested in horses and Jack remembered me and what I did and he contacted me and asked if I would get involved with his two girls and teach them what they needed to know and help pick out and train their horses. I was delighted, of course.

"Jack and the girls have been in and out of here quite a few times since I started a year ago. Jack had come to my husband's funeral, so it has been a bit more than the normal client relationship. I've gotten to know the girls quite well, and we get along great. The four of us have been to dinner quite a few times, and I always assumed it was for the benefit of the girls. Last night we all flew on his plane to Atlanta for dinner. Only the girls went to visit friends there. Jack and I ate alone, and Jack has asked me to come to Ocala to this new investment of his. He wants me to help him make sure everything is done right there plus continue to work with the girls. To be perfectly honest, Harry, he has also said he would not object to our relationship being more than just business. Harry, I was completely taken by surprise."

"How old is Jack?" Harry asked now becoming distressed.

"He is my age, Harry, but I hope you know that doesn't matter to me."

"Andy, when will you be back?" Harry inquired.

"I have no timetable."

"But Andy, what about your place?" Harry said almost pleading.

"Juan can handle everything and Clay has agreed to help. And before you ask, this truly has all just happened in the last few days and this is the first Clay knows of it."

"Andy, I don't know quite what to say. To say that I'm disappointed would be an understatement. I really felt like you and I were ready to take another step forward, but I guess I misread that." Harry said glumly.

"No, Harry, I don't think you did. There is just so much here to consider. The opportunities with the ranch are limitless."

"Not to mention a man with limitless wealth."

"Harry, that's unkind," she said in a defensive tone.

"Sometimes, Andy, the truth is what it is. But if this is what makes you happy, then God Bless you girl."

"Harry, I wish I could stay and talk, but I have to be at the airport in an hour," she said getting up to leave.

"Hey, I understand; you can't keep those private jets waiting," he said in his best monotone.

"Harry, we will talk again," she said, leaving without a hug or embrace.

"Sure we will," he said silently. For the first time, he noticed she was riding in a black limo. Harry stood at the door watching as the limo disappeared over the top of his driveway. He stood there paralyzed, couldn't move. His thoughts were jumbles. He had been transported into some other unreal world. He was jolted back to reality when he heard the door slam on the big Tahoe and see Clay climbing his front steps.

Clay opened the front door and let himself in as Harry just stood silently. "I know she's been here, Harry, I passed the limo on the way here. Harry, I know you must be pissed at me, but I wanted to see you and explain as best I can."

Harry looked Clay in the eye and said, "This must be a happy day for you Clay, too bad you had to come here and see me and mess it up. And, by the way, you don't owe me any explanation. If you want to turn around and leave, it's okay with me." Harry turned and walked to the kitchen without an invitation for Clay to follow.

But Clay did follow and without invitation, poured himself a cup of coffee and refilled Harry's cup without a word being spoken. "Harry, I want you to open your ears and your mind and listen to what I have to say. First, this is not a joyful day for me. I didn't know she was leaving until late last night; correction, it was early this morning. And to set the record straight, I advised against her going so fast. I told her to slow down, be sure she had carefully thought through everything.

"Here's what I know, Andy has known Jack Winstone and his two girls for quite a while. It's been more than a regular client relationship because of their past history. Jack and the girls have been coming to Andy's for well over a year. The girls are, I'm not sure, but 14 or 15, I think. A lot of the time, Jack would drop the girls off, leave them for a week or so at a time. The girls have been primarily raised by nannies because Jack travels so much. I know you will understand this; the girls have just fallen in love with Andy. They love being with her. Now Jack spoils these girls. Maybe guilt, maybe love, perhaps both.

"This is what Andy told me three days ago. She told me the girls were there with her and Jack would come by for dinner with them. He had told her he had bought this big ass thoroughbred farm in Ocala. In case you don't know, that's big horse county. He told Andy he, of course, knew nothing about horses or horse farming and he wanted her to come to Ocala and run the farm. He would give her free reign and an unlimited budget. The girls would relocate, and they could be together full time. Naturally, the girls were very excited about the prospects. He told her there was an estate house where he and the girls would reside but there was also an operations manager's cottage, which would be her residence. She could totally remodel it or tear it down and build exactly what she wanted.

"Harry, when they were alone, he told her how he had been attracted to her for quite a while and hoped after they spent more time together, she might consider a closer relationship with him, and maybe join him in the estate house and the four of them become a family. Harry, he is going to pay her a huge salary and she'll have free reign over this sizable enterprise. She was just blown away. So she had three days of these girls chipping away at her about how excited they were and how great it was going to be plus Jack putting on the big sell. Finally, the jet to Atlanta for a romantic dinner, it was just too much. Harry, she just was overwhelmed."

"Harry, the reason I didn't mention this to you when we had our conversations was that I truly did not think she would do this. I found out she was going in the wee hours this morning when she called to tell me the details. Please believe me, Harry, I made a misjudgment. If I had thought she would do something like this so fast, I would have called you and asked you to help me try to convince her to say no." Clay finally stopped talking and waited for Harry to comment.

Harry was sitting on one of the kitchen stools and just sat there staring at the floor.

Clay waited for Harry to speak but after a few minutes he spoke again, "Harry, I hope you believe I am telling you the truth."

Harry spoke, "It doesn't matter. That's not true, it does matter. You are my friend and I do believe you. Plus, the truth is, Clay, it's a hell of an opportunity. Think about it, she's going to be the boss of this substantial enterprise. It's something she loves and can make big money. She likes the girls and maybe she will end up as the wife of a very wealthy man. And Clay, he's not an old fart like me."

"Harry, that's nasty."

"Sorry, it just came out."

Chapter 39

Andy knew she had made a terrible mistake. She had handled the meeting and conversation in the worst way. God, how could she have been so cold and distant? She knew very well something was developing between them. There was some kind of chemistry, and whatever it was it had been growing, and no doubt would be taking the next step had she not upset the apple cart.

She said to herself, she was not having second thoughts about her decision to go to Ocala, but it was the way she had handled it with Harry. That was the problem she was almost sure. She decided to call Clay and get his update on his visit with Harry. She phoned but only got voicemail. This gave her no comfort. She asked the limo driver if they had time to turn around and go back to Harry's house. He told her no, that with morning traffic he would have to push hard to make it on time. Harry must think her to be an awful fickle person.

The whole thing had been unbelievable. To be her age and have an offer to be in total control of a world-class horse farm. To be associated with a dynamic businessman like Jack Winstone was a fascinating proposition. Even though she had casually known Jack from their past and then the infrequent visits to get updates on his girls, she never realized what a charming and personable man he could be. Not to mention the fact that he was also quite good looking. Then there were the girls, they had hit it off from the beginning. They were hungry for a mother figure and her having had no children of her own was the perfect fit. Surely Harry could understand, couldn't he? Maybe she thought if she had spent more time with Harry. Perhaps, if she had given him a chance to say more. She needed to make amends but not by phone.

As the limo was nearing the airport, her cell phone rang, and it was Clay.

"Clay, how is Harry? What did he say? Is he terribly upset? Clay, I handled it very poorly."

"Hold on sis, it will be fine. Harry is a tough old bird. He will get over it. Face it, y'all were just starting to get to know each other. It can't be that big of a deal. Can it?"

Andy paused, she could tell Clay did not understand the feelings she and Harry shared. Then she thought it was probably understandable based on what she was doing.

"Clay, would you mind keeping me updated on Harry?"

"Sure, but I don't think you are going to have much time to think about Harry. You will be so busy and be having so much fun with your new life, Harry will just be an old memory. By the way, I am going to the farm to meet with Juan today so we can get an understanding of how we will communicate and operate. It's all going to be fine. Andy, don't worry."

Chapter 40

Andy entered the lobby of the FBO at Ocala Jet Port where she was greeted by the Winstone teenagers, Jenny and Jane. They could hardly contain their enthusiasm to see Andy and have her at their new home.

The luggage was loaded in a big gray SUV with 'Shadow Lake Farm' written above the image of a lovely blue lake below the name. The drive took twenty minutes. The first thing Andy noticed was at least one-half mile of a bright white fence line that ran to an archway topped by the same logo as the big SUV. The paved drive was two-lanes at the arch for about a hundred yards before it narrowed into a standard sized two-lane roadway. There was fenced pasture on both sides of the entrance road. The land was slightly inclined and peaked at a circular drive that fronted a structure that looked to Andy as if it could be a small hotel. The SUV circled and stopped in front of massive double doors that were now opening to reveal a robust looking woman wearing a dull gray dress. She was accompanied by a man and young lady who were dressed in black and white. The girls told Andy the lady in gray was Ms. Spurgeon, who was in charge of the house.

The SUV doors were opened and Ms. Spurgeon introduced herself and her two assistants. The young man was starting to unload the bags when Andy stopped him, "Those bags need to go to the house where I am going to be staying."

Ms. Spurgeon had signaled the man to keep unloading and spoke to Andy, "Ms. Wilson, Mr. Winstone has decided you should stay here until Mr. Langley has completely moved out of that house and you have had time to do your remodeling."

Andy was caught off guard, "Who is Mr. Langley?"

"Dax Langley is the manager of Shadow Lake Farms."

"Is he continuing his employment?"

"Oh, yes ma'am, I doubt anyone could properly replace Dax. Mr. Langley has been here since the place was built 18 years ago."

"Well, where is he moving to?"

"Oh, he will displace one of his foremen. There are four employees houses here."

"I think you should tell him not to move any more of his things until I can talk to Jack. This is not what I expected."

"Miss you can tell him yourself. He will be joining you for lunch here in less than an hour. Mr. Winstone said it was best you two meet just as soon as you arrived." Ms. Spurgeon turned to the girls and said, "Jenny, Jane why don't you two show Miss Wilson to her room."

The two girls each took one of Andy's hands and led her to a big winding staircase. "Stairs or elevator? Which do you prefer?"

"Oh, let's walk, I get to see more that way." The stairs were double entry and formed a heart shape and overlooked the considerable foyer which was more like a giant lobby. When they arrived at her room, the young man with her luggage was already there. He had taken the elevator. They entered the room which was more like a suite than a room. There was a large sitting room with a desk and chair. There was a bar with four stools and a large-screened TV. Beside the bar was a powder room. On one end of the sitting room was a door that led to the bedroom and bathroom, the other end of the sitting room was another door which Andy would soon find out led to Jack Winstone's master suite. There, double doors leading outside to a porch from both the sitting room and the bedroom. When Andy walked outside, the view was spectacular.

Below, on the ground floor was a large patio which led to a swimming pool. On both, the left and right side of the pool, were massive gardens with flowers and plants that all seemed to be in bloom. Beyond the gardens that encircled the pool, she could see the large horse barn and the ¾ mile dirt track. Beyond that, the pastures ended on high ground. Andy assumed there was a lake and more pastures over the hill. She also noticed the porch extended to Jack Winstone's suite. As if reading her mind, the older girl Jenny said, "Daddy said he wanted you next to him in case you needed anything." The younger girl Jane chimed in, "Are you and Daddy going to have a romance?"

Andy blushed, "Jane, I'm here to work on the ranch and take care of horses and teach you two girls how to be fine horsewomen." Andy couldn't help but wonder what Jack had told the girls. She did not like the fact that she had been placed so close to Jack's quarters. And what about her private house? And what about Harry? She couldn't stop thinking about how poorly she had handled their last visit.

At that moment the young man who had brought up her luggage reappeared and announced it was time for her to go down for lunch.

"Are you girls joining me for lunch?"

Jenny answered, "No, Ms. Spurgeon said he wanted you and Mr. Langley to have a private lunch, so you could get to know each other better."

Andy responded without thinking, "Your daddy thinks of everything, doesn't he?"

Both girls started shaking their heads and Jenny said, "Oh yeah, you just wait and see."

Even though Christmas was nearing, the Florida weather allowed the lunch service to be set on a screened porch in sight of the pool and gardens. A table for two had been arranged with a fresh flower arrangement in the center of the table. The young man who led her there seated her and left.

Dax Langley was an imposing looking man. He entered the porch wearing a straw cowboy hat, western shirt, jeans, and freshly shined cowboy boots. As he entered, he removed his hat and the toothpick that had been in his mouth. He had a barrel chest and stomach. His spiny legs and rear end didn't seem to match his upper half. Dax was over 6' and had to weigh at least 250 lbs.

"Ms. Wilson, I'm Dax Langley, the manager of Shadow Lake Farm." Andy stood and offered her hand but before she could speak, Dax spoke again, "No, no, please sit we don't need to be too formal 'round here." He said this as he waved off her hand and sat himself down.

A server in the meantime poured water and offered mint iced tea. Dax spoke again, "Oh please, spare me the mint iced tea. Just bring me some black coffee if you can."

"Mr. Langley," Andy started but was interrupted. "Now Ms. Wilson, we ain't gonna have to be formal, I hope. I'm Dax to everyone who knows me."

"Okay, that's fine, and I am Andy to everyone who knows me."

Dax grinned, "Andy, I always thought that was a boy's name."

"It's short for Andrea."

"Oh, I see. okay."

"Dax, you and I have a number of subjects to talk about."

"Yes ma'am we do."

"Let's start with the house. Jack never told me you were living there."

"Yes ma'am, about ten years now."

"Please don't do anything else toward a move until I talk to Jack. I don't think this is right."

"Well Andy, Jack was pretty damn clear he wanted my ass out of there."

"Well just wait, okay, I want to discuss this with Jack."

"Whatever you say, but Jack don't seem like the type to change his mind much. But, of course, I don't know exactly what your relationship is with Jack." Dax said raising his eyebrows and smiling.

Andy said, "Let's move on. How long have you been at Shadow Lake, Dax?"

"Oh, about 18 years or so. When I came, Shadow Lake was just raw land with a big lake in the middle. I helped lay everything out. You know like where this house is, the stables, the track and things you can't see from here, like what I call the working barn and sheds, the growing fields, cow pastures, and even the airstrip."

"Airstrip, why in the world do you have that?"

"Well, from time to time we get supplies. We have a few folks that visit by small plane and sometimes we even make trips in our little plane."

"Tell me, Dax, what did Mr. Winstone tell you my role would be at Shadow Lake?"

"He said you would probably be doing several things. One, he said you were training two horses for his girls. Two, he said you were teaching the girls how to be good riders. He said you were going to remodel my house and might even live in it. Although he wasn't sure about that, since you might decide to stay here at the main house. He said you might have some suggestions for me on how to improve the operation here. Andy, can I be blunt and ask you some questions?"

"Of course."

"How much do you know about cattle ranching and raising cattle?"

"Very little, why?"

"Do you not know we have a sizable cattle operation here?"

"No, I guess I didn't."

"Do you know about farming, growing crops?"

"A little."

"We do that too."

"Do you know thoroughbred racehorses?"

"Well, I have done some work with them."

"I'm talking real racehorses."

"Not really."

"If I might say so, how the hell are you gonna make suggestions about things you don't know a damn thing about?"

Andy was saved by the food service. The conversation changed to food and halfway through lunch, she had no appetite. She stood and said, "It was nice meeting you Dax, but I am not feeling well and I need to be excused." She left without giving Dax a chance to speak.

She went to her quarters and locked the door. Her mind was in thought overload. How could she have been so naive? She had always been a thoughtful person. Her instincts had usually been good, cautious, and stable. She started to think when had she jumped before she was absolutely sure it was safe? Maybe with Harry a little bit. But she had nothing but pleasant, positive surprises with him.

One thing for sure, she had turned her brain over to Jack Winstone, and he had made her feel good about it until now. But she knew full well it wasn't Jack's fault, it was hers. How could she have not asked more questions and done more research? Why did everything have to move so fast? That, she was not understanding was Jack Winstone's world. She was at the double doors of her sitting room when she noticed a note on the bar. She opened it and it read, *Mr. Winstone apologizes. He has been delayed in South America and will not be able to be here for at least five more days. He wants you to relax for a few days and get to know Shadow Lake Farm. He looks forward to being here with you.*

Her first reaction to the note was not good, but after thinking about it for a few minutes she changed her mind. Yes, that's exactly what she would do. She would relax, spend time with the girls, and get to know Shadow Lake Farm.

Chapter 41

Harry spent the next several days preparing his speech for the Women's group and trying to make a dent in his Christmas shopping. Only three weeks away and a large part of his family would be descending on him. One thing he didn't have to worry about was introducing Andy to his clan. What a shame, he had looked forward to the introduction even though he knew there would be ruffled feathers and hurt feelings.

The day finally came for Harry's speech to the Women's Business Owners group. Harry was apprehensive, not because of his speech, he was well-prepared and had dealt with the subject for over 30 years. No, he was anxious because with Andy gone, he knew absolutely no one there.

The meeting was held in the banquet room of The Mountain View Inn and Restaurant. Harry arrived 30 minutes early as was his style. When he walked into the banquet room, he was met by a very attractive petite blonde who introduced herself as Betty Matthews, the current president of the organization. She explained the agenda and the fact that Harry would be last and could speak and then have a period for Q&A and later they would be dismissed for a group lunch which she encouraged Harry to attend.

There were twenty women business owners without Andy. Most brought at least one and some up to three of their employees. There were about 40 women, ten men, and then numerous representatives of the press. As Mack Peters had said, there were not many celebrities in Polk County and Harry was one.

Betty Matthews called the meeting to order, and Harry could see why she was chosen to be their leader. She was self-confident, knowledgeable and moved quickly, but thoroughly through their agenda. She had explained to Harry earlier that Andy had sent her the biographical introduction for Harry. She also added that she understood he and Andy were dating. Harry quickly responded they were just friends and he had wished her the best in her new endeavor. Betty added that they were all going to miss her as she was sure Harry would.

Betty introduced Harry and he was greeted with a warm response. Harry spoke on 'Standards' with a strong emphasis on the fact that it did not matter the sex of the owner, only that if it was worth the effort, it should be what the owner wanted it to be. Harry spoke in some detail for a little over 30 minutes. He got a standing ovation when concluded and opened the floor for questions. The questions, for the most part, were good and thoughtful. Betty Matthews closed the session with the final question.

"Mr. Blake are you available for one on one consultations?"

At one point in his retirement, Harry had considered consulting but had forgotten about it when he started writing. But with only a slight hesitation he answered affirmatively.

Before Betty could finalize the end of the meeting, someone from the press asked if they might ask some questions? Betty who was now standing next to Harry leaned up next to him and whispered, "If you don't want to do this, I can handle shutting it off."

Harry was impressed with her thoughtfulness and her self-confidence. He was also impressed with how good she smelled. He told her it would be okay.

Harry said, "I'll take a few, but remember I think everybody has heard enough from me and are ready to eat."

The first question was about the release of the mini-series which Harry explained there was no date set.

The second questioner wanted to know if he was still writing and if so, when would there be a new book. Harry responded that he was writing but too soon to know. He explained the subject and said the plot was still developing.

The third question, did he have any comments about his recent court case. Harry replied that results speak for themselves.

The fourth question was about the various attacks at his home. Harry stood silent for several minutes and then said, "No comment."

He turned toward Betty, and she immediately said, "We are dismissed to the dining room."

The reporters were now shouting for more questions, but Betty took Harry by the arm and escorted him to the dining room.

There were so many interruptions during lunch, it was hard to carry on a conversation. When the room finally cleared, Betty and Harry were the only ones left.

Betty said, "Harry I would like to talk to you about a consulting arrangement. I've known for a while my business needs some help, but after hearing you today, I know for sure I need some help. Maybe just a fresh set of eyes at what I have."

"Betty just let me know when you would like to sit down and talk, and I'll do my best to accommodate you."

"Are you free this afternoon?"

"I am, having never been to one of your meetings. I wasn't sure about the timing, so I didn't plan anything else. Would you like me to follow you to your business?"

"Actually no, I don't want to alarm any of my employees. I'm afraid they might think I'm going to sell the place."

Harry looked at his watch and spoke, "I understand. It's 2:30 in the afternoon; I bet the lounge is empty and quiet. Would you like to try there?"

"That's a great idea, Harry."

"Okay, we will see."

They walked to the lounge at the inn and sure enough only the bartender setting up for his afternoon happy hour.

Harry spoke, "Excuse me, would you mind if we used that booth in the back where it's quiet to talk a little business?"

The bartender said, "Help yourselves," but he was thinking business maybe monkey business.

Harry spent the next thirty minutes explaining how he would conduct business. He told her that in his business life he had been responsible for over 60 acquisitions. He had a good model for putting a value on businesses. As a part of this, he would expose the good, bad and ugly of the enterprise. He explained that he would start with one on one meetings with all of the employees to reassure them their jobs weren't in jeopardy and to get their input on the business.

When he finished, Betty was comfortable going forward but was concerned about Harry's fee.

Harry laughed and explained that he was not in the consulting business but if he were able to help, he would accept a nice dinner from her.

She laughed too, shook her head and changed the subject.

"Harry, did you know Andy and I were good friends?"

"No, I didn't."

"Well, we were. Polk County is not well-populated, and Lakeview is a small town. She was a widow, and I was a divorcee. My husband left me about seven years ago for a young sweet thing 15 years my junior. Johnny always loved to gamble. He could always find a card or dice game anywhere. Our vacations were always to Vegas or Reno. He finally went over the edge. He would disappear for days at a time. I had my fill and after another two days of absence, he showed up with divorce papers. I ended up with the business, the house, and the bank accounts. That's all I could hope for. I'm sorry I have really gone off subject. I'm sure you have no interest in hearing my sordid history.

"Anyway, Andy and I were close to the same age in a small town trying to run a business, although I'm pretty sure Andy's survival didn't necessarily depend on her business success. But Andy is Andy, and she worked at it like it was necessary. We met and got to know each other and decided to do the WBO groups which as you saw today has had a nice amount of success. Andy and I have done many nice shopping trips together. We have been to New York, Atlanta and several times to the state capital. We have had a lot of nice times."

Harry spoke up smiling, "I bet you have. You, two beautiful mature women, had to turn some heads."

"Thank you for the compliment, Harry. I can assure you we were always on our best behavior," she said tilting her head and batting her eyelashes.

"Oh, I'm sure you were," Harry replied laughing. "And, Betty, you have never remarried?"

"No, I guess I have been a lot like Andy. The pickings are slim out here in the foothills."

"How about a special guy?"

Betty's expression turned serious, "No, I just got gun shy after Johnny. I really thought we had a good marriage. I was doing a good job of taking care of him and then out of nowhere… Hey, it is what it is, as they say. Let me ask you something? I got the impression that maybe you and Andy were more than just friends. Any truth to that?"

Harry turned serious and stared at the bar. "Well, it may have been heading that way with more time. But let's just leave it at, we were just good friends."

"Well, Harry it seems we have both lost a good friend. Maybe you and I will turn out to be good friends," she said as she squeezed his arm.

"Maybe so," Harry said smiling.

Chapter 42

Two days after Harry had committed to helping Betty Matthews with a business review, he was ready. It had been a few years since he had been involved with any business other than his own personal issues. He had crafted an outline of what he would do and in what order. After several tweaks, he was ready to go.

He arrived at the location before business hours and began an inspection of the property and exterior of the building. Betty had assured him she had briefed all of her employees on why he would be there and sure enough, as they arrived for work, they all waved and gave him a friendly smile.

The business was the only equipment rental business in the county. Some of the big box stores offered some limited number of items but they were not really a threat. Betty's ex, Johnny, had opened the business after they were first married and his propensity for gambling and carousing put him in with a lot of 'good ol' boys' who were contractors, sub-contractors, builders, and tradesmen. They, in turn, were a solid base for his business. When Johnny had run off, they all felt bad for Betty and assured her not only would they continue to support the company, but they would also encourage others to do so. A number of them, mostly married, also volunteered to fill in for Johnny as far as her love life was concerned. Betty Matthews was a beautiful lady.

When Harry had finished outside, he had a half page of recommendations. Inside, Harry did one on one private interviews with each of Betty's employees. When he had completed the interviews, he did an inspection of the inside of the building. When that was complete, he went to Betty's office. He knocked on the open door frame. "Do you have time for me?"

"Sure, how much time do you need?"

"About a half hour or so for the interview and then I can tell you what I have found thus far. I have yet to look at your numbers."

"Harry, I was just about to go make a bank deposit and grab lunch. Would you like to join me and do the interview over lunch? I'll buy," she said smiling.

"That will work," he said smiling back at her.

Betty did a drive-thru for the deposit and drove to the Blue Moon Cafe for lunch. When she parked, she said, "I hope this is okay, I forgot to ask."

"This is fine, I don't think I've been here since I came with Maggie."

"Oh, are you sure it's okay, I can go somewhere else?"

"No, No, I'm fine, it's closing in on a year now."

They went in, got a table, ordered, and Harry began his interview. By the time they had finished their meal, the interview was complete.

"Betty, I have changed my mind. If you don't mind, I think I will go through the numbers before I say anything else regarding my findings and recommendations."

"Is it that bad?" she said fearfully. "I've known for a while I needed to change some things, but I have just kept putting them off."

"No, no, Betty what I will do in my final report will be to point out certain things. Some of these things you may already know or suspect, others, maybe not. Each recommendation I make will be accompanied by a why you should consider doing it. Please note I said consider. This is your business, and you should be the one to set your priorities. Betty, this is not meant to be painful," he said smiling and squeezing her hand.

"I hope that's the case, but I'm not so sure," she responded. Betty paid for lunch, and they headed back so that Harry could start the review of the numbers.

When the business day had come to an end, Harry came into Betty's office with a list of information he thought was necessary. He told her it was all here but not in a format that he could use. He told her there were things he thought they should be tracking and following and he explained in detail why.

"Harry, I never even thought of these things! You are breaking the business down into a piece by piece review."

"Betty, it's your business, shouldn't you know exactly what each part contributes?"

"When you put it that way, I guess it's kinda fundamental, isn't it?"

Harry just raised his eyebrows and shrugged.

"Betty, all of this is in the bowels of your computer. You need a programmer to put it together and pull it out."

"How much will that cost Harry?"

"No clue, but do you know somebody you can call?"

"I do, but…"

"But what?"

"I'll have to have dinner with him to get a reasonable price."

"So?"

"So ,this guy has been after me since Johnny left and he is a nerd. But he just doesn't seem to take no for an answer. I'm afraid this will just encourage him. But I will call him. I'll let you know what he says."

"Betty, when we get that, I will have what I need to finish my work."

A week later, Harry had all he needed to make his final report. He had done one page of bullet points to summarize what was detailed in the next ten pages and finally a two-page ending summary of the estimated cost to implement all of the recommendations. He had it typed and took it to the UPS store and had three nicely bound copies made.

He called Betty and invited her to lunch at his place. He told her the menu was fresh catfish sandwiches with apple, fennel and onion coleslaw and the beverage of her choice with a gelato dessert. Betty accepted and asked if she could bring anything.

"Betty, just bring yourself and an open mind."

Chapter 43

Betty was five minutes late and apologized. Harry led her into the dining room where the table was perfectly set with fresh flowers in the middle. He explained lunches were usually in the kitchen, but because of the special occasion, he thought this would be better.

"Harry your home is beautiful, and the view of the lake is magnificent. But explain the special occasion," she said thinking she already knew the answer.

Harry smiled and said, "Multi-part answer; you are my first consulting client, and it's your first time to visit my home."

"Would you mind giving me a tour after we eat?"

"Not at all, it would be my pleasure."

Harry served the food that he had already plated from the kitchen.

"Harry, where did you get the fresh catfish?"

"Compliments of my dock. It seems it sits over catfish heaven and I never seem to get shut out. I put out two lines last night and 'Voilà!'" he said pointing at the sandwiches. They ate, and both decided to pass on dessert. Harry cleared the table and brought out the report.

Harry read the report in its entirety out loud, and they discussed each point in detail. It had taken over an hour and two cups of coffee to complete the process.

"Harry, this is amazing. It looks like you know more about my business than I do. I can't tell you how much I appreciate what you have done, I just hope I can afford to pay you. I didn't see your fee listed at the end."

"Oh, don't worry about that now. What do you think or do you need time to let it sink in before you comment?"

"Oh no, no more time needed. I think you will find, when you get to know me better, I'm pretty quick on my feet. I can make decisions. I'm not always right, but it is not because I can't make a decision. Once we started this process, I realized, and I think I said this to you before. I have been putting off some things I know should be fixed or changed, but my gracious, you have opened my eyes about so many things I never thought about. Harry, you are truly amazing. And Harry, they all said you were just another pretty face." They both laughed.

"Harry, seriously, I want to do everything now. But Harry I don't have that kind of cash, and I have always run this business without any long-term debt. I really don't want to do these changes piecemeal as I can save cash."

"Betty, there is a way to do it all now. It may go against your grain but let me explain. You are right you have no long-term debt, but you own the property and building outright. With today's low-interest rates, you can cash in on them and set up debt payments that will not put your day-to-day operations in jeopardy. I have already run the numbers."

Harry went to his office and came back with some worksheets to show her what the actual numbers looked like.

"Do you think I can get rates this low?"

"I'm sure of it. If you want to do this, I'll go to the bank with you and help you if you want me to. It will be included in my fee." And he laughed.

She did not laugh, "Harry, I insist we discuss your fee. If I do decide to borrow, your fee will need to be included in the loan amount."

"Betty, I don't want to talk about my fee. I promise you will not have to borrow to settle with me. Let's take a break, and I will give you the house tour."

The last place Harry took her was the master bedroom.

"Harry your home is lovely. You know I think for people like us, you know living alone, the bedroom always seems to have a lonely feel to it. Does it seem that way to you?"

"I guess. It is what it is, though."

"Harry, are you over being lonely, and I don't necessarily mean your wife but just being alone."

"To be very honest, I miss having someone in the house with me. I miss sharing things you know, TV, food, wine, the boat, sunsets. God, I'm starting to sound melancholy, let's get back to work."

She said, "Harry, wait," and she gave him a hug. "Thank you for sharing that and all the other things you have done." She backed slightly away and looked at him in a way that froze him in his tracks, and she was gone back to the dining room. He followed finding her with the report in her hand turned to the cost page.

"Harry, I want to do it, and I want you to go to the bank with me."

"Okay, great. When do you want to do it?"

"When, well now of course. Can you go with me now?"

Harry laughed and thought, *'Pepper Pot' yessir this little lady is damn sure a pepper pot.*

"Absolutely."

She went to her purse and got her cell phone and called her banker. She had never borrowed any money for more than a week. Phil Jones was president of one of the three local banks in Lakeview. He, even though married, had on more than one occasion suggested he and Betty get better acquainted over drinks. Betty had resisted by saying she would be happy to have drinks with him and his wife anytime. This had always slowed him down and kept him at bay.

When she called, he accepted her call and was hoping for another opportunity. She told him she wanted to borrow some money and would like to come over now. He told her to come over now, that he couldn't wait to see her. She hung up and told Harry they could go now. Harry shook his head laughing, "The power of a beautiful woman."

She gave him that strange look again and said, "Well, thank you, Harry Blake."

They went back to town in separate cars. When they walked into Phil Jones' office together, the disappointment on his face was evident. Betty briefed Phil on Harry's work and offered him a copy of the report.

Phil thumbed through the report and looked up at Harry and said, "I thought you were a writer, Mr. Blake."

"I was a businessman long before and for far much longer than I have been a writer."

"Betty your property is more than enough collateral to cover the amount you want to borrow. There will be some paperwork of course. How long do you want the loan to be?"

She told him.

"No problem, I'll get someone started on the paperwork this afternoon, and you can come by tomorrow and sign and get the money put in your account." Phil was standing to indicate the meeting was over when Betty, still sitting, asked Phil about the interest rate on the loan. He told her he was giving her his preferred rate. She said she was hoping for 1% less. Phil laughed and sat back down. "Pretty lady," Phil said it before he realized he should not have said it. "She is a pretty lady, don't you agree, Mr. Blake?" he said trying to make it seem the comment was not negative. "Tell her, Mr. Blake, that's not a real number. Tell her she won't get that around here."

Betty looked at Harry without speaking.

"Mr. Jones, I think her request based on her record and her collateral is worthy of your reconsideration."

Phil was now becoming defensive.

"Nobody will go that low. You obviously have been out of the real world too long."

"Thanks for your time, Mr. Jones. I know you will understand when Betty moves her accounts," Harry said standing and holding out his hand for Betty to join him.

"Wait a minute, you can't threaten me and walk out just like that." Now Phil was standing and visibly upset.

"Look Phil, my attitude is, you local guys should take care of your good, local business people. You happen to have one of the best right here. I know there are two other local banks I believe would love to have her business. And as far as the loan is concerned, I don't have your assets, but I'll loan Betty the money for the term and rate she needs. Let's go, Betty."

An octave higher Phil said, "So now you are going into the banking business?"

"It's an interesting thought. I may have a knack for it," Harry said leading Betty toward the door.

"Wait, come back in and let's talk some more," Phil said beginning to sweat.

"I don't think there's anything else to say," Harry said standing still.

"How about we compromise on the rate, we each give a half point," Phil said almost begging.

"Have a good day, Mr. Jones," Harry said as he reached for the door handle.

"Okay, okay, you win, you get your way. It will be ready for you tomorrow Betty. And Betty, don't bring him with you anymore," he said sitting back at his desk pretending to go back to work.

When they got to the parking lot, she grabbed him and hugged him, "Harry you were great in there. I mean the line you gave him about lending me the money, I thought he might mess in his britches."

Harry smiled.

"It was a line, wasn't it?"

"Absolutely not, but I was sure he was not going to let it happen. My experience is most of those guys are all the same," he said as he realized she was staring at him.

"Betty, are you okay?"

"Harry, you were really considering loaning me that much money?" she said not smiling.

"Of course, I would," he said, and he saw her eyes starting to get leaky. He quickly decided to try to get out of the serious moment. "But Betty, you have to understand I would want you as my collateral. You would have to be my slave until you repaid the loan," and he laughed and added, "Betty, just kidding. Hey, are you happy?"

Betty felt like her throat was in a vice. The thought of this man she barely knew to loan her that sum of money had really grabbed her heart but then when he added the slave part, it made her smile. What the hell was wrong with Andy Wilson?

Chapter 44

Andy had made the decision not to take on any official duties until Jack arrived at Shadow Lake Farm. He, unfortunately, kept sending messages that he had been detained in South America, Columbia specifically. The business deal he had been working on had become much more complicated than he had anticipated.

So for the last several days, she had been doing self-guided tours of the entire 700+ acres. She and the girls had gotten their horses settled into their new surroundings and used the tours as a way to exercise their horses and spend time together. Everywhere people were working; she stopped and introduced herself. With no exception, everyone seemed to know who she was. She was somewhat surprised by this, but the girls told her that their father is very detailed in all that he does.

Andy was sure about two things. One, she was sure she was not sure this is where she should be. How she had initially envisioned being the manager of Shadow Lake Farm did not match what she had found here. The second thing she was sure of, she felt terribly guilty over how she left Harry Blake. Maybe there was a third thing, she missed Harry. Perhaps this would change when Jack finally arrived.

She was not sleeping well, and this morning she was awake just after 5:00 am. She and the girls were going Christmas shopping today, but that was later. She decided to slip out and take an early morning ride. When she stepped out of the back of the house, she was met by a man she had never seen before who was obviously some sort of security personnel. When she told him she was going to the barn to get her horse for an early morning ride, he used a radio and immediately a man showed up in a golf cart to drive her to the barn. When they arrived at the barn, her horse was already being saddled. The service was like being at an exclusive resort, but something struck her as eerie about it.

She rode out to the highest point on the property. She stopped there, and now there was just enough light for her to see hands working the herd of cattle. The men were separating the calves from their mothers. It was like watching a choreographed dance the way the quarter horses responded to the movement of the cows and calves. She was fascinated by the whole scene. Her attention was broken by the arrival of an open top Jeep driven by Dax Langley. He pulled up on her right side so close and so fast, it made her horse skitter quickly to the left. Dax always looked the same, cowboy boots, blue jeans, western shirt, straw hat, and the ever-present toothpick sticking out of his mouth.

"Sorry 'bout that, I got a little close. Would you like some coffee?" Dax said holding up a shiny thermos.

She shook her head no without speaking.

He was reading her mind, "Fun to watch the horses work. It's shot day for the young ones. Oh, before I forget Ms. Spurgeon says to remind you the vehicle for you and the girls needs to leave promptly at 8:30 am."

She nodded affirmatively, turned her horse without ever saying a word and left. She supposed she had been rude, but she didn't like him and especially didn't like the way he looked at her.

At the appropriate time, the three women were in front of the house when the big black SUV pulled up. A man dressed in a dark blue suit got out and introduced himself as Harmon without defining whether it was a first or last name. He was obviously fit, tan and wore a flat top haircut of black hair. When he opened the door for the women, Andy noticed his shoulder holster and weapon. He was apparently more than just a driver. When they were on their way, he spoke.

"Ladies we are hopefully going to have a great Christmas shopping day. We are headed to the International Plaza in Tampa. It is supposed to be great shopping and some excellent places to eat. Now there are a few rules I am going to have to insist you follow. First, I will be accompanying you wherever you go. I try to stay away as far as I can. I will pay for all your purchases. There are no limits on your purchases in either volume or cost. We must stay together; by that I mean we, or you, do one store at a time. You must all stay on the same floor of the store at all times. We must be able to communicate with each other at all times. I have here a phone that services as a walkie-talkie so just push the button and speak and I will answer and expect you to do the same for me."

He saw them in his mirror, and they did not look happy.

"It will not be as bad as you think, I just need to be able to see you."

Andy smiled and spoke up, "I'm sure it will be fine."

Jenny looked at Andy and said, "I told you Daddy doesn't miss anything."

Jane followed with, "He's awful," and laughed out loud. They all laughed. It was going to be a fun day.

When they arrived, Harmon valet parked the SUV and explained that there would probably be numerous packages during the course of the day that would be sent to the SUV. He gave the attendant a $100 bill to make sure it all got handled properly.

After two hours of successful heavy shopping, the trio was able to follow the rules and still have fun. They decided it was time for a break and lunch.

An hour earlier a man in a black suit and open-collar shirt had visited some restaurants supposedly to check menus, atmosphere, etc. He finally found the one he wanted and bought a $100 gift certificate.

The three women and Harmon were standing in an open area near several upscale eateries. They were discussing where they would eat. The man in the black suit approached the group, and Harmon stepped forward to meet him.

"Excuse me, I don't mean to interrupt or be rude but could I talk to you for a minute?"

Harmon looked at the ladies and Andy was saying sure, so he said, "Go ahead."

The man spoke good English but with an obvious Spanish accent. "I am considering investing in that restaurant," as he pointed it out, "and you seem to be trying to decide where to eat. I have for you a $100 gift certificate if you will eat there and simply tell me what you think after lunch. I will be out here when you have finished."

Andy spoke up, "Oh, I think that would be fun. How about it, girls?" They all agreed. Harmon took the certificate, and the group entered the restaurant and got a table for one and another for three. Andy tried to convince Harmon to join but he refused. When they were settled and had ordered, the girls were ready to freshen up before they ate. They decided to all go together. They walked by Harmon's table smiling and waving their walkie-talkies at him. When they went down the hallway to the ladies' room, they were surprised to find two men standing at the end of the hallway at the entrance to the ladies room. One of the men was the same man who gave them the $100 gift certificate. The other man was also dressed in a black suit and an open collar shirt and definitely looked Hispanic. The original man smiled at them and spoke, "Ladies, please come with me," and he opened an exit door to the outside.

Andy said, "Why would we do that?"

The man pulled a pistol and said, "No time to talk now, hurry, go!"

Jane yelled into her walkie-talkie, "Harmon."

The second man started shoving the group out the door. Then he heard Harmon running down the hallway toward them. The man held up his left arm and hand indicating he wanted Harmon to stop. Harmon was opening his coat to retrieve his weapon when the man's right hand came up and he tasered Harmon sending him to the floor where he was jerking and moaning.

The two men herded the women into a white panel van parked in the alley outside the door, engine running. The girls were in the back, the man with the taser was driving, the other in the passenger seat still holding his weapon. There were no dividers between the front and back of the van and the man with the gun turned back and spoke, "Ladies, we are not going to harm you. You are in no danger as long as you behave and follow my instructions. Now, I am going to put my gun away and take out my phone and take your pictures." He was smiling now.

Andy sat forward and said harshly, "What's going on here, what's this about?"

"Picture first. Please get close and smile."

They closed up but nobody smiled.

"Okay, I will tell you. The girls' father is being very difficult to deal with on a business transaction. My friends thought the girls' father might not be so difficult if he knew his daughters were visiting with us," and he laughed.

Their plan had been a good one, almost perfect, almost. Andy leaned back in her seat and slid her pocketbook up between her legs. She put her finger to her lips to let the girls know to be quiet. Then she pulled the girls close and they appeared to be huddling together. She slipped her hand into her purse and pulled out her snub-nosed .38. Years before, Clay had taught her to be proficient with handguns and helped to obtain a carry permit. Why, she and Harry had even done some target practicing at her farm. If Harry could defend himself, so could she.

The driver was in traffic trying to get them out of the main shopping area of the International Plaza. The other man was texting and sending their pictures to their associates and ultimately to Jack. Andy leaned forward and stuck the barrel of the .38 into the back of the man's head which halted his texting.

"Okay, I'm going to ask you once. Stop the van and let us out or I will have to shoot you."

The man placed the phone in his lap and started to turn his head and reach for his gun.

"No, no, don't turn around. Pick up your phone and tell your friend to stop the damn van."

He spoke, "Lady, killing someone is very difficult for most people to do and quite frankly I don't think you can do it."

Before he could say more Andy said, "You know you could be right, but I know I can shoot you in the shoulder. You are right handed, aren't you?" She said this as she jammed the gun into his right shoulder. Then she spoke again, "And after I shoot you, I am going to shoot your partner in the leg. Now stop the van or the shooting begins."

The two men looked at each other and then heard her pull the hammer back into the cocked position.

"Lady, please don't do that. A little bump and it goes off."

"You are right, a little bump and bang! So, you better stop the van."

They felt the van slowing and pull over to the curb. The women jumped out, but Andy wasn't through.

"Girls memorize the tag number please," and she leaned toward the passenger open window sticking the .38 still cocked in the man's right ear.

"You two drive away from here and never let me see you again. If I see you or the van, I will start shooting the gun into the air to attract attention. I hope you know I mean what I say. Now get out of here."

The van pulled away never to be seen again.

Chapter 45

In less than 15 minutes Harmon was on his feet. He was greeted by two Tampa police officers who had been called by the people in the restaurant when all the commotion started. Harmon had explained the three women had been abducted by two men who he described in detail. He, unfortunately, was unable to provide any information on the type or description of the vehicle they used or which direction they had gone. As he was finishing his dialogue with the police, his walkie-talkie came to life. It was Andy telling him they were okay and still in sight of the International Plaza. One of the officers left immediately to pick them up.

They were all reunited and took a private dining room to do a debriefing. Andy provided the commentary and details. When she reached the part about the photograph and how it was to be used against Jack, Harmon stopped everything. He had to get the information to Mr. Winstone that his children were safe. Hopefully, it would not be too late.

When Harmon had sent his message, Andy continued. She explained that the two men had not taken her purse and the fact she had her carry permit and her handgun. She then offered a very vague explanation of how the kidnapping ended. Jenny insisted she give them a detailed blow by blow description.

When Jenny finished, Harmon asked if he could see Andy's handgun. She carefully took the weapon from her purse and handed it to Harmon. The two police officers gathered around Harmon to get a close look. Harmon opened the revolver cylinder revealing all empty chambers. He looked at the two officers and then at Andy, "You unloaded it?"

Andy looked at the empty cylinder and flushed red, "Oh shit! I'm sorry, forgive my language. The bullets are in the inside pouch in my purse. I forgot I unloaded when I packed to come to Florida." The policemen were smiling but Harmon was not.

"What the hell would you have done if he had forced you to shoot him the shoulder?"

Andy stared away from the group and finally said, "I really don't know. Maybe I would have hit him in the head with the gun. I truly don't know."

One of the policemen said, "I bet those two guys would truly be pissed off if they knew you stopped an abduction with an empty weapon." Everybody laughed, except Andy, who was still flushed and concerned about what might have happened.

Harmon said, "If you don't mind, I think I'll keep this for you," holding the weapon up in front of Andy.

"Oh, but I do mind. I'll take it back, thank you."

Harmon pulled the gun away from her reach, "I think Mr. Winstone would prefer I keep this."

"That's too bad, I want my weapon, and I don't give a damn what Jack wants. I am capable of making my own decisions about my own things." Andy was starting to get angry.

Harmon nodded his head, "I am very sure Mr. Winstone would want me to be in control of this weapon."

"Frankly Harmon if we are going to be honest then let's be honest. First, why would I want you in charge of my weapon when you sir could not keep us from being abducted. Second, I don't give a flying flip whether Jack likes it or not. I will not be treated like a child by you or him. This whole control thing is absurd. I can shop, and I can pay for what I buy. I don't need you or him to hold the money. I am not twelve. Now, do I make myself clear, and return my weapon."

Harmon was now turning red and the two policemen were having a difficult time not laughing out loud. The two girls were smiling at each other as Andy tore Harmon apart. Harmon now bowed his back, "Well, little lady, what do you intend to do if I refuse to return your weapon?"

Andy opened her purse pulled out her permit and showed it to the two policemen, "Would you please have this man return my property to me?"

The two policemen looked at each other, smiled, and one held out his hand to Harmon for the weapon. Harmon shook his head and reluctantly handed over the gun which was immediately given to Andy.

Andy then opened the pouch in her purse and loaded the weapon. She then turned to the girls, "Young ladies it's time for us to resume our day. First, ladies room, second lunch, third complete our shopping." She then turned to Harmon, "We will let you know when we are ready to go back to Ocala." She thanked the police and led the girls out of the room.

Chapter 46

Betty Matthews was ecstatic. They were two days into the implementation of Harry's recommendations. Her employees' attitudes had virtually changed overnight. Not that it had been bad, but now there were more smiles and enthusiasm than she had ever seen. They had only completed about a third of their list. She could hardly believe how insightful Harry had been. He not only had provided the detailed plan but he had shown her how to pay for all their changes.

It had become obvious to her he was a self-confident leader. He had joked about his age, but she saw no issues. His enthusiasm was that of a much younger man.

She decided to call him and invite him to dinner. "Harry, it's Betty Matthews, do you have a minute to talk?"

"Betty, yes, for you, I will always have time. What can I do for you?"

"Harry, things are going so well here, I wanted to celebrate by inviting you to dinner. Plus, Harry, we have to discuss your fee."

"Betty, please don't worry about my fee, but, yes, I would love to have dinner and celebrate. When?"

"How is your schedule for tomorrow night?"

"It's reserved for you. What time?"

"How about 6:30 at the Lighthouse? I have heard too much about your power in the kitchen, and I would not embarrass myself by trying to cook for you."

"Betty, don't be silly. I am easy to please. You would never have to be uncomfortable with me. Betty, if I make you feel uptight or uncomfortable, I apologize. I'm really a very down-to-earth guy."

Betty was silent. She didn't know what to say. Before she spoke, Harry started again, "I didn't mean to put you on the spot, Betty. When you get to know me better, and Betty, I do hope we get to know each other better, you can relax and feel comfortable being with me. Betty, would you want me to pick you up?"

"Harry, that's not necessary. I'll just meet you there. And Harry, I'm not uncomfortable about being with you, and I too look forward to us knowing each other better."

Harry showed up 15 minutes early and asked for a table for two. They asked if he had reservations? He told them to check under Blake or Matthews. They told him they had one for a Betty Matthews. He confirmed that was the one, but he would wait on her in the bar.

When Harry went into the bar, there was Clay Hardaway and a reasonably attractive woman having drinks. Harry walked straight to their table and spoke to Clay. He immediately introduced Harry to Vicki Noble. Clay invited Harry to join them, but he declined and said he was meeting Betty Matthews for dinner.

Clay said, "I heard you'd been helping Betty with her business, but I also heard you were through."

"You heard correctly, we are just having a little celebration dinner."

"Well, Betty is a lovely person to celebrate with."

Harry excused himself and turned to go sit at the bar when Betty walked in. She looked great, dressed perfectly for the occasion. She was petite, with a perfectly proportioned body. All the men in the bar were giving her the once over. She gave Harry a big smile and then surprised him when she walked over, hugged him, and kissed him on the cheek.

She spoke first, "You want to stay here or go to our table?"

"Oh, the table's fine with me," Harry said as they left the bar. Harry looked back and saw Clay smiling at him and shaking his head approvingly.

When they were seated and had ordered drinks, Harry asked: "Did you see Clay in the bar?"

"I did, he's with Vicki tonight. She is one of Hardaway's Harem. That's what they are called. Clay has four, I think, maybe five women who he beds on a regularly rotating basis."

Harry asked, "Is this common knowledge and does everybody know about this and who they are?"

"Well, maybe not everybody, but I do know they all know each other on some level, and nobody seems to be bothered by the sharing. Their thought is, it satisfies a mutual need without having to make a commitment."

"Betty, do you mind me asking how you know all this?"

"No, I don't mind. I went to dinner with Clay a few times and we got along well, and then he offered me the opportunity to be one of his partners. I politely declined. Harry, I don't mind dating more than one man at a time, but I will not have a serious relationship and see other people simultaneously."

"Do you mind me asking, Betty? Have you had any serious relationships since you have been divorced?"

"Harry, no I don't mind you asking. I've had one, and it was a serious mistake. I was lonely, and my judgment vanished for a while. Thank goodness I came to my senses."

The waitress brought their drinks, and Harry offered a toast to her business success. After the toast, Betty asked, "Harry do you mind if I ask you a question?"

"Not at all, please ask."

"Would you call your relationship with Andy serious?"

Harry didn't hesitate, "Betty, I thought we were on the verge of being very serious. I was sure it was a mutual thing and then she showed up at my house one morning and said she was off to a new life in Florida. It sounded like a great opportunity for her, but it was just so sudden. I guess she knew what she wanted. I was not seeing or pursuing anyone else, and I did not think she was either. But at my age, it's hard to be surprised."

"Harry, do you miss her?"

"Yes, I have missed talking to her and doing things with her."

"Harry would you agree that it is easier to be with someone than to be alone."

"I think I would agree but not at the expense of being with the wrong person."

"Boy, do I know that is true."

She then changed the subject and started talking about the changes she had seen in her business. They finished their dinner, as the check came, Harry picked it up and pulled out his credit card.

"Oh, no Harry, this is my treat, and we haven't even talked about your fee. This is my check."

"Okay Betty, but let's kill two birds with one stone. You pay the check, and that will cover my fee."

"No, Harry, that's not right."

"Why Betty, I now consider you my friend. Friends don't charge to help friends."

"But Harry, we have just started to get to know each other."

Harry leaned over to put his hand on hers and said, "Betty, I don't want to pressure you, but from my perspective, I would like to get to know you better. I would like to spend more time with you." He removed his hand and waited for her to respond.

She sat silently for a minute and looked Harry in the eye and said, "Harry, will you marry me?"

Harry was shocked, "What!"

Betty laughed, punched him in the arm, and said, "Just joking, Harry, just joking. Yes, you and I need to spend more time together and if I ever feel pressured, I will not hesitate to tell you. And Harry, you should do the same. Now I have to go home. I have another big day of change in the morning. What are you going to be doing now that you have solved my problems?"

"Unfortunately, I have to decorate for Christmas. I have a lot of family coming. Maggie always loved doing the decorating, and she was good at it. I hardly know where to start."

"Oh good Lord, I love decorating even though I'm normally by myself, I decorate my little home. Harry, would you like for me to help you?"

"Really? Would you do that for me? I would truly appreciate your help and guidance in that department."

"Absolutely, your home is so beautiful, I am excited already."

"Betty, how about after work tomorrow. Bring some real casual, comfortable clothes, and I'll cook a hamburger on the grill, and we can do this thing."

"Harry, I can't wait. This is going to be so fun!"

She gave Harry another kiss on the cheek and left.

Chapter 47

It was shortly after 4:00 pm the next afternoon, and it had started to rain hard. Harry's dad had called this kind of rain a "frog choker." He decided to call Betty, "Betty, it's Harry."

"Oh, Harry I was about to call you. I think I can get out of here in a few minutes, and, if it's okay, I thought I would come out early."

"Terrific, I called to tell you to honk your horn when you arrive, I will open a garage door, and you can park inside so you won't drown getting to the house."

"Harry, that is so thoughtful. Yes, I will do that, see you soon."

"Betty, please be careful, it's really coming down out here."

"I will, I promise."

A half-hour later Betty honked her horn and Harry raised the door and let her in. She came in carrying an overnight bag that contained her casual clothes. When she was inside, she put her bag down, walked over to Harry, hugged him, and said again, "Thank you, Harry, that was such a thoughtful thing to do."

He led her back to his bedroom so she could change and took her drink order. She chose a beer. Harry left for the kitchen, and she changed out of her business attire into more appropriate clothing. When she arrived in the kitchen, she brought a huge smile to Harry's face. She was wearing well-fitting blue jeans, a white oxford blouse with the top three buttons undone and tennis shoes. Harry had always had a thing about a woman in blue jeans and this woman only reinforced his feelings. She was a knockout.

"Are you going to be able to cook out with all this rain?"

"Not a problem, my grill is on the porch."

"My goodness, Harry, are all these boxes and bags Christmas decorations?"

Harry had brought everything up from the downstairs storage but the big two-piece Christmas tree.

"Betty, we can be thankful, Maggie gave our kids about this much more when we moved here."

"Wow, I would have had to stay a few days if this was doubled."

Harry looked at her, smiled, and said, "Well, maybe we should have kept them."

Betty didn't respond, but she did smile.

"Betty, would you like to eat early or wait a while?"

"If it's okay with you, I would like to wait. Right now I would like to go through these boxes and see what we have to work with."

"No problem, but first let's go downstairs and get the tree, it's a two-person job."

They spent the next hour and a half setting up the tree and removing the decorations from the storage boxes. They took a break and decided it was time to eat.

Harry took the burgers to the porch and Betty sliced tomatoes and onions; then put a pan of frozen sweet potato fries in the oven. When Harry came back inside, he said, "I'm afraid I have some bad news."

"Oh no, did you burn our burgers?"

"No, the meat is fine but it is now sleeting, and I think the temp may be below freezing. I want to check the weather app on my phone."

After a few taps, "Uh oh, this says it gets no better not only in the next hour or so but looks like this might last a couple of days."

"Do you think I should leave while I can?"

"I think it's already too late. I think you are trapped here."

"Harry, you wouldn't take advantage of me, would you?" she said batting her eyes and smiling.

"Be careful what you ask for, Ms. Matthews."

That seemed to end that part of the conversation when Harry added, "Let's eat, I'm starving."

As they sat down to eat, they both had the same thought...what did that just mean?

After they finished their burgers and fries, Betty took over. She was in complete command. Two and half hours later the inside of the house was complete. The only thing not finished was the outside wreaths. Harry walked to the front door and turned the outside lights on and motioned for Betty to come and look outside. He guided her in front so she could get a good view. It was beautiful. It was a combination of sleet and snow falling hard. The driveway looked like a frozen pond. Harry put his hand on top of her shoulder. She glanced back and said, "It's beautiful, isn't it? I think you are going to be stuck with me tonight."

Harry turned her toward him and said, "Good, how about a glass of wine." He took her by the hand and led her to the sofa, then got the fire going. He got their wine and turned out all the lights except for the Christmas tree.

"Betty, the place looks great. You did a wonderful job."

She turned to him, "We did it together Harry, now come sit beside me."

"That I will do, but I was just your gopher." It made her smile. Harry sat down beside her and made a toast, "To doing good things together."

Betty said a silent prayer, "God, thank you for sending Andy to Florida."

They finished their wine, and Harry asked if she wanted more, she declined. He then asked if she would like some music and again she said no. She said she would just like to enjoy the atmosphere and the quiet. Moments later they were both asleep.

Harry woke first. His watch said it was after 2:00 am. He eased off of the couch and went to his bedroom and got his big flannel robe which he never wore, a pair of his boxer shorts and a pullover long sleeve shirt. He turned down his bed, got an extra blanket and pillow, and went back to wake her.

She had been in a deep sleep; Harry led her back to his bedroom. He showed her the things he had laid out and told her to go back to sleep.

"Harry, where are you going? This is your bed; if anyone leaves, it should be me."

"Betty, it's late, don't worry I'll be fine." And Harry left closing the bedroom door behind him. Walking through the house, extinguishing lights, he ended up back on his favorite spot. Harry loved his recliner, and he leaned back into its most horizontal position. With the pillow behind his head and covered with the blanket, he was asleep in a matter of minutes.

Harry thought he must be dreaming, he heard a bell ring. He opened one eye and saw that the morning light was starting to appear over the lake. Then he heard a bell ring again. It was his doorbell. He crawled out of his chair and saw Clay Hardaway standing at his front door wearing a fur cap and a heavy coat. Unlatching the door to let him in, he noticed the weather had changed little. It was still sleeting and snowing, and his lawn looked like a scene from Vermont and not South Carolina.

Clay came in apologizing, "I am sorry to wake you, but I knew you had a generator. Most of the county has no power. The roads are deplorable and as you can see, it hasn't let up. The forecasters say even if it stops today, the temp is going to be too low to give us any relief on the roads. My team chained up our vehicles, and we have been trying to do what we can for emergency situations. It's a mess. I thought I could count on you for some much-needed coffee 'cause there's nothing open. And my friend, maybe even a little breakfast." As he finished, he said, "But Harry, please put some pants on first."

Harry got his pants and then thought about Betty, maybe, hopefully, she would sleep through Clay's visit.

"Harry what did you do, go to sleep in your chair and not wake up?"

Harry held his hand up in the air trying to think of the best way to respond when Betty came walking into the kitchen wearing Harry's flannel robe. "I thought I heard voices, but I didn't see any vehicles in the driveway. Hello Clay and good morning Harry." When she finished speaking, she smiled and stared at Harry for just a moment.

Clay couldn't take his eyes off of Betty. "Betty Matthews, wow, you two sure know how to celebrate. What this starting the third day. Harry, you must have done one helluva consulting job." Clay was laughing.

Before Betty could respond, Harry spoke, "No, no, Clay, it's not what it looks like. Betty came out to help me with my Christmas decorating, and the weather kept her from leaving. By the way, take a look at her work, she did a great job."

Clay was still smiling and looking at Betty, "I'm sure Betty is good at everything she does. Did Harry bring you out here?"

Harry answered, "Her car is in the garage, Clay." Harry was starting to get irritated and changed the subject to breakfast. Clay still staring at Betty told her why he was there, explaining at best it would probably be two more days before she could get out.

"Of course, I could take you out, and you could come back and get your car."

Harry chimed in, "Clay, why would she want to go home to no power when she can stay here with all the comforts."

Clay laughed, "You are so right, Harry. Let the celebration go on and on." Then Clay added, "I got a crazy call from Andy last night. Listen to this, she and those two young girls went Christmas shopping in Tampa and with a bodyguard. The three of them were abducted by two men. They put them in a van and left the mall. I guess according to Andy they tasered the bodyguard, but they did not take Andy's purse. Now, Betty, you may not know this but Andy always carries a .38 revolver with her. Anyway, Harry knows this, so she slips the gun out of her purse and makes them stop the van by threatening to shoot them. The girls escaped and later when they are with local police, the officer asks to see her weapon. She gives it to him, and he says, 'I see you unloaded it.' Now, Andy about faints because she unloaded it about a week ago and totally forgot. She was one lucky lady. Oh, by the way, Harry, she told me to tell you she misses you and wants to talk to you soon. And, I said to her I had just seen you at the Lighthouse."

The conversation changed back to the winter storm as the three finished breakfast. Clay told Harry he was a life saver. He thanked him profusely, and his parting words were, "You two have fun and don't get bored."

Chapter 48

The two police officers left International Plaza headed back to their station and the junior officer said to the senior, "I think I know why you didn't ask those women to come back to the station and look at mugshots."

"Okay, smart guy, why?"

"Frank Martinez and his cousin."

"Excellent recognition, A+ for you. What do you know about Frank and his cousin?"

"Well, I know that obviously, they are plainclothes detectives in the narcotics division. I know there have been all sorts of rumors that they're connected to the boys in South America, and I know the description the woman gave fit them perfectly. They even gave the description of the white van with no tag which, to me, might even be the one from the motor pool that they use on a regular basis."

"That's what I call being very observant. And yes you are right, I didn't see the need to waste everyone's time coming to the station not to mention what might happen if they saw each other. It could be very embarrassing for the captain. But, hopefully, we are wrong. We can have some fun with this and probably know for sure if we are right. When we know they are in the building, we will find an excuse to go and see them and tell the story of the two inept abductors who were fooled by a woman with an empty gun. If it was them, we should get some kind of reaction. First, I want to swing by the motor pool."

When they arrived at the motor pool, the senior officer spoke, "Is that white van by chance available?"

The man in charge said that it had been checked out for a couple of days by Frank Martinez in narcotics.

Meanwhile, with their shopping complete, the three women and Harmon headed back to Ocala. It was a quiet ride. Even the two teenagers who always talked stayed quiet and to themselves. Andy's head was spinning. What kind of business was Jack doing in South America that would put her, much less his two daughters, in jeopardy? She was pissed. Not to mention the fact that she was being treated as if he, Jack, was in charge of her. She had been treated as if she were one of his children. This whole thing from the beginning had been nothing like she expected. She had accepted the fact that she had been wrong to move so fast. She had not asked nearly enough questions. She had gotten swept up in the money, glamor, and private jet. Maybe, she thought that's why she was treated like a teenager. In her mind now, she accepted the fact that she had acted like one.

If she could have a do-over, she would surely take it. But she knew she had to try and work through it. And what about Harry? She was sure she had hurt him. And truthfully, she missed him. What a mess.

Chapter 49

Harry and Betty sat at the kitchen island silently for a few minutes after Clay left. Betty finally spoke, "Are you going to be able to handle this, Harry?"

"Handle what?"

"Harry, you do know, don't you, that Clay is the biggest gossip in Lakeview. He's much worse than the women."

Harry was stunned, "No, I guess I didn't."

"Clay's a great guy, but he just can't keep his mouth shut. I am truly surprised Andy never mentioned this to you."

"No, she never did," Harry was still reeling.

"Harry, by the time this town thaws, you and I will be the talk of the town. How do you feel about that, Harry?"

"Betty, I don't think this is so much about me. I mean everybody sorta has seen me as some kind of wild guy. You know gunfights, civil lawsuits, Hollywood movies. I think this will be more about your reputation than mine. Maybe you are wrong. I would hope Clay wouldn't make this out to be more than it is."

"Oh, I'm not worried, Harry. I told you we had a relationship after I was divorced. It was a huge mistake, but I survived it. People in Lakeview and Polk County tend to overlook or ignore romances by single people. An awful lot of times they end up in marriage. And, by the way, I hope this doesn't cause you a problem with Andy. Clay was very clear that she misses you and wants to talk to you."

Harry stared at Betty who had turned toward him. His flannel robe had opened at the bottom, and he could see his plaid boxers she was wearing.

"Betty, you and Andy were good friends. You took trips together, you were close, right."

"Yes, we were friends. Close may be going a bit far. Did we confide in each other, not often."

"I'm curious, Betty, did she even mention me?"

"I'm sorry, Harry, she never did."

"Oh, don't be sorry. You know, it does bring up a point. I think it's easy when a man and a woman begin to be friends, and maybe one, or both, for that matter, begin to think about next steps. You must be careful about thinking you know what the other person wants or expects. When you have been out of the single life over

40 years; you were young then, and now you are older, I find it now to be very confusing as a mature adult. Listen, I am not angry with Andy, disappointed, yes. Having said that, it takes time for people to get to know each other really. I think that's why so many young people live with each other before they marry. I don't agree with that, by the way, but I do understand it. But before I hear your thoughts, let me say this: 24 hours after Andy left, I realized I was just an old fool, and I moved on. I learned to do that a long time ago. I can empty the box and move on. Now please tell me your thoughts."

"I had heard you were a tough old bird, Harry, and the more I am around you, I can see why people think that. Don't take that the wrong way, but I'm not so sure you are over Andy. She was or is my friend. She is a beautiful woman with a great personality and a good sense of humor. She did have an impulsive side. She has surprised me on our trips with her impulsiveness. It was just ever so often she would just jump out of her conservative thinking model. When I saw this just the few times, I thought she was funny. But occasionally it bothered me."

"What do you mean? Expand on that."

"No, I don't mean she would rob a bank on anything like that. When I said it bothered me, it aggravated me. Maybe it was my mood at the time. Anyway, I haven't talked to her, and quite frankly I doubt I'll hear from her.

"As to your other thought, I think I understand what you are saying. You already know I made a mistake with one relationship after I was divorced. I have tried not to make another. As I have dated, I have found a number of men I just didn't care about being around. It seems the ones I saw, maybe seemed only to want one thing. I am no longer a young woman with raging hormones. I have had one marriage that turned out bad. If I ever have another, I want to have no doubts about its success. I can't remember if I told you, but I have one son, John Jr., who lives in Japan. He is married to a local, and says he will never come back to the States. I made one try to visit, and I have no desire to go back."

She stood up, realized the robe needed tightening, apologized, and started cleaning up the breakfast dishes. Harry stood to help, but she insisted that he stay seated.

"Let me ramble a little more. I think too many marriages at our age are for convenience or for financial security or for loneliness. And I know a lot of people make them work. I also know some women who have done this and feel it's too late to start over and just grit their teeth and go forward. I think the problem is honesty. I think an awful lot of people just can't be honest with themselves much less honest with someone they are seeing. My feeling is that if I can't be honest with someone, I could never have a relationship. Plus, I would have to know he was being honest with me."

"But, Betty, how would you know for sure he was being honest?"

"I think that's a difficult one to answer. I think it takes some time. I think it's a matter of both parties opening up and revealing their thoughts. I don't know if it happens that often, but, at least right now, that's what I think. In the meantime, I want to enjoy myself and have good friends. And, Harry, I hope you and I will be good friends."

"Betty, you want honesty, I think we are already good friends, and we are about to spend two days together alone in this frozen setting. Our friendship will either grow or fade in the next two days."

"Harry, I hope it grows but are you willing to try an experiment with me?"

"Maybe, what is it?"

"Let's you and I be totally honest with each other while we are together. No tiptoeing around it. Let's just be truthful and see what happens."

Harry thought about this for a moment and said, "Are you sure about this?"

"Only if you are a willing participant."

"Betty, I think I can do this."

"Okay, I want to start with two truths. One, I don't want you to get the wrong impression about what I said about Clay. Clay does gossip, but, Harry, Clay is a good man. He is a good law officer. And, Harry, Clay really likes you. Some of his gossip is talking about you, and it is all good things. I found out a lot about you from him. Harry, I like Clay, and you know we all have faults.

"My second truth, since we have nowhere to go, I would like a Bloody Mary and watch one of the morning shows. As a businesswoman, I never get to see them except on weekends."

Harry smiled, "My truth is I think it's a great idea. And, one more truth, you know we really haven't known each other very long. And, Betty, you have been very open in the discussions we have had. Maybe, because we spent so much time on the business. I don't know, but I want you to know I've really enjoyed it."

"Harry, you are right. But you get a lot of the credit. You are very easy to talk to and to be with. I hardly believe I'm sitting here in your underwear and robe and having a drink at 8:00 am in the morning. I mean I probably should not be doing this, but I am comfortable with you. And, Harry, don't take this the wrong way; this is not an invitation for anything more."

Harry laughed, "Don't worry, I haven't taken this the wrong way and, Betty, don't take this the wrong way. I think you are a very attractive woman. I feel lucky to be able to spend time with you."

Chapter 50

The next couple of days were uneventful at Shadow Lake. Andy had a routine with the girls. They worked in the covered ring for an hour from 9:30 till 10:30 am, and they rode the property from 10:30 am till noon. After lunch, the girls spent the afternoon working on their studies. Andy spent her afternoons reading the latest equestrian periodicals and watching cable TV news.

On this particular day, Ms. Spurgeon informed the girls their father had returned and had requested a private lunch with them and then a meeting with Andy at 3:00 pm. Andy was surprised that Jack would not include her in the luncheon or at least come out and tell her hello. Andy asked Ms. Spurgeon where she could find Jack so that she could at least welcome him back.

"Your lunch is being served in your suite. Mr. Winstone has requested no visitors until your meeting at three. Someone will come to your suite and take you to Mr. Winstone," she said this curtly and turned to begin talking to the girls.

Andy was now angry and stepped in between Ms. Spurgeon and the girls. "Are you telling me I'm restricted to my quarters until I am summoned?"

Ms. Spurgeon spoke without any change in expression, "I believe that would be preferable to Mr. Winstone."

Andy was now pissed, "Ms. Spurgeon, I will have my lunch by the pool and not in my suite, and I will let everyone know where I will be after lunch."

Ms. Spurgeon almost cracked a smile, "I am afraid not ma'am. The pool has been reserved for the luncheon of Mr. Winstone and his girls, and, your lunch has already been delivered and set up in your suite."

Andy turned and walked away without saying another word. She went to her suite, ate her lunch, showered and put on fresh clothes to await her summoning.

Andy was seething. At a little after 2:00 pm, she left the suite and headed for the pool area. When she arrived, she saw that lunch had been taken away, and Jack and the girls were still at the table. She didn't hesitate walking straight to their table. "Jack, welcome back, it's so good to see you."

Jack's face began to flush as he stood, "It's good to see you, and it is good to be back. But didn't you get my message that I would send someone to get you for a meeting at three?"

Andy smiled, "I did, but why so formal?"

"I have to stay organized, it's the way I am." The two girls began to giggle, and Jack turned and gave them a nasty look.

No hug, no embrace, no warmth; it was fuel on Andy's fire.

"Well, excuse me, Jack. Far be it for me to be the one who keeps you from being organized." She turned and walked away.

The girls laughed again as Jack shouted, "Andy come back here." Andy never paused as she left the house and headed for the barn.

Jack turned to his two daughters, "Since when did rudeness become funny? What kind of nonsense is Andy putting into your heads?"

Jane looked at her father with a puzzled look on her face, "Dad, I don't think Andy is used to having all her decisions made for her. She even said to Harmon that she would not be treated like a 12-year-old."

Jack did not smile, "Yeah, I have already heard about all the things she said to Harmon. He was there to serve and provide protection for you and not to be questioned or berated."

Jenny then spoke, "Heck, Andy is the one who protected us."

Jack put his hand on Jenny's shoulder and angrily said, "Young lady, Andy almost got you killed. You don't know what you are talking about."

"All I know, Daddy, is that Harmon was laying on the floor when the two men forced us in the van. And only Andy got us free."

"You are wrong, Jenny, now please don't say that again," he said as his anger was clearly showing.

"Daddy, what part is wrong?" Jenny was becoming defiant. Jane put her hand on Jenny's arm and started negatively shaking her head.

"How dare you talk back to me, young lady. This conversation is over. Now both of you to your rooms."

"We have studies now, Dad," Jane said as she led Jenny away from the table and their angry, frustrated father.

Andy arrived at the barn and wanted to take her horse and disappear in the 700 acres of Shadow Lake Farm. But she had dressed to impress Jack and not ride horses. Her shoes certainly were not ones she could walk far in, and that left her one choice. She asked one of the men if he would get her a Jeep. She wanted to drive around. He informed her he would have to contact Mr. Winstone and get his permission. Andy exploded. She ripped the poor man apart. She told him in no uncertain terms, that if he didn't get her the Jeep now, he was fired. The poor man was terrified and left and was back in minutes with a vehicle. Andy took the Jeep and disappeared into a grove of trees at the far end of Shadow Lake. She was out of the Jeep pacing in the trees talking out loud to herself. She was praying; she was crying. What a mess. She was beginning to doubt herself. Was she overreacting? Was she acting like a spoiled teenager? NO! She was mad. She had been disrespected. Her biggest problem was not knowing what to do next. She looked at her watch; it was half past four. She had been there for several hours. It was then she heard a vehicle approaching. It was Dax. He parked beside her vehicle and got out and walked over to her, "Damn, I was about to decide that you left the property."

"I would have, but I didn't have my purse."

"I've been riding around for a while trying to find you."

"I didn't want to be found."

"I can see that. Well, I found you, and Mr. Winstone says you and he were supposed to parlay at three."

"I decided not to go."

Dax took off his hat, pulled a handkerchief from his back pocket and wiped the moisture from the inside band. He sucked on his ever-present toothpick and spoke. "Now, Andy, I know you don't like me, but let me say a few things that, if you don't already know, you should. Mr. Winstone is the third owner I have worked for here. All three had a load of money. Most men like that are used to having things their way. Even if it's wrong, they want their way. He ain't no different. I don't know what your problems are, and, to be honest, I don't really give a damn. And while I'm going that way, Andy, I don't give a damn whether you like me or not. I don't give a damn whether you go or stay as long as you don't stop me from keeping this ranch running the way it's supposed to run. My thought is, if you want to stay, you ought to get your ass off your shoulders and get on back there and take your medicine and move on. But hey, that's me. Now I'm going to get in my Jeep and go back to tell him I found you. If you decide to follow me, then I'll peel off and let you handle it. And again I don't give a damn what you decide." Dax turned and walked to his Jeep and left, never looking back. It was a moment of reckoning for Andy.

Chapter 51

It was almost midday; Betty and Harry were still in front of the TV watching the morning shows. They were having a fine time together. They had laughed, talked politics, religion, and even some sports. Harry had made a giant pitcher of Bloody Marys, but he had had only one. Betty had now gotten very quiet, and Harry noticed that the Bloody's were gone. She turned away from the TV and looked at him and said, "Harry, I think I am blasted," and then she laughed. "I think I called you Hawy," and she laughed again. Harry was now grinning and could see her eyes had gone glassy.

"Oh my, I haven't been this way in thirty years," and she laughed again. She started to stand but sat right back down. "I have to pee," and she was starting to laugh harder. Harry jumped up. "Let me help," he said, as he helped her off the couch and started walking her to the powder room.

"I don't need your help to pee," she said trying to be serious, but she couldn't stifle her giggle.

Harry was smiling trying not to laugh out loud. "I'll just take you to the door, and you're on your own."

She came out in a few minutes to find him waiting at the door. "Oh Harry, I'm smashed," as she reached out to him for support.

Harry was leading her down the hallway, and she said, "Where are we going?"

He said, "I have a plan. I'm going to take you to bed."

Before he could finish, she said, "Oh my, you devil," and she was laughing again.

"No, no. I'm going to let you have a nice nap and I am going to shave and shower, and then think about what I am going to make you for lunch when you wake up."

"You can take a nap with me," she said with a mischievous grin.

He was now laughing, "No, I need to shave and clean up. You sleep for a while, and then you will feel better."

She put her hand on her breast and said, "But, umm, I think I feel good now."

Harry was beginning to feel anxious. "No, it's nap time for you," and he helped her into the bed which was still unmade and covered her. He grabbed some fresh underwear and headed for the door. He closed it without looking back.

He got fresh clothes from his hall closet and went into bath, closing the door behind him. He shaved smiling at himself in the mirror thinking about what a tempting situation this was. But he knew he would never take advantage this way. He was in his walk-in shower when he heard the bathroom door open, and his first thought was she was headed for the water closet. A moment later she was standing at the shower entrance wearing only his robe, which was wide open, revealing her naked body. Harry was beginning to panic. His only cover was a washcloth and a bar of soap.

She was steadying herself on the entrance and smiling. "I thought you might like me to wash your back, and if I did a good job you might like me to wash your front," and she laughed again.

"Betty, Betty, please, please go back to bed," he was pleading.

"I don't think you like me," she said, pretending to pout. He was trying not to look at her.

"Please go back to bed, and when I've finished with my shower, I promise to come to the bedroom."

"You promise?" she said.

"I do, now go back to bed, and let me finish up in here."

"Okay, Okay," and she left.

Harry left the shower running, but he exited and dressed. He was trying to take as much time as possible. He finally had to go to the bedroom and when he was halfway down the hall, he heard her. He walked to the now open door and saw her snoring away. She was only covered to the waist, and he was afraid to change anything. He closed the door. He had promised her he would come to the bedroom, and he kept his promise.

Harry went to his office and started working on his notes for his new book. The winter storm was no longer raging, but the temperature was well below freezing. After working for a while, he was getting hungry and looked at his watch, and it was after one. He walked to the bedroom and stood quietly, wondering if he could hear if she was up and about. After waiting a couple of minutes and hearing only silence, he went to the kitchen for food. After he ate, he went back to his office to continue his work.

Two hours later he heard her and came out of his office. She was walking toward the kitchen fully dressed and obviously showered. He greeted her with a smile and when she saw him, she began apologizing. "Oh Harry, I am so sorry. You must think I am awful. I am so embarrassed."

"Betty, it's okay. You don't have to apologize. Just forget about it."

"No, I can't forget about it. I was so enjoying myself, and the Bloody's were so good. I didn't feel anything coming. It was like I was instantly smashed. I only vaguely remember some of the things that happened. What really frightens me is what I don't remember. When I woke up, I had no clothes on. Did we..." she hesitated.

"No," Harry said beginning to laugh, "I would never take advantage of you in that condition."

"Did you undress me?"

"No, that was your doing."

"I have vague memories of a shower. Did we shower together?"

"No, absolutely not."

"Well, what about the shower, did I try to shower with you?"

Harry paused, "Uh, well, sort of."

"Oh, good Lord. Did you see me without any clothes?"

He hesitated, "Sort of, well, I guess, yes."

"Oh no! I am so sorry. I can't believe I have done this. Will the weather let me leave?"

"No, and you don't have to leave. It's going to be okay. How about some food and coffee and maybe some hair of the dog? It's been a long time since I was hungover, but as I remember, my best remedy was breakfast, coffee and a bloody."

"The coffee and breakfast sound okay but I doubt I'll ever have another Bloody Mary. Let me say again how sorry I am. I hope this doesn't ruin our relationship. I am sure you must be more than ready for me to be out of here."

"I don't know about that. I bet most single men would be thrilled to be iced in with a beautiful woman running around their house naked." He was smiling a wicked smile as he said this.

"Oh my, please don't speak of this to anyone. Promise me, please."

Chapter 52

Dax was almost out of sight when she pulled out of the trees headed in the same direction. He was parked and walking toward the house when he heard her Jeep approaching. He turned, paused, and walked back to his Jeep shaking his head.

When she was close, she could see Jack sitting alone at a table beside the pool. She was finally ready to meet with him.

Jack stood when he saw her come into the pool area and stepped around the table to greet her. He spoke first, "Andy, I'm sorry you got so upset. I hope you will sit and let's talk."

"I'm ready to talk, Jack," she said coolly.

They sat and he spoke, "Why don't you tell me what your problems are and let me address them."

"I'll do that, but I don't think you can change my mind."

"What do you mean, 'change your mind'? Change your mind about what?"

"Leaving, I won't be staying. This has been a terrible mistake on my part."

"Leave, my God, Andy, you just got here. You can't even think about leaving. That's ridiculous. There is nothing I can't fix. Now let's go through issues one by one."

"Jack, let me first say the first big problem is me. I jumped too quickly. I didn't do enough research. I didn't ask enough questions. All this is my fault."

"Andy, what's the big deal? What did you not ask about?"

"Jack, this is not a horse farm in the terms that I have always considered. This is a complex, multi-faceted operation that includes raising cattle, farming, and thoroughbred racing. I am not nearly qualified or trained to handle this."

"If Dax can handle it, I'm sure you can do it better. Plus, he'll be around to help with anything you don't know until you can get your arms around it."

"Don't underestimate Dax. He has spent his whole life doing this work. Besides, I don't like him, and he doesn't like me."

"That doesn't bother me a bit. I learned a long time ago people who work for you don't have to like you, and you don't have to like them. They must respect your position, and you must respect their work."

"That just won't work with me, Jack. I don't like the way he looks at me. I won't be put in that position every day."

"Look, Andy, if it's that big a deal for you, I will fire him, and you won't have that issue."

"No, absolutely, no! You don't understand. You are not hearing what I am saying. I am not capable of doing his job."

"Okay, here's what we will do. I'll let Dax run the cattle and farm operation and you handle all the horse things. Will that make you happy?"

"That's a thoughtful try, but I think everything is too closely tied together. I think it could create some real operational issues. It appears to operate efficiently now, but I am afraid that would create problems."

"Well, what do you want me to do?"

"Nothing, I am going to go back home and try to resume my old life."

"Just put a hold on that thought; what other issues do you have?"

"I have been treated like one of your teenage daughters. What I can do, what I can't do when we go shopping. I can't even pay my bills."

"That was for your own protection and to make it easier on you. That was a perk."

"Not to me it wasn't, and Harmon even tried to take my revolver. He would have too, if not for the police."

"You don't need a weapon when you are under my control."

"Your control?! I will not be under your control. And speaking of that, what kind of people do you do business with that would abduct your daughters and me? And luckily I had my weapon, or we might all be dead."

"They weren't going to hurt you. It was to force me into a certain position on the deal I was working."

"Well, that's pretty easy to say now that we are free. Who were these people? What kind of business were you doing?"

"You don't need to know about my business so don't even ask. Everything is okay now, so let's just move on."

"Listen to you. So every time there is a shopping trip, do the girls have to worry about being abducted?"

"Andy, families of men of wealth have always been targets, and precautions must always be taken. Enough of that, what else?"

She chuckled shaking her head negatively, "And there's the house, it belongs to Dax. He's lived there since it was built."

"Correction, the house belongs to me, and I decide who lives there."

"And then, there's my suite adjoining yours. I thought that was bold, Jack."

"Andy, I am a bold person, and I told you I hoped our relationship might turn into something more. I just wanted to make it convenient," he said, smiling at her.

"It's just too much, Jack. I do thank you for the opportunity, and I am genuinely sorry, it's just too complicated. I plan to work with the girls and their horses tomorrow morning as scheduled. I will talk to them and explain my decision. I will expect to leave after lunch."

"Andy please slow down. Take at least a week to reconsider. Maybe I can come up with a plan to change your mind."

"I don't think so, Jack."

She got up and left.

Andy skipped dinner with Jack and the girls opting to dine in her room. When Jack informed the girls at dinner that Andy intended to leave, there was chaos at the table. Jenny, the youngest, started crying and she said, "If Andy's leaving, so am I. If she's not here, I want to go back to my old house and to my school and to my friends. Daddy, you ruin everything. You think you are so smart. Well, you're not. You treated Andy like she was a child. Daddy, you were so wrong."

Jack turned to Jane, the oldest but before he could respond Jane spoke, "Dad, Jenny is right. This whole thing has not been good for her since the beginning. And, I feel the same as Jenny, if Andy is leaving, I want to go back to our old home, our school, and our friends."

Jack was stunned, "I can't believe you two would talk to me like this. You sound like ungrateful brats. You both know I do everything for you. You live a fine lifestyle, one that other girls your age would love."

Jane spoke again while Jenny sat and sobbed, "Dad we know you have been good to us but, you have treated Andy poorly. Everyone is afraid of you and nobody questions you. But Andy is different, she is not afraid of you."

"Girls, I promise I will find someone just as competent to replace her."

Jenny stopped sobbing and almost yelled, "No, we don't want anybody else. You go tell her you're sorry, and you get her to stay," and she resumed her tears.

Andy was in her room lining up flights and transportation to the airport. She would absolutely not ask Jack for anything. She called Clay and told him she was coming home. She asked him to call Harry and let him know. That's when Clay told her about the ice storm and Betty being iced in for two days with Harry. She immediately rescinded her request to tell Harry she was coming back. She was shocked Harry already had connected with someone so quickly. Maybe they weren't where she thought they were.

Chapter 53

It had been a night of anxious thoughts for Andy. She had hardly slept, and now it was time for her to go down and meet the girls for breakfast for the last time. She wasn't looking forward to this because she knew how upset the girls were going to be.

She walked into the breakfast room expecting to see the girls, but it was Jack alone who was waiting to meet her.

"Jack, good morning, I normally meet the girls for breakfast. Have you seen them this morning?"

"Andy, good morning, the girls are eating alone this morning so that I might have some time with you."

"Jack, I don't have anything else to add to what I said yesterday. I'm packed, and I have all my travel arrangements made. Other than spending the morning with the girls and the horses, there's nothing left to do or say."

"Andy, I understand what you're saying, and I'm pretty sure I know why you feel the way you do. I don't want you to talk. Just please give me the courtesy of having your breakfast while I do all the talking."

"Okay."

They sat down and Jack began, "Andy, I can't tell you how sorry I am. I think my behavior has almost cost me my relationship with my girls. When I told them that you were leaving, any inhibitions they had about telling me what they really thought disappeared. They pulled no punches. They were brutally honest with me.

"One thing I readily admit is I have done a poor job of transitioning between my work and my personal life. I come back from a business trip, and I treat everyone as if they are my employees. I have done it so much; it has become my standard operating procedure. I have been terrible, and I promise you I do regret it. Andy, after the girls got through with me last night and some hard reflection on my part; I realize what an apology I owe you. This was a major lifestyle change for you, and I just dumped you down here with a bunch of people you didn't know and who didn't know you with a poorly planned set of instructions. It was terrible on my part, and I am truly sorry. I would give anything if I could do this over. It is easy for me to understand how you feel. I was just plain wrong.

"Andy, I am a businessman so let me get to the bottom line. I am about to lose my girls. They both say if you don't stay, they want to move back to our old home, old school, and friends. I don't think that's in their best interest, which is why I brought them here with you. I know you must know how they feel about you. After last night, I think if they had to choose between the two of us, I would be their second choice. They haven't had a mother influence in their lives. You are the closest thing they have had, and I see how important that is. Maybe if they were boys, it would be different, I don't know. It just seems that since they have become teenagers, there is so much I don't know. We are a week away from Christmas and then the New Year's holiday.

"I'm asking, no, no, I am not asking, I am begging you to delay your decision to leave until after the New Year. Andy, I don't expect you to do this for me. I know for sure their Christmas will be ruined if you go. So, please do it for them. I know you care for them and I know you want what's best for them. Please use this extra time to enjoy the holiday with the girls and if you won't change your mind about leaving, at least help me convince them that this is a better place for them than where they were."

Jack had finished and he was obviously distressed.

"Jack, I have all these travel plans in place."

"We can unwind those, no problem. Besides, if you do decide to leave, I will take care of that for you." When he said this, he realized he might have said that the wrong way and he quickly added, "I know you are quite capable, I just meant, I brought you down here and I will return you if necessary. I don't want you to have any expenses related to this experience. And one more thing, if you could find it in your heart to give me one more chance, I promise we can sit together and go through every detail and find a way for you to be happy and function here with the girls."

Andy sat quietly finishing up the last of her breakfast.

Jack continued, "Well what do you say?" As he said that, the two girls appeared. They were both staring at Andy.

"Are you ready, girls?" Andy asked as she stood up from the table. The girls didn't answer, they switched their eyes to their father's who was staring at Andy.

"We will see you at lunch, Jack," and she led the girls out of the room. Andy and the girls spent the first hour not riding but talking. The girls influenced by their father were trying not to be emotional, but it was hard. They said all the things to her they had said to their father. They did not want her to leave. Their father had promised them Andy could have whatever she wanted if she would stay. Andy tried to explain how complicated the whole thing had become. She did miss her farm and she missed her friends. She didn't talk specifically about Harry but he was definitely on her mind. She couldn't help but wonder if Harry was now lost to her. Could he already be that serious with Betty? What would happen when she got back? Was she forgotten?

The girls interrupted her wandering thoughts. Their final request was that she at least stay until after the new year. They told her their Christmas would totally be ruined. They had bought her gifts and they wanted to see her open them. She understood, she too had gifts for the girls and would like to see their faces Christmas morning.

At this point, her big concern was Harry and Betty spending a romantic Christmas and New Year's together.

Andy finally relented and agreed to spend the holidays with the girls at Shadow Lake. Jack had told her he would not be traveling until after the New Year so this would give her a chance for an extended amount of time with his presence.

Chapter 54

Betty finished her breakfast and the mimosa Harry insisted she have. She admitted the food and the mimosa had her feeling much better. Harry told her they would have a late dinner since it was now mid-afternoon.

"Harry, the storm has stopped. I think I should get out of here before it gets dark."

"I don't think you can. You're right the storm has stopped, but the temp has not gone up. From the looks of the driveway, I don't think you could get out and that probably means the roads are still pretty slick. Plus, we need to check on your power. There's no sense going back to a cold dark house."

Harry called Clay for an update on the roads and power. Clay laughed and wanted to know if Betty had worn him out? He wanted to know if Harry was trying to get rid of her. He said this laughing, but he gave him one more sarcastic jab, "Hey, Harry, I'm envious man," and he laughed again. The good news, he told Harry, was there was a warm front that should hit the area around midnight and by noon the next day the roads should be clear. He also told him that about half the county now had power, but he had no clue if that included Betty's neighborhood.

Harry hung up and relayed his conversation with Clay. Meanwhile, Betty called a neighbor and was told that the power company had promised restoration by noon the next day. So she was destined to be there with Harry until midday tomorrow.

"Harry, I am sorry, you are stuck with me until midday tomorrow."

"Hey, it's not your fault, and are we still taking the truth serum?"

She shook her head in the affirmative.

"Okay, well, I don't feel I'm stuck with you."

She looked at him and almost in tears said, "I just feel like I have probably ruined what was starting to be a very nice friendship."

Harry walked over to her and embraced her. "I told you to forget what happened. It's oaky." He held her tight for several minutes and finally said again, "It's okay. Remember it's truth serum time."

She gently pushed him away, smiled, and kissed him on the cheek.

Harry asked her what she usually did on Christmas day. She said usually one of her friends or neighbors felt sorry for her and invited her to share their Christmas meal.

Harry asked her to join his family and share Christmas with them. He told her it would be a real mob scene. He said the celebration started after a church service on Christmas Eve. The family tradition was pulled pork and Brunswick stew for which he was responsible. He told her they had always invited friends who had no family to join them. In her case, she was invited to come back Christmas day for their big Christmas dinner.

"I want my children to know my really good friends. You should know I have also invited Clay since he will not have Andy to be with this year."

"Harry, that's so nice of you but are you sure you want them to meet me? Will they be defensive? I mean have they ever met Andy?"

"No, but being truthful, I would have invited her if she had not left."

"How do you think they will react?"

"I don't know, for sure, but probably, two of the boys will be okay. The two girls may be a little annoyed with me. The other boy and his family will not be here."

"There won't be a fight, will there?"

"No, I don't think so. My family is reasonably civil," he said half laughing. "And if it turns bad, we will have the sheriff there," they both laughed. "So do you accept my invitation?"

Betty paused, "Yes, yes I do, and thank you."

The rest of their day and early evening Harry stayed in his office and worked on his book. Betty had insisted he do this and she borrowed a book from his office and read. She chose 'The Cuban Affair' by DeMille.

At a little after seven, Harry came out and suggested cocktails and food. Betty opted for a cup of tea and suggested something light for her. She said the mid-afternoon breakfast had filled her. Harry suggested BLT's. Afterward, they found an old movie on TMC to watch 'The Quiet Man' with John Wayne and Maureen O'Hara. When the movie ended, Betty was sound asleep still fully dressed. He was a little unsure of exactly what he wanted to do so he opted to leave her alone. He got comfortable in his big recliner, turned on the news, and promptly went to sleep.

He was awakened by the sun coming across the lake. Betty was no longer on the couch. He went back to his bedroom and found her fully dressed and asleep on top of his bed. He slipped out, went to the kitchen, and made coffee. He looked outside and saw ice melting everywhere. The warm front had come in during the night. Things would be back to normal soon.

Betty was up about the time the coffee finished brewing. There was no mention of Betty's intoxicated antics from the night before. Betty passed on breakfast after Harry called Clay about road conditions. He gave the all clear and Betty said she was going straight to her business. They parted as friends, with a hug and a peck on the cheek. When she left, they were both thinking what might have been if she had not gotten drunk.

Chapter 55

The storm had passed, and Lakeview was getting back to normal. Lakeview had two Mexican restaurants. One was where most of the gringos ate and was in a prime spot in the town. The other place was on the edge of the Hispanic community and where the Hispanics ate. It was called Casa Grande. At 10:00 pm, a Cadillac pulled into the back of Casa Grande, not visible to the street. The driver was a huge black man who opened the back door of the car allowing Roscoe Abernathy to exit. The driver/bodyguard was named George. George opened the back door to the Casa Grande and was met by two armed Hispanic men. They asked George for his weapon. George turned to Roscoe and said, "I ain't givin' up my gun." The voices of the three men grew louder and a door opened off the hallway, and Freddy Lopez appeared. Freddy calmed everyone down and invited Roscoe to come in alone. He said something in Spanish and then in English to George,

"You wait out here and try not to shoot each other. They will bring you food and drink."

Freddy closed the door to the private room and shook hands with Roscoe. "Freddy, thank you for meeting me. It's been a while since we've seen each other."

"You are right and now I hear you want to be a senator. That's a big step."

"I do, and yes, it is. I think the timing may be right. I think a lot of people are disgusted with the guy who has been there so long. That's part of the reason I wanted to meet with you. They'll begin to do the first real polling after the New Year, and I need to be able to show I can win my home county. I need the full backing of all the minorities, and that includes the Hispanics. That's where you come in. Freddy, I know all you have to do is pass the word, and I'll be golden."

Freddy smiled, waved his hand, and started to speak. Before he could, Roscoe continued, "I'm not asking for something without something in return. With this run, there will be a lot of jobs. Some full time and a lot more part-time. Since that's your business, I would expect you to handle all of this for the campaign. I expect my first big check to come in from the NAACP in the next couple of weeks. Plus, I have some big money from the entertainment world. Money, will not be a problem. Can I count on your support Freddy?"

"Of course you can, my friend. I have many people who need to work, and they are generally favorable to my suggestions at the voting booth," he said, continuing to smile at Roscoe.

"You are too modest. We both know you are like the Godfather to these people."

"This is a small town, and everyone needs a helping hand." Freddy stopped smiling and became serious, "There must be something else I could do for you?"

"Winning this county is going to be critical for me to get support around the state and in the party. Believe it or not, one of my biggest worries is one man."

Freddy frowned, "Which opponent?"

"Oh, it's not an opponent. I know you at least know of this guy, Harry Blake."

Freddy nodded.

"He and I have had several run-ins. One made a lot of news in court. There is no doubt in my mind the man is a racist. He is also selfish and unreasonable. The bottom line is; he has threatened to campaign against me. He has threatened his money and his time against me. He has become a celebrity of sorts and could be a real thorn if he carries out the threats he made."

Without a smile or change of expression, Freddy said, "Do you want him to go away?"

"Whoa Freddy, I'm not that kind of guy." Roscoe paused, "I mean if something happened to the guy, I probably would not send flowers. But I would never hire a hit."

Freddy now smiled, "Just asking."

"The guy is no candy ass. He has killed a number of men who tried to take those damn gold coins of his. As a matter of fact, as I think about it, they have all been minorities. Two of my people and four of yours."

Freddy corrected Roscoe, "The four were not mine, they were Guatemalans."

"Okay, okay but you know what I mean. I don't know of anything specifically you can do in that regard, but if he were distracted in some way, it could be helpful."

Roscoe stood and said, "I have a case of 15-year-old single malt in the car for you. I'll have George get it, and we will be on our way."

Freddy walked to a cabinet and retrieved a box of Cuban cigars and handed them to Roscoe, "I know how much you like these." The two men embraced, and the meeting was over.

When Freddy was sure Roscoe was gone, he reached under the table and unsnapped the tape recorder. He played it back for just a couple of minutes to check the sound quality. He decided it was time to have a visit with Harry's housekeeper, his sister Ruth.

Meanwhile, Roscoe sat in the backseat of his Cadillac on the ride home tinkering with his NAACP lapel pin which wirelessly connected to the thin line recorder in the inside pocket of his suit coat. He was amazed at the sound quality.

Chapter 56
Christmas – Shadow Lake Farm

After a lengthy emotional exchange, the two girls had not only convinced Andy to stay until the week after New Year's, but she also committed not to make her final decision on leaving until then. Andy had reluctantly changed her mind solely on the emotional plea made by the two girls. She had admitted to herself, it had been fun being with them and sharing their excitement about Christmas. She had convinced herself that another two weeks wouldn't matter in the big picture of her future.

Christmas Eve dinner had been planned for late because Jack had things to do. He had told the girls that he and Santa had final details to work out before the big day. Everything Andy needed to do had been done. She decided to take a late afternoon ride to have some quiet time to herself. Even though she had made the decision to stay through the holidays, she really and truly was not sure what her long-term future should be.

Andy rode to an isolated hill that overlooked the airstrip. She was just thinking she had never seen or heard a plane use it. As her thoughts were about to shift, a small single-engine airplane lined up and drifted down slowly and quietly on the end of the runway. Immediately, two Jeeps pulled up at the end of the runway. One was driven by Dax alone, and the other had three workers. They were obviously there to meet the plane.

Her first thought was that it was strange to see this happening on Christmas Eve. Then she realized there was another vehicle coming down the service road that led to the airstrip. It was a white van. Since the day of the abduction every white van she saw, she did her best to see what the passengers looked like. She watched the scene unfold.

The plane taxied to the end of the runway, where it did a U-turn and was ready to take flight. Dax was out of his Jeep talking to his three workers. The white van pulled up next to the plane, and two men got out. One went over to speak with Dax and the pilot, who had now joined Dax. The other man opened the side door to the van while the second man from the plane opened its side door. The three workers went immediately to the plane and began moving bundles of packages from the plane to the van.

Andy stared in disbelief. The two men from the van both wore dark suits with open collar shirts. Her mind was racing. It was the same two men or was it. Yes, it had to be them. It was them, wasn't it? One the men from the van began to look around, and when he got to the direction of the hill she was sitting on, he turned to Dax and pointed at her. Dax turned, looked in her direction, and stared for a moment and then started talking to the man. Andy turned her horse and made a fast retreat to the barn where she turned her horse over to one of the workers, and she headed back to the house.

She was shaking. What did this mean? What was that all about? As she reached the entrance to the house, she heard the little plane take off and disappear into the clouds. She decided to keep quiet about this until after Christmas when she could have a private conversation with Dax.

Dinner was to be served at 8:30 pm, and after getting ready, she noticed it was only 7:30 pm, she decided to call Clay. Poor Clay, for the last number of years she and Clay had rotated houses on Christmas Eve and Christmas day. They enjoyed each other's company, and after all, they were the last of their family.

When Clay answered, she could barely hear him. The background noise was people talking and laughing and obviously having a good time. Clay had her hold while he walked outside.

"Where are you, Clay? It sounds like a party."

"I guess I forgot to tell you. I am at Harry's. Most of his family is here. They have this tradition of pulled pork and Brunswick stew on Christmas Eve. As usual, when it comes to food, Harry is the best. His family is a hoot. They are really good people. Much better circumstances than when I first met them. They are all so curious trying to figure out if Betty is for Harry or for me."

"Betty Matthews is there?"

"Oh yeah, the guys think she's pretty neat, but the girls are a little standoffish. It's funny."

"Clay, I just called to check on you. I'm glad you are not alone and are having fun. What are your plans for tomorrow?"

"I'll work in the morning, but I'll be back here in the afternoon for Christmas dinner."

"Will she be back tomorrow?"

"Oh yeah. Are you jealous?" he said laughing.

She said no without thinking, wished him well and headed downstairs to dinner.

After dinner, the girls spent their time picking out their gifts. They shook them, checked for noise and weight, and made guesses about what was in the packages. They kept Andy and Jack entertained entirely. Jack insisted on getting everyone to bed; he said they all had to rise early for their Christmas surprise. The girls did their best to get a hint from their father, but he was steadfast. They all relented and settled into their rooms for the night.

Andy was awakened by a female voice. She looked at the bedside clock, and it registered 4:15 am. Maybe someone on staff was outside to wake Jack. The voice continued, it was squeaky, and it was coming from the outside deck. She got out of the bed without turning on the lights and pulled the curtains back to see if she could tell where the voice was coming from. The light from Jack's suite clearly showed Jack and the female flight attendant both clothed in robes standing on the deck. She closed the curtains and got back into the bed. After tossing and turning for an hour, she decided to go to the kitchen for coffee. Before the coffee had finished brewing, she heard voices in the hallway. It was the flight attendant with the squeaky voice telling Jack goodbye.

At 6:00 am her cell phone rang. It was Jack telling her she had 45 minutes to get ready to go on a trip. He told her what to pack and to be on time. She was to take only personal items, no clothes, other than what she was wearing. She thought this was strange, but she complied. She was the last one down, and the first thing she noticed was all the gifts under the tree were missing. Jack hustled everyone into a waiting car; they headed to the airport. When they had boarded the plane, he told them they were headed for a surprise destination. The female flight attendant served everyone a beautiful Christmas breakfast. She was young, good-looking, and had a terrible squeaky voice.

They landed in the Caribbean, then were boated to a private island with a magnificent villa that was decorated for Christmas with all the presents under the tree. The villa was located on a beautifully manicured piece of property adjoining a wide white sand beach. There was also a large pool and an adjoining guest house where Jack had decided to house the pilot, copilot, and flight attendant. The villa had six bedrooms, three on each side of the villa. Jack put Andy and the girls on one side, and he had taken a suite on the opposite side of the villa, the one next to the guest house.

They had no unpacking to do so they quickly gathered in the main living room by the tree and the presents. Jack explained that his gift to Andy and the girls, in addition to the trip, was a complete wardrobe for the trip; everything from swimsuits, underwear, and clothes for all other occasions. He said they hoped he liked his taste. He also told them they would be going back to Shadow Lake Farm on New Year's Day.

Chapter 57
Christmas – Pine Lake

It was almost 6:00 pm on Christmas Eve, and the family that was coming for Christmas had arrived, settled in, and had just returned from a Christmas Eve service at Harry's church. Four of the five children and spouses were all in the kitchen having drinks and munchies as Harry prepared the food. Only Pete and his family were unable to come. It was a strange year in that all of the grandchildren ended up at their in-laws in the same year. It was a tradition of many years past that Harry always cooked pulled pork and Brunswick stew on Christmas Eve. He cooked Boston butts for six hours the day before, and while they were preparing, he made the stew. It had also been a tradition of Harry and Maggie's to invite any friends who had no family around to join their family.

It seemed everyone in the kitchen was talking at the same time, so Harry had to bang his big wooden spoon on the side of the stew pot to get their attention. "Everyone knows that Maggie and I always invited friends who were going to be alone to join us. This year is no different. I have invited Clay Hardaway to come. I think you all probably remember Clay from Maggie's funeral. Clay and I have become really good friends since then."

Paul, their youngest son, spoke up, "After all the shootouts you have been in Dad, he probably considers you a deputy." Everyone laughed.

Paul spoke again, "Hey, isn't he the one who has the sister you are really friendly with. Is she coming also? She's the redhead who is a lot younger and hot." This provoked laughter again.

"Partly correct, Clay does have a redheaded sister that I became friends with, but that's the reason Clay is coming. They usually spend Christmas together, but she has taken a new job and moved to Florida."

Paul spoke again, "That sucks for you, Dad, I'm sorry."

Millie and Sally looked at each other and rolled their eyes. They weren't ready to talk about female friends for their father, especially younger, hot ones.

Harry held up his hand and spoke again, "In addition to Clay, you will meet Betty Matthews. Clay and Betty have been friends for years, and I met Betty when I spoke at a women's business conference, and then I ended up doing a consulting job for the company she owns and runs. She's divorced for eight or nine years or more, I'm not sure, anyway, she has one son who lives in Japan, and she would be spending Christmas with no family. They should be here anytime, so I know as always, you will make them feel comfortable."

Paul could not hold back, "So Dad, does Betty replace the redhead?" The men laughed and the women stared at Harry waiting for a response. Just then the doorbell rang. "Saved by the bell." Paul added and headed for the door. Harry followed to avoid any further conversation on the subject.

Clay and Betty were together. Clay was wearing his uniform and Betty was dressed like a million dollars. She was wearing black silk slacks and a Christmas red silk blouse. She wore shiny black high heels, so she looked taller. The slacks and blouse fit perfectly to accent her attractive figure. Add the blond hair, and she was a knockout.

Paul looked at Betty and then at his father and just shook his head. The men were smiling and lining up to introduce themselves to her while the women were focusing on Clay. Harry stood back and watched almost laughing out loud. Betty finally got to Harry where she proceeded to put her hands on his shoulders and kiss him on the cheek. She turned and realized everyone in the room was watching them and said, "My goodness, Harry, what a beautiful family you have. I want to thank y'all so much for allowing me to share this holiday with you. Thank you, so much."

She then stepped back by Harry and put her hand on his arm. He stood for a moment then pulled away and said, "I have to stir the stew. Will someone take care of our visitors with something to drink."

Clay spoke up, "Don't bother, Betty and I have spent enough time here to be able to serve ourselves." Clay and Betty proceeded to the bar where they served themselves.

As usual, Harry's family made their guests feel welcome even though Millie and Sally were still a bit standoffish to Betty. Harry hoped he was the only one who noticed. He was just about ready to announce that it was time for the blessing when he saw Millie whisper something in the ear of her husband, Dave. Dave immediately walked to the center of the room and called everyone to attention. For a moment, Harry thought he was going to offer a blessing. Instead, he proposed a toast, "To Maggie, who is missed by all of us." For a moment the conversation completely died, until Harry spoke.

"Thank you, Dave. I know we all miss Maggie, especially at this time of the year; we all have so many good memories of our family at Christmas time. Now, allow me to bless the food, it's time to eat."

Everyone loaded their plates and found a place to sit. Casual dining tonight, no formal seating for this meal. Some sat at the dining room table, some at the big kitchen island, and others in the sitting area between Harry's office and the kitchen. Harry was the last to fill his plate. He was looking around for an open seat when Clay spoke, "Hey, Harry, why don't you come over here with us, it appears Betty has saved you a seat."

Harry joined the group at the dining room table at the only open seat which was beside Betty. Harry put his food down but remained standing. "Could I have everyone's attention? I have a very important Christmas question. How did y'all like the way I decorated the house?"

Everyone spoke at the same time, "Good job, Dad. It looks great. Mom taught you well."

Harry spoke again, "I lied. Maggie never taught me, she just used me as her instrument. Put this here, put that there. It was always her skill, never mine. This year would have been a disaster, but I had a volunteer whose skill you see displayed. I want to formally thank Ms. Betty Matthews for making this happen. A toast to Betty."

Everyone toasted, but the accolades were somewhat subdued.

Clay could not resist, he had to speak, "Y'all probably don't know this, but there is a real backstory to this Christmas decorating story and Betty." Clay had everyone's attention, they all had stopped eating. "Betty came out here to help Harry, and it had been a cold nasty rainy day. Well, being in the foothills of the mountains, we occasionally get these surprise winter storms that unexpectedly pop out of the mountains and nail us. Well, it happens on the evening that Betty is here to decorate. The bottom fell out of the thermometer, then sleet, snow, wind, it was a mess. Trees down everywhere and the county lost power. Most for two days and some for about four days. For my department, it means all hands on deck 24/7. Your father is a smart man, and he has a full blown GenSet generator, so the loss of power had no effect on him and his guest. I mean they couldn't get out of the driveway but when your refrigerator, freezer, and bar are stocked like Harry's always is, who cares. Let it storm, let it storm, let it storm. I came by and checked on them, and they had no problems. What a perfect time to decorate."

The women were speechless, and the men were doing their best to suppress smiles.

Dave finally spoke, "Thank goodness for that generator, Harry."

Betty spoke up. "Yes, thank goodness for the generator. My power stayed off for two and a half days. But my business boomed."

Dave spoke again, "Your business boomed. Tell us about it."

Betty explained, and everyone at the table listened but everywhere else other conversations resumed. Clay looked at Harry and smiled while Harry just rolled his eyes.

Chapter 58

It was New Year's Eve afternoon at the island villa. The night before had been crazy. It started when it appeared everyone had retired for the evening. Andy was dressed for bed when there was a knock at her door. It turned out to be Jane and Jenny. They said they needed to talk to her.

Jane, the oldest, began, "We know the week is almost over and we think you probably know what you are going to do. We want you to be honest with us and tell us. Please don't make us wait. Tell us, please."

They were all dressed for bed and sitting in her living room. Andy tried to put them off, but they said they weren't leaving until she gave them the answer.

She sat quietly for a few minutes trying to decide how she wanted to answer them.

She finally began, "This has not been an easy decision. There are a number of different issues I have had to consider. First and foremost is you. I love you girls, and I love being with you. If that were the only consideration, the decision would be easy."

Jenny jumped in, "Well, what else matters?"

Jane said, "Shut up, Jenny, let her finish."

Andy smiled at the girls, "Let me talk about me for a minute and I will tell you what I see that is very real. After you two, what I came for was an opportunity to take on much more responsibility. I wanted to be a part of managing a big horse farm. That can never happen at Shadow Lake and let me be clear, that is nobody's fault. Actually, had I done the proper research, I would have never accepted your father's offer.

"Also, it is now evident to me that your father may find the right woman and it would make our situation very awkward."

Jenny interrupted again, "Andy I think you and my dad would make a great pair. It would be perfect for us. You just need to be patient. We will talk to our dad and encourage him to get moving."

"Absolutely not! When you get older, you will understand. Even on this trip, your father has shown where his interest probably lies. He leans toward women younger than me. That's okay, he should follow his heart."

Jenny again, "If you're talking about Ms. Squeaky voice, I'm sure that's just poolside flirting with my dad. I'm sure it would never go beyond that."

Andy smiled and realized how innocent she was.

"I think you are wrong, Jenny, you are just too young to understand, and there is another fact. You two will be off to college in just a few years, and I will be out of your lives probably forever. Girls, please understand I want more out of the rest of my life. Truthfully I miss my farm and my friends."

Jane spoke, "So you are leaving."

Andy looked sadly at the girls but did not speak. Jane got up and pulled Jenny out of her seat, "Let's go to bed little sister." No further words were spoken as they left the suite.

Jane went to her room, but Jenny headed to the other side of the villa and her father's bedroom. When she got there, she could hear music. She pounded on the door calling loudly for her dad. She heard the music sound disappear and then she heard Ms. Squeaky voice call her dad's name. She was shocked as her father opened the door and stepped into the hall closing the door behind him. He was wearing a robe, and she could see he had no shirt or shoes under the robe.

"Sweetheart, what's wrong, why aren't you in bed?"

"I need to talk to you about Andy. I want to come in and talk."

"No, not tonight. It's too late. We will talk tomorrow. Now you, young lady, go back to your room and sleep."

"I want to talk now!"

"I said no, vamoose!"

"I guess Ms. Squeaky voice is more important than I am."

"What did you say? Now I am not going to tell you again out, out of here, back to your room and I mean NOW!"

Jenny turned walked away but had a parting shot for her father, "Have a good time, Dad."

Jack's first thought was to chase her down but decided to leave well enough alone and go back to his friend. His last thought was what she called her Ms. Squeaky voice. It made him smile.

Meanwhile, Andy could not sleep, and she decided to call Clay. He filled her in on the events with Harry's family. He told her how much he and Betty enjoyed Harry's family and playing the game of trying to keep the family from knowing if he and Betty were a couple or if Betty was there for Harry. His impression was the family was unsure either way. He finished the story by saying how much better he had gotten to know Betty and what a great gal she was. Andy thought this was odd.

She told Clay she had forgotten to mention to him about the incident with the small plane and the two men with the white van, and how she couldn't be 100% sure, but she was pretty sure they were her abductors.

Clay responded, "What the hell is Jack involved with?" He told her never to go anywhere without her weapon and to stay alert. He said he wanted to think about it and would be back in touch.

As she finished her call, she heard Jenny in the hall pounding on Jane's door. When Jane opened the door, the only words Andy heard were, "Dad's got Ms. Squeaky voice in his suite, and I know he must be doing the ugly with her."

Chapter 59

It was New Year's Eve afternoon, and Harry was at his desk trying to work on his book, but his mind kept wandering. His family had all gone back to their homes and friends too. Ruth Lopez and her team were finishing up the week's worth of cleaning. It had been a longer than usual work day for them since all the guest bedrooms and bathrooms had to be cleaned and remade.

Harry smiled as his thoughts shifted to Christmas Eve. Clay and Betty had gone home, and the family had all retreated to their rooms. He was finishing up a nightcap in his office when Johnny and Paul appeared. They wanted to know if they could talk. They wanted to talk about Betty. They said they were a little unsure about whether or not Betty was Clay's friend or their dad's. They were both sure she was beautiful. And what happened to the horse lady friend. They both laughed saying they had talked and figured that the two of us had become 'real close.'

Harry explained for the second time about Andy and how he came to become friends with Betty. Both sons listened intently, and then Paul started smiling and said, "What I want to know is what it was like to be snowed in for a few days with Betty. She's older than I am but I think that wouldn't bother me one bit."

Harry shot back, "Hey, I don't think your wife would appreciate that remark."

"I'm sure you're right, but I was just making a point."

Johnny spoke, "Dad I just wanted to tell you, and I know Paul feels the same that if and when you find someone you want to spend the rest of your life with, you have our support. And Dad, if it's Betty you have not only our support but also our admiration." Both boys had big grins on their faces. Harry thought it was hilarious.

Then he thought about early Christmas morning. He was first up, so he made the coffee and retreated to his computer to check emails. There was one that came in at midnight from Betty telling him what a wonderful time she had. She said she loved his family and couldn't wait for Christmas dinner with them.

Then, there was a second one that came a little after one in the morning, it was from Andy. She wished him a Merry Christmas and told him she thought of him often. She was sorry she didn't get to meet his family. She closed by saying she looked forward to seeing him. She made no indication when that might be.

He then remembered Sally and Millie standing at his door in their robes with coffee. He got up and gave them both big hugs, and they then entered his office, closed the doors and sat down. Millie started, "Dad, we want to talk with you and tell you how we feel about," she paused, "about your situation. I hope you know how much we love you and loved mama. We still miss her, and we don't think it's been long enough since she's passed that you should be out of your mourning period."

He remembered beginning to feel angry, but he contained himself but interrupted her to say, "There is no set period for mourning. It varies with everybody. I've already met with Ray Andrews on the subject. So don't tell me how long I should mourn."

"Okay, okay, well then, let's call it a period of respect."

Harry interrupted again, and now he was getting very defensive, "Do not tell me you are setting a timetable for me. I will not have it. Listen, I loved Maggie and I always will, but hopefully, I have some time left to live. I'm not trying to find someone to marry, but I enjoy companionship. I enjoy being with someone besides Clay. I enjoy female company. And if something were to come from that, so be it. I appreciate your concern, but my feeling is this. You should be concerned about the living, not the dead. Maggie is in her eternal home, don't worry about her and I think you two should be praying for me to have a good companion whether it be as a friend or whatever."

As he thought back about how serious the conversation had become, he could now smile at the look on their faces as he put them in their places as he had done so many times when they were growing up. He remembered Sally finally spoke, "Well, I think Betty is lovely, but Dad, she is just too young for you."

He remembered laughing and telling her he would try to find an older blue-haired model maybe even one with a walker to make them happy. He remembered them both getting up, smiling, and telling him he was hopeless. God, he loved his family.

All in all, he thought it had been a great Christmas and he had really enjoyed being with his family. He was also a little curious about how Clay had handled the two days with Betty. They had agreed beforehand that he, Clay, would be non-committal about whether Betty was with him or there for Harry. Harry felt like Clay's behavior made them seem more like a couple. Clay could be quite the ladies' man, after all, Hardaway's harem. It was what he hoped, the family all went home not really sure if he and Betty or Clay and Betty were a thing. Beautiful!

Ruth came to his office having finished with all her work. Harry thanked her, paid her, and wished her a happy New Year. Ruth and Clay were the only people who knew the location of the hidden house key. His rule with Ruth was all doors always locked which kept the alarm triggered. Ruth had been gone for about five minutes when he heard the front door open. Ruth must have forgotten something, but why retrieve the door key when she could have just rung the bell.

Harry got up from his desk and walked outside the office speaking loudly, "Ruth did you forget," but before he could finish, he saw two masked men running toward him. Harry turned to rush back to his desk to get the .38 he always kept there. Just as he jerked open the desk drawer, the first man through the door hit him with what appeared to be a rubber hose but much heavier. The hose slammed hard against the left side of his face and left ear.

The blow was hard, it knocked him to his knees, and he could hardly hear for the ringing in his ear. He tried to stand and turn to look at his attackers. The man with the hose hit him again, this time across the front of his face smashing his nose and upper lip. He felt his nose crunch and blood starting to pour down into his mouth and down his neck and the front of his shirt. This time Harry was all the way down knocking his desk chair across the room. The man with the hose walked over and began kicking him in his side. He heard the other man speak with a distinct Hispanic accent, "Stop, the man said we cannot kill him." The man kicked him again, and the last thing Harry saw was black cowboy boots with silver tips.

Chapter 60

Harry had talked to both Betty and Clay about New Year's Eve. Clay was committed to working, citing that typically it was a busy evening for his group. Harry explained to Betty that he had done so many black-tie celebrations that he was going to spend a quiet evening, make a good dinner, have a great bottle of wine, and watch the ball drop on TV. He told her if it was not too tame for her, she was invited to join him and also to stay the night to avoid driving while drinking plus avoid all the drunks who were sure to be out. She said she was thankful for the invitation. She too had done all the big parties in the past. She also took him up on the overnight and promised not to repeat overindulging again.

Betty arrived at seven as planned and was surprised to see the house dark with no visible lights. Her first thought was that she had the time wrong and that maybe he had run an errand. But even then he would have left some lights on. She walked to the front door where she could see light for the first time. There was a small amount of light coming from the kitchen or maybe his office. Her next thought was perhaps it was candlelight. Maybe Harry had planned a romantic setting. She rang the doorbell, but there was no answer. Harry's doors were always locked, but she tried the handle anyway. The door opened, it had not been locked. Maybe this was his surprise for her. She walked in and toward the kitchen calling, "Harry it's me, I'm here." When she reached the kitchen, she could see the light had come from his office. "Harry, are you there?" she said as she entered the office doorway. She immediately saw his desk chair sitting sideways across the room. Then she saw one of his legs on the floor sticking from behind the desk and not moving.

"Harry!" she screamed as she rounded the desk and saw him lying on the floor in a pool of blood. He was on his side and his face, neck, and front of his shirt were soaked in drying blood. The side of his face had a huge blue bruise, and his bloody nose was no longer straight. She was immediately beside him trying to get him to speak. She got up and grabbed a pillow from his couch and placed it under his head. He was breathing, he was alive. Finally, he opened his eyes, tried to speak but could only moan. She grabbed her cell phone, dialed 911, and explained the circumstances. They all knew Harry and set in motion the ambulance and the officer on duty. Betty hung up and called Clay. When he saw it was Betty, he answered immediately, "Hello beautiful, I was just thinking about you."

"Not now Clay, I am at Harry's, and it looks like he has been beaten badly. There's blood everywhere, and he is barely conscious. If you have any influence over the ambulance, make sure they hurry."

"Done, I'll be there as fast as I can."

Harry's quiet street was once again a parade of flashing lights. Clay first, with flashing lights and siren blasting, followed by the EMT's and a second deputy's car.

Clay tried to talk to Harry, but he was unable to speak, only moan. When they loaded him into the ambulance, Betty insisted she go with him. As she started to get in beside him, she turned to Clay and said, "The front door was not locked."

Clay knew that something was wrong. He walked back into the house and straight to where Harry kept the gold coins. They were gone. Clay kept everything in the house sealed off. He had a team there to check for prints and any other clues that might identify the attackers. Clay was furious and frustrated. He felt he might have let his friend down. He wasn't sure why he felt that way, but he did. He had begged Harry to secure the coins, but his friend was a hard-headed man. Maybe some guilt came from the way he was beginning to feel about Betty.

He called her at the hospital to check on his friend. Betty said he was now in ICU with a broken nose, cracked cheekbone, one rib broken, one cracked and a possible concussion. The doctors were keeping everyone away from him until the next day. They wanted him to have complete rest. She told him she was taking a taxi back to Harry's house to pick up her car. She convinced Clay to call either Millie or Sally to let them know what had happened.

Chapter 61

It was New Year's morning, and Jack's plane was already in the air. This special New Year's Eve party had been a bust. His girls had hardly spoken to him. They were mad about his obvious affair and they, at least partially, blamed that for Andy's decision to go back home. They left the party around ten o'clock. They not only avoided talking to their father but also hardly spoke to Andy.

Andy felt like she was the odd person out and left shortly after the girls. This left Jack and the flight crew for the band and the food. Jack was ticked, but Ms. Squeaky voice made his troubles disappear.

Andy moved from her seat and asked Jack if she could join him. She had a topic she hoped he could explain. She told him about the plane, the two men, the white van and the fact she was almost sure they were the abductors from the mall. Jack responded, "I hardly think that they were the same men. One of my clients asked if he could send some materials for one of his jobs to our place. He promised he would have someone there to pick them up and he would make sure they caused us no inconvenience. I talked to Dax, and he said it would be no problem. I didn't know they had come and gone until Dax informed me. Maybe you have a little paranoia after the incident. That's understandable, but I don't think you should worry. Especially now, with you going back home. And, by the way, I am so sorry this did not work out the way we had all hoped. I have your transportation lined up from the airport to your house."

"You think of everything, but, let me set the record straight. I have no paranoia! Thanks for everything Jack. You have been more than generous."

Before he could respond, she was up and back to her original seat. When they had landed and walking to the FBO, she heard her phone buzz. She had missed a call, and it was from Clay. She listened to the voicemail and heard Clay describe the attack on Harry and that he was in bad shape in the hospital. She needed to be back as soon as she could get there.

Chapter 62

Betty picked up her car and went straight back to the hospital. She had brought a change of clothes for New Year's Day, so she changed to be more comfortable. She checked in at the nurse's station and said she would not be leaving until she could talk to a doctor and see Harry. She said she was representing his family who all lived out of town.

A nurse came to the ICU waiting room and told her that they had taken him to the surgical floor. They were going to work on his nose to try to improve his ability to breathe. She said his vitals were stable, but at his age and the beating he had taken, they were being extra cautious. She moved to the surgical waiting room and stopped at the chapel on the way to say a prayer for him.

It was now after midnight. She knew because all of the people at the nurse's station were toasting each other with coffee and water. At near one in the morning, Clay showed up. She stood up when he entered the waiting room. She spoke first, "Oh, Clay, I'm so worried about him. He looked so bad," and then she broke down and began to cry.

He put his big arms around her and did his best to console her. "I know, I know. He's too damn old for this. He is just such a damn hard head. But I promise you this. I will find the bastards, and they will be punished."

She was regaining her composure and trying to separate herself from him when he spoke again, "This is probably a bad time, but I have had this on my mind for a while now. I want you to know as I have gotten to know you better, I have started having some strong feelings about you. I know when we went out before, I was sort of cocky and said I had three other women and all that, but I now see how much happier I could be with just one woman. I have been very envious of you and Harry and the things you have done together. And, by the way, Andy will be back tomorrow. She'll be back permanently. I was thinking the four of us could really have some good times together. I want you to think about it." As soon as he said this, he realized it was a mistake. Awful timing.

Her mind went into overload. Harry was in surgery. She was beginning to be so attached to him. Andy was coming back. Clay wanted her. It was too much for her to handle. "Clay, not now, please."

She held up both hands in front of her and nodded her head negatively. Just then the nurse came in and said Harry was out of surgery and his breathing was much better. The doctors had still said no visitors until morning. She suggested they go home and come back then.

Clay thought that was a good idea and offered to buy her breakfast before he went back to work. He wanted to apologize for his bad timing.

She absolutely did not want to be alone with Clay now. She said she was not leaving and wanted to lie down on the waiting room couch and try to rest. As hard as he tried, he could not change her mind. Before he left, she asked him which of Harry's daughters he called. He told her it got late and he decided to wait until morning to call when they had more definitive information on his condition. He said he was going to call the oldest, Millie.

Chapter 63

Andy was packed and ready to leave. She had one more task before she left. She had asked Dax to stop by so she could tell him goodbye and ask him a question. He showed up right on time and met Andy by the pool where she was having a last cup of coffee.

As he approached, he removed his straw hat, "On your way huh? Sorry it didn't work for you. I'm sure the girls will miss you."

"I'll miss them too, but they are young and adaptable, they will be fine. I wanted to tell you goodbye and say it has been interesting meeting you. I also have a question."

He didn't speak, he just nodded.

"The plane that landed here before we left town was met by a white van and two men who were wearing dark suits and no ties, do you remember?"

He again nodded.

"I believe they were the two men who were our abductors. Did they identify themselves to you?"

"They did," he said now grinning.

"Do you find this humorous?"

"Well, I do. You see, they showed me their IDs. They are detectives working for the Tampa police," he said ending with a chuckle.

"I seen their badges and IDs."

"Are you sure?"

"O' course. I wouldn't have said it unless I saw 'em with my own eyes."

Andy was stunned. She got up from the table, told him to have a nice life, and left.

When she landed in South Carolina, she instructed the driver to take her straight to the hospital. She called Clay to tell him her plan. Clay was just entering the hospital and said that he would wait for her. She wanted to know about Harry, but he said he had not talked to anyone yet. He told her he would stay until she arrived.

Earlier in Harry's room, Betty had pulled a chair up close where she could hand him his water. His arms worked fine but when he moved his torso, the ribs were painful. He was trying to limit his pain medicine to be able to stay alert to talk to Clay about the attack. He had tried to get Betty to go home and get some rest assuring her he was fine. With all the bandages and tubes in his body, he wasn't very convincing. Clay had posted a deputy and told him nobody but medical staff and Betty were to be allowed in his room. The press had already gotten wind of the attack and two different reporters had attempted entry.

Clay finally arrived. He nodded at Betty and said, "Old man, you look like hell. You are too damn old for this lifestyle you're living."

Betty said, "Clay."

Clay smiled and said, "I'll say one thing for you, friend, you have the prettiest nurse in the building."

Harry tried his own humor, "Have you caught the bastards yet?" He said it smiling even though you could not see it through all his bandages.

"Can you tell me what happened? The only thing I know other than the obvious is your gold is gone, and Betty said your front door was unlocked when she got there."

Harry spoke in a stilted speech. "Two men, Hispanic, heard them talk, accents, one man, big, had a hose like thing weighted on one end, hurt like hell." As he talked more his mouth and jaw loosened so he could talk almost normal. "The man with the hose kicked the crap out of me. He wore black cowboy boots with silver tips on the points of the toes. His right boot had a rip in the side of the sole. The other one told him to stop because the 'man' said they could not kill me. They came in through the front door. Thought it was Ruth. Thought she must have forgotten something. They were on me before I could get the gun out of the drawer."

Harry's body went limp, he was obviously exhausted even though his speech had gotten better.

She said, "I think that's enough Clay, he needs to rest."

"One more thing. Has Ruth ever left the door unlocked before?"

He shook his head no.

"Freddy Lopez's sister, right?"

"Yeah."

"Well he is Hispanic and the SOB is a crook. It's a place to start."

"Hello everybody. I'm back." Andy was standing in the doorway. "Harry, Harry, look at you." She was tearing up and walking toward the bed and kissed him on the head and picked up his hand.

"Hello, Andy, it looks worse that is." His last words before he drifted off.

Clay looked at Andy, "You look good, it's great to have you back. I'm sorry, but I have a lot to do so if you want a ride, we need to go now."

Andy looked disappointed, Betty spoke, "If you want to stay for a while, I will take you home."

Clay had not been gone five minutes when the nurse came in and said, "You need to go now ladies. I'm going to increase his meds so he can get some rest. The doctors have done all they needed to do, and now it's just rest. These bodies take longer to heal when we get older. He should probably be able to talk much better by tomorrow or maybe even tonight."

They left and loaded Betty's car with Andy's bags and headed to Andy's farm. "We didn't talk before you left, but Clay told me about your great opportunity. It must not have been so great."

"Oh no, it was great, too great. It was beyond my capabilities. I jumped too quickly. I didn't do near enough homework. You know me, sometimes I just kind of leap before I look."

Betty didn't respond.

"Tell me about you and Harry. You must have made a move before I landed in Florida."

"That's not fair and not true, you actually made it possible for me to get to know Harry."

"How so?"

"You set him up as the speaker for our women's group. Without you to be his host and show him around the task became mine. His talk was so impressive, I asked if he would do a consulting job for my business. He agreed and we spent a lot of time together. He did an amazing job."

"I didn't know he was doing consulting."

"I'm not sure he had ever intended to, but with the response he got from our group, I think it got him back in business mode. I think he truly enjoyed his work at my business. And then one thing led to another, and I volunteered to help him with his Christmas decorations, and then the winter storm hit and the next thing you know, we have spent two days and two nights at his house."

"Was he a good lover?"

"Whoa, I'm not saying that we slept together. But even if we did, I would not tell you."

"A simple yes or no was all I wanted."

Betty, shocked, "Everything between him and me is strictly our business."

"I'll ask him, he will tell me."

"Are you still interested in him? You just dumped him pretty abruptly."

"It was part of my overall mistake. It was wrong but, yes, I am still very much interested in him."

The rest of the trip was silent. When they arrived, Betty helped her get her things into her house.

"It's nice to have you back. I'm sure we will see each other soon."

Chapter 64

Betty called Clay on her way home to inquire about his call to Harry's daughter. He told her he had left a message telling her that her father had been assaulted and was in the hospital. He said he had not heard back from her.

He also said, "I was just about to call you about dinner tonight. We could either go before or after we go to the hospital."

"No, not tonight. I haven't had much rest and I think I need to spend some time with the daughter if she comes. Give me her number so I can call her."

"Well, you have to eat, I don't see why we can't eat together."

"No, I'm going to offer my time to the daughter, or I'm going home to rest."

He gave her the number, and his last words were that he would probably see her at the hospital. As soon as they hung up, his phone rang again, this time it was Andy. "Hello, brother, are you glad to have me back?"

"Lord of mercy, yes, I am."

"Good, I'm glad to be back home. Let me buy you dinner, my pantry is empty. We can catch up, and I have some interesting things to tell you."

"Well, at least someone will have dinner with me."

"What?"

"I'll tell you later."

"Do you remember I told you about the two guys and the airplane that landed at the farm and I told you I thought they were our abductors?"

"Oh, yeah."

"Well listen to this. They identified themselves to the farm manager as two Tampa police detectives. He saw their IDs and badges."

"What? What's that about?"

"I don't know, but it's starting to smell like a day old fish."

"Hmm, I've got an idea. I'll tell you about it at dinner."

They set the time and place and hung up.

Meanwhile, Betty made a call to Millie, Harry's oldest daughter who was now on her way to Lakeview. She gave her the latest update on her dad and offered to take her to dinner so she could give her a detailed account of everything she knew. Millie was hesitant at first but then agreed. They would meet at the hospital first and then have a late supper.

Clay and Andy had settled into their table at the restaurant and Clay opened a file folder and handed it to her. "These are pictures of all the non-uniformed officers at Tampa PD. See if you recognize anyone."

There were four pictures per page and on the last page she said, "Here they are, it's them, these two," and she pointed at two of the pictures.

"Are you sure?"

"99.9%, I know it's them."

"What the hell has Jack gotten himself into?"

"Why do you say, Jack?"

"The plane, his airstrip, the abduction of you and his daughters. The abduction and nobody hurt. Too many coincidences. You have to be positive of the men, that's critical."

"I'm sure ,but I have an idea. I'll put the pictures on my phone, and I'll send a text to Jane and ask if she or Jenny recognize anybody in the pictures, and that's all I will say."

"Good idea."

She sent the message and the pictures to Jane. In less than five minutes the girls texted back that they were their abductors. She texted back and asked if they were both sure and they said they were positive. She then forwarded all of the texts to his phone so he could have a record of their identification of the two men.

"I'm going to call a contact at the DEA and go over this with him."

"Why the DEA?"

"Well, there is all this info that points towards drugs. First, the guys are narcotics agents. Second, a private plane comes into a private runway and delivers unidentified material. Third, Jack is in South America, and the abduction was to persuade Jack to make the deal. Is that not what you told me?"

"Yes, you are right, but, oh my goodness. You think Jack is involved?"

"At this point, I don't know what to think."

Their dinner was served, and the conversation changed to Clay's new infatuation with Betty. "You know I was becoming envious of you and Harry and how much fun it looked like you were having. At first, I didn't like it. I thought he was too old for you, but then I saw how happy you were and then you up and left. Then the Betty and Harry thing starts up and I see two people again really happy, and I'm thinking I bounce around with three or four women, have sex and momentary fun but not anything beyond the moment. Then I get to know Betty much better, and I see why he has taken to her. I admit I was jealous again. Then I find out you are coming back and I think this is perfect. You and Harry and Betty and me, the four of us could really have some fun together. Don't you think I'm right about this?"

"I see why you say that, but, I'm not sure where Harry is. I didn't treat him the best when I left. And then there is Betty, and I'm pretty sure she has slept with him and I never did."

"Really, I assumed y'all were there."

She didn't respond. They had finished with their dinner and her phone buzzed; it was Jack. She motioned for Clay to stay quiet.

"Hello, Jack. I didn't expect to hear from you so soon."

"Andy I just met with the girls, and they told me, showed me the text and pictures you sent. What the hell do you think you are doing? I'm telling you in no uncertain terms, drop this, stop this. My girls are minors and will not be allowed to testify or be witnesses. Besides, I think they made a mistake when they said what they did. They are not sure of anything anymore. Listen nobody has been harmed, please let it go. If you don't, you are asking for trouble not only for my family and me but also for you. Do you understand me?"

She was stunned at his tone. She had turned the phone on speaker and Clay had heard every word. He was red-faced and pissed and wanted to take the phone away from her, but she wisely kept control of it.

"Jack, I understand every word you said, but I make no promises about anything. What kind of mess are you in?"

"Just drop it, and it will go away."

"Goodbye, Jack."

"He threatened you. That SOB threatened you. Who the hell does he think he is?" Clay caught his breath, relaxed and sat back in his chair. "Jack's in big trouble, and I believe now even more than what I thought earlier. It's probably drugs and probably one of the cartels."

Chapter 65

Harry watched as Millie and Betty left his hospital room headed for dinner. He had hated that Millie had to come back so soon after Christmas. She was the oldest and she had the most flexible schedule but still not a fun visit. The medication and sleep had made him start to feel human again. As long as he was relatively still, the pain was under control. Only when he moved, did his face and ribs hurt. After some thought, he felt like he was lucky to be alive. A blessing. He hoped he had persuaded Millie to go back home in the morning. He was hoping to go home the next day, and Betty had insisted she would make sure he was properly cared for.

Betty, he had seen the look on her face. He had watched her interact with Millie. What a change between the two of them since Christmas and now dinner. It would be interesting to see if Millie left and trusted Betty to be his caregiver. His thoughts kept going back to Betty and how caring she had been. She had stayed overnight. Even though her face showed fatigue and stress, he could also tell they were becoming bound together. He loved the interaction he saw between the two women.

Then his thoughts turned to Andy. Betty had told him she was back for good. At least that's what she said Andy had told them. He thought he remembered seeing her, but maybe it was a dream. The previous night had turned into a fog. He wondered what her expectations were regarding their relationship. Did she think they would pick back up where they were when she so abruptly left? He truly was not sure about her expectations. And then the question entered his mind; what did he expect or want? Was he going to have to choose? He tried to take his thoughts somewhere else, somewhere more pleasant. But right now his thoughts were not pleasant. He thought about the two bastards who came into his house, beat him, and stole his coins. He thought about Ruth and the fact the one and only time she forgets to lock the door there are intruders there just to walk right in and Hispanic intruders. It could not be a coincidence. He would have bet a thousand dollars Ruth would never betray him the way he believed she had.

Chapter 66

As Clay and Andy walked from the parking lot to the hospital, Andy stopped. "Clay, maybe we should do what Jack suggested, just drop this whole thing. He was correct in that nobody was hurt. Maybe we should just move on."

"I can't believe you would think or even say that. These are bad dudes. Maybe the next time somebody gets hurt or killed. Plus, as sure as we are standing here, there are drugs involved. That plane, private airfield, in and out in a hurry. The police don't do things that way. Hell no, we are going to stop those two bad cops and maybe even more bad guys."

"But Jack says he will not let the girls testify. It will just be my word."

"We've got pictures and text messages from the girls, and I'll let my friends at the DEA worry about all that. We need to get on in and see how Harry's doing, but I have one big question before we go. Are you expecting to be back in the same place with him before you left?"

She paused then started walking again, "We will see…we will just have to wait and see."

As they started through the entrance, they ran into Millie and Betty on their way out and to dinner.

Clay introduced Millie and she responded, "Oh, you must be the redhead I've heard about." Andy smiled and glanced at Betty. They got a quick update on Harry's condition, and each couple moved on.

*****

Harry was resting when he heard someone entering his room. When he opened his eyes, he saw her, red hair, big smile and as beautiful as ever.

"Andy, you're back and still as gorgeous as ever."

"And you, Harry Blake, no matter your condition you never change, still a charming rascal."

She came to his side grabbed his hand and kissed him very gently on his lips.

Clay walked in behind her and said, "It looks like nothing has changed." He said that wanting it to be so.

Harry looked at her and said, "You didn't have to come all this way to check on me, I'm fine." He said this knowing he had been told she had come back for good.

She smiled mischievously and said, "After I heard what happened to you, I realized I should have never left. You need a responsible person to take care of you in your old age."

"Oh, that hurts, maybe more than my body," and he chuckled.

"I'm going to interrupt you two. Harry and I need to talk, and then I'm going to leave and y'all can catch up. I know you must have a lot to talk about."

"Did you arrest anybody?"

"Not yet."

"Did you talk to Ruth?"

"No, but listen to this. She disappeared. We couldn't find her anywhere. We tried to see Freddy, but, he too, was nowhere to be found. Then late this afternoon I get a call from our mutual friend and attorney Roscoe Abernathy. He says he knows we are looking for Ruth Lopez, and that she is now his client and will be available at his office tomorrow afternoon."

"Well, if there was any doubt, she left my door unlocked accidentally, I guess that answers that question."

"I would say so, but I would also guarantee she's not going to be providing any help on anything. I think this is Freddy's way of locking her down."

"I think she will talk to me. I'm sure I can make her talk."

"Maybe, but you aren't going to get that chance. Roscoe wouldn't dare let her come here."

"I'm sure, but I'm going with you to see her and Roscoe."

Andy exclaimed, "What? You can't do that." She jumped in, "Harry that blow to your head must have scrambled your brain. You have to stay here and recover. A person your age has got to take the proper time to heal and regain your strength."

Harry stared at Andy and spoke, "You haven't been here ten minutes and that's the second time you have commented about my age. It didn't seem to bother you before."

She blushed, "You know what I mean," her response was sharp.

Clay responded, "Hey, even if I wanted to take you, the hospital is not going to let you out of here."

"You are both wrong. I am going to get released in the morning to go home. I am going home with one stop to see my old friend, Roscoe, and my housekeeper, Ruth."

"Never gonna happen, my friend. But I tell you what, if they let you out, I'll take you with me," and he smiled smugly.

"Clay!" Andy jumped in, but before she could say more, he held up his hand in her direction and spoke, "Don't worry, I've made a good decision. Now I'm out of here so you two can get caught up."

Clay left, and Andy started thinking. She could tell she had touched a nerve with her comment about his age and she wanted to recover.

"Hey, listen, I'm not worried about your age. You and I have talked about it, and you know it has never been an issue for me. The point I was trying to make was our bodies heal slower, and take more time to recover as we get older. It's obvious you took quite a beating. So please don't be mad at me on our first visit since I have come back!" she said smiling and putting her hand on his arm.

"Okay, forget it. But just so you know, I have one more concussion-related test in the morning, and if I pass, I'm out of here. They have done all they can for me. I just need time and to finish some antibiotics."

She did not respond to what he had said but she did begin, "Can we change subjects?"

"Sure."

"I need to apologize for the way I left. It was wrong. I owed you more than that. When I walked out of your house, I knew I had made a big mistake. We had something that was starting to be special, and I just pulled the plug on it.

"I was impulsive and wrong. I've always had this impulsive streak. I have usually gotten away with some stupid decisions but not this time. Do you think you could ever forgive me?"

"Of course. Look we weren't married or even engaged. You had this big opportunity. I'm sorry it didn't work out. By the way, do you want to tell me what happened?"

"It was nobody's fault but my own. I didn't do the research and check it out. It was a great place. It was way over my head. Jack tried to accommodate me in every way possible, but it just wasn't right. I needed to come back here where I now know I belong. My small town, my lake, my farm, my family, my friends, and you, Harry, if we can start over."

"I will always be your friend. All my memories before you leaving were great. I'll admit I was hurt. I couldn't believe you left like you did, but it made me realize I was probably a good bit ahead of where you were. I also realized you were the first woman in my life since Maggie and maybe I was lonely and trying to move too fast. I'm not sure, but those were some of my thoughts."

She was now beginning to fend off the tears, "What about Betty?"

He smiled, "I certainly wasn't looking for anyone else. The speech that you set up at the women's luncheon was where we first met. She was terrific. The speech went well, and so we ended up spending the better part of a day together. She then asked me if I would do a review of her business. I had always wanted to consult, but it just never worked out. I decided to take the job, and it turned out really good for both of us. By this time, we were very comfortable with each other, and we enjoyed the others' company. Anyway, I mentioned I had to decorate the house for Christmas before my family came and that Maggie had always handled it and I didn't know where to start, and she volunteered to help and then the winter storm and two and half days stranded alone, and now we are close friends."

"I can see how it happened, I'm just disappointed. I really thought you and I would be together. Is there any chance we could start over? I know you have slept with her, but sometimes that doesn't necessarily work out."

He frowned, shook his head negatively, and spoke, "Why do you say you know we have slept together?"

"Well, Clay, and two days stranded in the storm. Are you saying you haven't slept with Betty?"

"That, my dear, is nobody's business. I would not respond one way or the other."

She decided to drop the subject. She decided there was hope. Time to move onward, but slowly.

Chapter 67

Betty arrived at the hospital early on her way to work, but Harry was not in his room. The nurse said they were running their last test to see if he could be released. She said he was insisting he be allowed to leave.

Betty wrote a note that told him to call if he was released and she would pick him up and take him home. She said if she didn't hear from him, she would be back to see him at lunchtime. She left the note on his pillow and went to her office.

Her morning passed quickly and as she was getting ready to go back to the hospital, her cell phone rang. It was Harry. He thanked her for coming by and told her he was leaving now with Clay for a meeting with Roscoe at Roscoe's office. He said he would call her back after the meeting. She cautioned him about overdoing it. He needed more time to recover.

Harry had been taken to the hospital entrance by wheelchair as was their policy where he carefully climbed into Clay's big SUV.

As they headed for Roscoe's, Clay said, "You know he's going to be pissed when you show up. He may not let you participate."

"I know, but you must insist. I need to see Ruth, and she needs to see me. I need to ask her questions in a certain way, and I need to hear and see how she reacts."

The two men walked into Roscoe's office, and when he saw Harry, he exploded, "Get him out of here, this is totally wrong."

When Ruth saw Harry's face, her eyes got as big as silver dollars, and she looked as if she were about to cry.

Harry spoke, "Ruth, are you upset with me?"

She shook her head from left to right and before Roscoe could speak, Harry said, "Then you don't mind if I stay, do you?"

Again, she shook her head from left to right. Roscoe looking at Ruth said, "Please Ruth, you need to listen to me, we can't allow him to be here."

Harry spoke quickly, "Ruth, are you afraid of me?"

Again, she moved her head from left to right.

Clay quickly spoke, "Well I guess that's settled. Look, we are here only to talk and ask some questions. We are not here to charge Ruth with any crime."

Ruth could not stop looking at Harry's face. He looked at her and said, "It's not quite as bad as it looks." She didn't appear to get any relief from his remark.

Clay and Harry sat, without being invited, in the two chairs in front of Roscoe's desk. Ruth was seated in a straight chair beside Roscoe's big leather desk chair. Roscoe was still standing, trying to decide his next move.

Clay ignored Roscoe and turned to Ruth and started speaking.

"Ruth did you and Mr. Blake have a disagreement, or did he hurt your feelings in some way?"

"No."

"Has he tried to take advantage of you in any way?"

"No."

"Do you like working for Mr. Blake?"

"Yes."

"How many times have you forgotten to lock Mr. Blake's door in the past?"

Roscoe interrupted, "Don't answer that. That is an improper question. If she forgot to lock the door, she wouldn't necessarily remember."

Clay was not to be denied, "Harry how many times has Ruth failed to lock your door when she left?"

"Never."

"You mean, never before the other day, right?"

"Correct."

Roscoe started to speak but stopped himself.

"Why did you leave the door unlocked Ruth?"

Roscoe answered, "Hey, it was a mistake. She's human, we all make mistakes."

Harry leaned over and whispered in Clay's ear. Then Clay spoke, "Was it a mistake, Ruth?"

She was beginning to tear up, "Yes, it was a mistake."

Roscoe smiled, "I told you."

"Do you wish you had not made the mistake, Ruth?"

"Oh, yes," and now she was quietly sobbing.

"You can see, Mr. Blake took quite a beating, and his gold coins were stolen. And you know and we know, it was a mistake."

Harry leaned over and again whispered to Clay.

Again Clay stared at Ruth and said, "Ruth it wasn't a forgetful error. You have proven you're way too efficient for that. No, it was a mistake, a mistake in judgment that could have cost Mr. Blake his life."

Roscoe stood up and almost shouted, "What are you trying to say? You are upsetting my client, and I must ask you to leave. This is outrageous!"

Clay now stood and leaned over the desk toward Roscoe, "No, this isn't outrageous. What is outrageous, is that five minutes after the mistake, two Mexican thugs broke into Harry's house, beat the hell out of him, and stole his gold coins."

Both men were nose to nose and breathing hard. The confrontation was broken by Ruth who was now openly crying, "I'm so sorry, Mr. Harry. Please forgive me. I wish I could take it back."

"Shut up, Ruth," Roscoe shouted, "You have upset her, so she doesn't know what she's saying."

"Yes, I do! Please forgive me, Mr. Harry."

Harry stared at Ruth but did not speak. He simply stood and walked out the door. Harry's mind was racing when he walked out of Roscoe's building. He needed to think. He walked past Clay's vehicle headed nowhere, just thinking. He turned the corner to the back of the building and saw a big SUV parked with two men in the front seat. The front windows were down and they were both smoking. As he got closer, he could see they were both Hispanic. He knew immediately the car was for Ruth and it had to belong to Freddy. They saw him walking toward the vehicle and they threw out their cigarettes and rolled up the front windows. Harry wanted to see their feet. He was looking for the black cowboy boots with the silver tips. He was almost to the front door when Clay rounded the corner and spoke, "Harry, what the hell are you doing?" He stopped and waited for Clay to join him. He told him he wanted to see if they were wearing boots. Clay insisted now is not the time, if the men realized the objective, then they would know we are looking for boots. "We've done enough for this trip. Let's get you home and resting."

Harry called Betty and told her Clay was taking him home, and he wanted to spend some time with Millie. She told him Millie had gone back home. They had agreed that Betty would take care of him and provide daily updates on his status. She told him to have Clay drop him off at her office.

Harry told Clay the new plan and leaned back, closed his eyes and thought, *Millie and Betty.*

Chapter 68

Betty transported Harry to his home and settled him in his big easy chair after he refused to go to bed. She sat down beside him and offered to get him food or something to drink, but he was just too tired and wanted to rest, maybe even sleep some.

But before he closed his eyes, he wanted to know how in the world she had convinced Millie to leave him in her hands. She smiled and told him that she and Millie had never had a real conversation during the holidays. They had only talked about superficial things. She said when she called Millie to talk about her father's condition, and what had happened, that the conversation had shifted to her relationship with her father. She told him she had been completely honest with Mille about how they had met and how their relationship had evolved. She admitted that for her seeing him on the floor that day with all the blood, the whole event took her a step forward in her feelings for him. She said she felt a bond developing between Millie and herself.

Harry was amazed. He sat silently. Then he told her he needed to rest and he closed his eyes. She got up went to the kitchen and started planning their dinner.

He had been asleep for a couple of hours when the phone rang. Betty answered on the first ring hoping it would not wake him.

"Betty? I was expecting to talk to his daughter. Is she available?"

"No, Andy, Millie has gone back home. I'm here taking care of Harry."

"Well, I called to say I have made my lamb stew which is one of his favorites. What time are you leaving now that dinner is taken care of?"

"I'm not, my deal with Millie was that I would be staying and taking care of him."

"But Betty, you must be exhausted; you hardly had time to rest. Listen I'll come over, take your place, handle dinner and you can get some rest. I'm sure Millie would not mind as long as someone is taking care of him."

"Absolutely not, I promised her, and if something were to happen, I would feel as if I had broken my promise."

"Nothing is going to happen."

"No, I'm not leaving, end of discussion."

"All right then, don't worry about dinner. I've got stew and bread; the three of us will eat together. Everything is ready, I will be there by five," and she hung up before Betty could reply.

He was awake by now and had come to the kitchen where she met him and they started to embrace when he gently pushed her away telling her no squeezing. She told him about Andy's phone call and what was going to happen for dinner. He decided he wanted a shower, fresh clothes, and a drink.

Harry was now clean and refreshed. Even though he was in pain, he was starting to feel like a human being again. He put on some Ella Fitzgerald and headed for the bar. Betty stopped him, made him sit down at the island and started making him a drink when the doorbell rang. It was Andy loaded down with their dinner. They let her in, and she also had to be reminded of no squeezing. She put her stew on the stove on low and preheated the oven, so when they decided to eat, she could bake the bread.

They had just settled on the stools at the kitchen island when the doorbell rang again. This time it was Clay who had come by to check on Harry, and to give Andy an update on his meeting with his DEA contact. He made himself a drink and gave Betty and Harry a brief summary on what had happened with Andy's abduction and the two Tampa detectives. He told them the DEA had decided not to make arrests now. They wanted to put surveillance on the two men in hopes of landing more and hopefully bigger fish. Clay finished and had agreed to stay for dinner when the doorbell rang again. This time it was Johnny Blake, Harry's oldest. He came in, saw his father, and said, "Dad, you are too damn old for fist fights, you need to stick to guns."

Harry grinned, "Now you tell me. Where were you a few days ago?" He wanted all the details, and Harry asked how long he was staying. He told him mid-morning, and he told his son he would fill him in later since everybody there had already heard the story.

When everyone had finished their drinks, they were ready to eat. As Andy dished up the last bowl of stew, she looked at Harry and said, "Sorry no leftover or seconds." They all laughed.

Andy thought at least Harry will not be alone with Betty tonight.

Betty wondered if Millie had solicited Johnny so her dad would not be left with her. She also knew at some point something had to give between Andy and her.

Dinner was over, the kitchen was clean and Clay spoke. "Okay, ladies it's time we let the Blake men have some time together. So let's get out of their hair."

Betty didn't hesitate, she walked over to Harry, kissed him and whispered in his ear, she would see him at lunchtime after Johnny was gone. She told everyone good night and walked out to her car where she waited to make sure Andy followed.

Andy also went to Harry, gave him a kiss and told him to enjoy his son.

Clay had watched both women say goodnight and as he left, he just walked out shaking his head saying, "Harry, Harry."

Harry went to his easy chair to recline and finish the last of his dinner wine. He then gave a detailed picture of what had happened including the meeting in Roscoe's office. He concluded by saying he felt between he and Clay they would get the perpetrators.

"Dad, the redhead is a real looker. What are you going to do? There was so much undercurrent in that room between those two women we could have all been sucked out to sea. Are you ready to break somebody's heart? How will you choose? On the one hand I don't envy you having to decide but, on the other hand, you sure can't lose."

Johnny waited, but his father didn't respond. He just sipped his wine and stared at the fire that had been started earlier in the evening.

Chapter 69

It was almost noon the next day. Johnny had left mid-morning after a late breakfast with his father. The older he got, the more he enjoyed spending time with his children especially when it was one on one. Andy had called an insisted on making dinner for him. She wanted them to spend some private time together.

Betty arrived just after noon with a batch of chili from the local diner. The place was a greasy spoon, but their chili was thick, meaty, and spicy, just perfect for a cold winter day. They ate at the kitchen island, and he assured her he was making progress in his recovery. He had taken no pain pills since the day before. His headaches were gone. The side of his face now only hurt when touched. His ribs were still sore and tender when he moved. They were going to take a while to heal. She told him again, she had promised Millie that she would see to it that he was taken care of, until he had healed and she intended to keep her promise and she would not be passing that responsibility on to anyone else, and they both knew to whom she was referring.

She poured him another cup of coffee and told him she needed to have a serious conversation with him, "I didn't sleep very well last night. I was trying to sort out my thoughts about my present situation. I decided I needed to talk to you and be as open an honest as I could. Yesterday evening was very uncomfortable for me. Andy and I have been friends for a long time, and all I felt was tension between us. It was like, okay, we both know we are competing with each other."

He tried to interrupt, but she stopped him, "Let me finish before you say anything. Let me say one of the things I know for sure is, I do not want to be in a competition. And here's where I was unsure of saying this, not because I wasn't sure of what I said, but whether I should say it. Our relationship has been growing, and for me, it has been great. I truly had not thought too much about where it was going, or if it was going anywhere. It's just been great. But, when I saw you down in your office and the blood, it broke my heart. At that moment I realized how much I cared for you. It wasn't feeling sorry for a hurt friend; it was the emotion of caring so much for you, I hurt.

"Having said that, I also know that you and Andy had a special relationship because you told me so. You said that you were ready to take a next step in the relationship when she bailed. I know she is back and it is very clear she wants to pick back up where you left off. I understand, and that's where I am going. I can't,

I mean, I will not be in a competition, at least not willingly. You now know how I feel about you, but if you still have strong feelings for Andy, it would never work. I will keep my promise to Millie, but I will not fight with Andy for your time."

They sat silently staring at each other for a few minutes, and he broke the ice, "Thank you for your honesty and sharing with me. I agree, there should be no competition. By the way, she has called and is bringing dinner for two again tonight."

She did not respond but only again stared at him.

He continued, "I have a lot going on. I want to help Clay catch the bastards who did this to me. I want to get my coins back. I want to have a private conversation with Ruth and hire her back if it goes well."

She looked surprised, "Are you sure that's wise? Can you ever trust her again?"

"After seeing her face to face, I think I can, depending on how she responds. I would like for you to be here when I call, as a witness. I'll do it on the speakerphone."

"When do you want to do it?"

"Now."

They went into his office, set the phone on speaker, and he called Ruth. She answered and was shocked that he had called her. Before he could start, she spoke, "Mr. Harry, how are you? How do you feel? I am so sorry, Mr. Harry."

"I am improving every day. Ruth, I have questions for you, but I must know you will be totally truthful with your answers."

"Of course, yes, I will."

"Would you like to continue working for me?"

She was silent for a moment, "You would let me? Oh yes, yes, of course."

"I must know you will always be truthful and never deceive or betray me again."

"Never, never again is my promise."

"I know it was your brother, but I must know that if he asks you to do anything involving, me you must say no."

"Yes, yes, it was a bad mistake by me, never again."

"Okay, can we keep our same schedule?"

"Oh yes, thank you, thank you."

"One other question. Do you know a Mexican man who wears black cowboy boots with silver tips?"

Again she was silent for a moment and then spoke, "Yes, I do."

"Do you know more than one man who wears boots like this?"

"No, only one."

"What is his name?"

"Henry Delgado."

"Does he work for your brother?"

"Sometimes he does, yes. Can I ask why you ask about him?"

"No, and I need to trust you will not mention my inquiry to anybody. Can I trust you on this?"

"Yes."

"I'll see you in a few days, everything as before."

"Yes, and thank you again, Mr. Blake."

He immediately dialed Clay.

"Clay, Henry Delgado is the man in the silver tip boots, and he works for Freddy. I want this to be an anonymous tip. I want to protect my source."

"Is it Ruth?"

"Keep me posted, Clay."

He thanked Betty for everything, and they promised to stay in touch. She kissed him on the cheek and left.

Chapter 70

Clay wasn't happy that Harry would not confide in him, but that was outweighed by his excitement of having a concrete lead in the case. He contacted his favorite judge, Felton Henry and explained the details and was told to come immediately and get his warrant to search the home and auto of Henry Delgado.

With warrant in hand, Clay and Morris Canady went directly to Delgado's home. They finally had caught a break. The low rider that had been identified by the DMV as to belonging to Delgado was parked in his driveway.

Clay sent Morris to the rear of the house, and he knocked on the front door. At first, no one answered and then finally a voice from inside answered, "Go away, I'm busy."

Clay knocked again and said, "Open up, it's the sheriff."

There was no response and Clay spoke again, "If you don't open the door, I will knock it down."

"Hold on, just wait a minute. I ain't done nothing," Delgado said this as he led his half-dressed girlfriend to the back door where they were met by Deputy Morris Canady. With handgun drawn Canady led them back through the house to the front door where they opened the door for the sheriff.

Delgado was wearing only blue jeans. It was obvious that they had interrupted their afternoon delight.

"Hey man, why you here? I ain't done nothing, I told you."

"Mr. Delgado, you have been listed as a suspect in the attempted murder of Mr. Harry Blake."

"I ain't tried to murder nobody."

"We have a warrant to search the premises and your automobile. Why don't you get dressed and we will begin our search."

Canady smiled at Clay as he realized he wanted him to put on the boots as confirmation of ownership. They began looking around the house for any weapons and especially the weighted hose Harry had described. After a few minutes, Delgado joined them fully dressed and wearing the black cowboy boots with the silver tips.

"Hey, nice boots," Morris said.

Delgado answered, "Yeah, expensive, and the only pair like them in these parts."

Canady leaned over and said, "Let me look closer."

"Oh, too bad, looks like you have a cut on the sole of the right boot."

"Yeah, happened a while back."

Without saying anything else they went to the bedroom and began to search. The bed was unmade and a mess. Canady spoke, "Mr. Delgado, are there any firearms in the house?"

"Oh, no."

About then Clay lifted the mattress and discovered a .357 magnum handgun and a .12-gauge shotgun.

"Oh yeah, I'm sorry, I just forgot."

They finished searching the bedroom, and the deputy went to check out Delgado's car. In less than five minutes he was back inside where Delgado and his girlfriend were sitting on the living room couch. The deputy was carrying a black rubber hose full of lead weights on one end.

"Hey man, I keep that for protection. There are some bad dudes around, you know."

Clay looked at Morris then turned, faced Delgado and said, "Mr. Delgado, I am arresting you and charging you with the attempted murder of Mr. Harry Blake. Cuff him, Morris."

"Hey man, you can't do this. I ain't tried to kill nobody. This ain't right." He looked at his girlfriend and told her to call Freddy.

"Freddy can't save you from this one. Only you can save yourself by telling me who put you up to the robbery and murder attempt."

Henry Delgado was in a state of shock. How could this be happening?

Chapter 71

After Betty left, Harry tried to work on his book, which had gotten little attention during the holidays and all the other confusion going on in his life. It was not just the book he wanted to avoid thinking about, this whole thing with the two women was invading his thoughts as well. Betty's confession had not made things any easier, and then tonight he would have to deal with Andy alone for the evening.

After a few hours in his office on the book, he was tired, and he moved to his recliner to close his eyes and rest for a while. In less than a minute he was asleep. He went into a deep sleep and now was awakened by his doorbell. Had he slept so long that Andy was already here? He hoped not. He came out of his sleep stupor, straightened up, exited his chair, and realized, to his amazement, it was Ruth Lopez at his door. He let her in, "Ruth what a surprise."

It was more than just her presence that amazed him, she was wearing makeup, and her hair was different. She was carrying a big wicker basket which was filled with food. He took the basket and led her into the house and headed toward the kitchen. When she removed her long winter coat, he was surprised again. She wore perfectly fitting grey slacks and a maroon silk blouse. It was the first time he had ever seen her made up. She always wore no makeup, frumpy clothes and hair when she came to work. This was quite a change, a pleasant one at that.

He wasn't speaking, just staring.

She smiled at him and spoke, "Is everything all right? I hope you are not mad. I fixed food for you. Hopefully enough for a few days. I thought it was the least I could do. I want to apologize again. I am so, so sorry for what I did." She was sorting out the various pots and bowls she brought as if her presence was a regular thing.

Harry's mind jumped to what Maggie had said on several occasions about the woman. He could still hear her voice, "Hey, I see you checking her out. Nice body, put some makeup and nice clothes, and she would be a fine looking woman." He would always deny, but they both knew what she said was true.

"I'm sorry Ruth, I was asleep when you came to the door and I, I mean, you really surprised me. "

"Oh, I'm so sorry I woke you. I know you need to get plenty of rest."

"No, no, I needed to be getting up, I slept long enough."

"If you like, I will be happy to stay until you are ready to eat. I can serve you and then clean up. Is there anything, I mean anything at all, I can do for you while I am here, I don't know if there could be enough that I could do for you to make up for the pain I have caused."

"It's okay. What is done is done, and we both have to move on. You didn't have to do this, but I can't tell you how much I appreciate this, and as far as you staying, I would not mind but the way you are dressed, you must have plans for the evening."

"No plans, other than you. I thought you should know, there is another side to me other than housekeeping, I am prepared to stay the evening if you needed or wanted me to."

He wasn't sure how he should respond. Then he remembered Andy, "Actually, a friend is bringing dinner. When you surprised me, I almost forgot."

"Again, I am so sorry. I just barged in, took over the kitchen, and started warming food without asking if you had plans. Forgive me."

"It's fine, don't worry, I know what she is bringing, and it will keep. It's fine."

"Mr. Harry, I should have called and asked before coming over, I'm sorry." She was obviously distressed.

Harry walked over to her put his hands on her shoulders, "Don't be upset, it was a wonderful gesture. But I think it's time to drop the 'Mister,' just call me Harry."

"But you are my employer, I must show respect."

"Make me happy and drop the Mr."

"I will do whatever I can to make you happy."

It was the first time he had ever been that close to her and the first time he had ever touched her. Her smell was intoxicating.

Then the doorbell rang. It had to be Andy. He dropped his hands from her shoulders and stepped back. He motioned for her to stay and he went to the door to find Clay.

"Big news friend, let me fix us something to drink, and I will give you the details. By the way, who's car is that?"

He motioned Clay toward the kitchen, and when Clay saw Ruth, he was shocked. He had only seen Ruth at Roscoe's office, and she had appeared to be a frumpy housekeeper, plus the fact she never got out of her chair.

"You two obviously know each other."

Clay spoke shaking his head, "Damn Ruth, if I had passed you on the street, I don't think I would have recognized you." She smiled but did not speak.

Clay spoke again, "This kitchen smells great."

"Complements of Ms. Lopez."

"I thought Andy was making your dinner."

"She is, it's complicated."

"I should leave," she said.

"Ruth, you don't have to go, you can stay as long as you like."

"No, I think I better go."

He walked her to the door just as Andy appeared. She came in, and for a moment the two women just looked each other over.

"Andy this is Ruth. Ruth this is Andy."

Neither spoke until Andy said, "You are the housekeeper?"

Ruth did not hesitate, "Why, yes, I am."

"The one who left the door unlocked?"

Harry couldn't believe she said that but before he could speak Ruth answered, "Yes, it was a terrible mistake."

"I guess," Andy said sarcastically.

"Why don't you join your brother in the kitchen, I need to speak to Ruth, I'll join you in a few minutes."

She turned and walked to the kitchen without saying another word.

He helped Ruth with her coat and again put his hands on her shoulders, "I'm sorry about that. She was very rude. I will see you at the regular time tomorrow, right?"

"Yes."

"Thank you for thinking about me, Ruth."

She smiled at him and left. He stood at the door and watched her go. He could hardly believe what just happened.

Chapter 72

When she was gone, he went back to the kitchen. Clay was smiling like a Cheshire cat. "What was that all about? Man, I never saw a housekeeper that looked like that."

Andy was not smiling.

Harry held up both hands, "I don't know exactly. I think it's about a guilty conscience. I've never seen her dressed up like that before. I think she is doing what she thinks she needs to do to make up for the beating I took. There is nothing romantic going on here. What is she, forty-five, maybe fifty? She didn't even look like the woman who takes care of my house."

Andy could not contain herself, "Why in the world would you have anything to do with her? You should be charging her with a crime, and you should be arresting her."

"Think about what you just said. Arresting her for forgetting to lock his front door. I don't think so."

"You both know that's not true."

"You are right, but we could never prove it in court," Harry answered. "Besides, she knows she was wrong, and she has apologized."

"You could have been killed. I think this is crazy."

"Hey, it's done, it's over, I made my decision and have moved on. Tell me about Delgado."

Clay gave them both the play by play of the Henry Delgado search and arrest. He told them he has Delgado sweating. He had never expected the charges to be attempted murder. Plus, it appears Freddy has vanished. Roscoe is going to represent Delgado, and he was heard telling Delgado that Freddy was gone and he doubted either of them would see him again. Clay had decided to let him sweat it out overnight and start to put the pressure on again in the morning. He finished by telling them they not only had the boots but also the weighted rubber hose which by the way still had traces of dried blood on it. They had sent it to the lab in hopes they could tie it back to Harry.

"What a great job you have done. All we need now is his partner and his boss."

"Nothing would have been done if you had not seen those boots and gotten your so-called anonymous tip. Delgado never dreamed you could identify those fancy boots. Without the boots, we would be chasing our tails."

"Good work and you are welcome to stay and eat. We have lots of food."

"Thanks, but no thanks, I'm going back to work. Lot's going on in our little town."

While he walked Clay to the door, she fixed them both drinks. He returned and started apologizing for all the food.

"I never dreamed in a million years she would show up here tonight dressed up and bring all this food. It was a real surprise. But I think we should eat hers. I think yours will be easier to freeze and save for later."

"Does this mean I can come back again tomorrow?"

Harry smiled, "I guess if that's what you would like."

"You know you are a very unpredictable man, don't you?"

"I didn't, but I think that's good. But please explain."

"How you could forgive that woman amazes me, let me rephrase that. I can see how you can forgive her but allowing her to work here still is surprising."

"It's very simple. I did not want to have to retrain somebody and let's face it, she's nice looking and easy to be around," as he laughed out loud, "Gotcha!"

"That's not funny, Mr. Harry Blake."

"Oh, it hurts to laugh, so no touching and no joking," he said with a huge grin on his face.

"One last word on the subject. I hope you forgive me that easily and hire me back the way I was before," and she pushed his shoulder.

He grimaced then smiled and said, "No touching, remember?"

They ate Ruth's food, and it was delicious. She cleaned up and suggested they start a fire and watch a movie. She had decided it was better not to push him too hard or too fast. She wanted him to feel comfortable with her again. She settled on the couch next to his recliner and watched the movie.

The excellent food and wine, fireplace and his physical condition had him asleep halfway through the movie. She lasted only minutes longer. They were awakened by his phone. It was Clay, he wanted to come back. When they looked at the time, they realized he had been gone for over three hours. In minutes Clay was at the front door.

"I hope I didn't interrupt anything important."

She answered, "Oh, but you did. You woke us both, sleeping through an old movie we had both probably seen twice."

"Can I impose and have a nightcap? You are not going to believe what I have to tell you."

She fixed them all a drink and they sat down in front of the fireplace. They were both staring at Clay.

"Okay, I told you they were going to surveil the two Tampa cops. Well, they did, including phone taps. They were able to identify the main guy in Miami. When I say the main guy, I mean he controls the whole southeast for this cartel. Well, they raided his place and caught him with his pants down. He was having some kind of big meeting with his people, and they got everything he had; detailed records of contacts, routes, money, the whole nine yards. You will not believe where his distribution in the upstate comes from? Our own little Lakeview. I told you there was lots going on in our little town. We had no clue. Now here is the icing on the cake. Guess who controls things in Lakeview?"

They, of course, had no clue.

"The one and only, Mr. Freddy Lopez."

"That's unbelievable, but you knew he was crooked," Harry said.

"True, but I sure didn't know this."

"Is this Miss Housekeeper's brother?"

"Absolutely," Clay said.

She looked at Harry, "And you still want to have her in your house?"

"It's not her, it's her brother." Harry shook his head amazed she would make the comment. He had said it harshly and decided to try to quickly change the tone, "Just because your brother is a weak and passive law enforcement person, doesn't mean you are too." And he laughed and pointed his finger at Clay, she laughed, but Clay said,

"You two, leave me out of your fight."

"What happens now?"

"My guess is we will never see Freddy again. I suspect between Delgado being caught and now this, he will slip across the border never to be seen or heard of again. Plus, I wouldn't be surprised if Delgado's partner isn't gone with Freddy. By the way, the DEA will raid everything related to Freddy at daylight."

"You know whose face I would like to see when they find all this out?"

"Who?"

"Our good friend, Roscoe."

Both men laughed.

Clay said, "I got to go grab a few hours of sleep before the big raid." He looked at his sister and said, "Are you staying or going?"

"None of your business, now get out of here."

"Okay, but one last thing, Andy, you are the new hero of the DEA. Thanks to your tip, it was one of their biggest busts ever."

Clay left the pair standing at the front door. He looked at her and said, "I'm beat, I've got to get some sleep."

She smiled, "I brought clothes so I can stay over and make you a nice breakfast."

"Thanks, but I need to work, and I've reached a point I can fend for myself."

"Are you sure? I don't mind staying, as a matter of fact, I would like to stay."

"Look, you have been so kind with the food and everything, but I really do need to spend some time alone. I need to have some quiet time to think."

"Well I hope some of your thinking time is about me," and she smiled, kissed him on the mouth, retrieved her coat and left. She was pretty sure Betty would be his chosen one.

Chapter 73

Harry slept hard and late, it was after nine in the morning when he pulled himself out of bed and headed to the kitchen to make coffee. He was glad to be alone. He seemed to have so many unresolved issues on his plate. He had his book which had been virtually ignored since before the holidays. He received an email with the final draft of the mini-series script which he was committed to approving. He had the open item of catching and solving all involved in his beating and of course trying to recover his coins. And last, but certainly not least, what was he going to do about Andy and Betty. When he thought of them, the other issues seemed easy.

He moved, and it was 11 am before he made it to this office to start work. His phone rang, it was Betty, wanting to bring lunch. He told her that he had a late breakfast and he needed to work. She had restated her promise to Millie, and he assured her he had talked to Millie and all was well. She was thinking, *Andy is back and I am out.*

As he worked into the early afternoon, he realized Ruth and her crew had not shown up for their housekeeping duties. He tried to call her but got voicemail. This worried him, he thought he might have to add another item to his open item list. Within minutes, Ruth called to apologize and explain why she wasn't there.

Clay had been correct, Freddy Lopez was gone never to return. He had given the property he maintained for himself to Ruth. Roscoe had Ruth come to his office and handle the paperwork. It seems she now owned the Mexican restaurant in the building where Freddy had his personal residence and office. Roscoe had shown her the records from the restaurant, and it was a very profitable place. She would now receive income in place of Freddy. The building and land which involved about an acre had no debt. The labor company Freddy had operated out of his office would also be hers. This enterprise also offered a substantial income which would now be hers. She said she wanted him to know all this to help him understand why she would not be coming back. But she would keep the crew that basically knew what to do the same and provide a new supervisor. She also said she had heard that he had helped Mrs. Matthews with her business, and wanted to know if she could hire him to help her. She now had two new enterprises.

Harry had been pleasantly surprised. She didn't even sound like the old Ruth. She had suddenly been thrust into a new role, and sounded as if she was adapting quickly. He told her he would be delighted to help her and she said she would bring his new head housekeeper out the next day, and if he had the time, they could discuss how he could help her. He agreed, and they terminated the call and he leaned back in his desk chair thinking what a surprising turn of events.

Andy called and wanted to know if she could come over and warm the stew for him for dinner, he insisted that he was working and did not want to stop, plus he was very capable of warming the stew when he wanted to eat. She seemed to understand. She wanted to ask if Betty was coming over but decided it might be a mistake.

It was after six in the evening when he stopped working and decided to warm the stew and fix himself a drink. His phone rang again, this time it was Clay wanting to know if he could stop by on his way home and give him an update on the investigation.

He showed up a few minutes later. "How are you? How do you feel?"

"Just sore, I worked a good bit today, so now I'm sore and tired. I don't have all my energy back."

"That's understandable, you just need to take it easy for a while, don't rush it."

"What's happening in the investigation?"

"Well, the DEA raid was a bust. It probably was ruined by your ID of Delgado and his arrest. I think Freddy already had a detailed escape plan in place. I mean he left most of his personal possessions behind, but there were no records or evidence of drugs anywhere. More people are missing than Freddy. Delgado's partner in crime is gone, plus a few more, probably his drug team. I think he was a smart guy. Nobody left behind to testify about drugs. Oh yeah, and listen to this, your hot housekeeper has inherited all Freddy's stuff. She is now in high cotton. Amazing."

"I know, she called me and told me everything plus she wants to hire me to help her with her new ventures."

"What, are you kidding me?"

"No, it's the truth. What about Delgado?"

"He broke today. Roscoe's representing him and they want a deal. I held strong and said tell us everything, and if it's good enough, we will tell you what we will do. Roscoe was pissed, but I said you don't talk, we have a strong case for attempted murder and robbery."

"And?"

"He spilled his guts, told us who his partner was. He told us the order came directly from Freddy, but he swears after they gave the coins to Freddy and got paid, he didn't know what happened."

"What about Ruth?"

"He says she didn't know anything other than to leave the door unlocked. They were parked outside of your neighborhood and when they saw Ruth and crew leave, they drove in and did the deed. He said Freddy said hurt you, but not to kill you. As I said before, I don't think we will ever see Freddy or Delgado's partner again. I think that we will put Delgado away for a while, but the rest will be done."

"You want some stew before you go?"

"I thought Andy was coming to eat with you."

"No, she did offer but I'm trying to catch up on some work, and I need some alone time."

They ate their stew without much talk. Finally, Clay spoke, "Can I ask you what you are thinking about Andy and Betty?"

"There have been so many things going on in my life, I haven't had time to try and sort through everything."

"Well, I know for sure Andy would like for you two to pick back up where you were before she left."

Harry did not respond.

"And I've told you if that happens, I would like to try to start something with Betty."

Harry still did not respond.

"Anyway, you know that's on the table."

Chapter 74

The black SUV pulled off the main road and onto a narrow dirt road and continued until it was out of sight. It was almost dark, but the man in the car had been there the day before and knew exactly where he was and where he was going.

The call had come two days earlier. Fortunately for him, he had been in Hilton Head playing golf with some of his old military buddies. The drive across the state was much easier than coming from Boca where he lived.

The man who he believed had called him was from South America, but he could not be exactly sure. It would be the sixth job he had done for the man. The man was the most generous of his clients. The fact that he did not know who he was, made it even better. The man said the woman had cost him dearly. He said, even though she had been warned, she still acted against him and now she must pay. He was very specific about pinning the note on her chest.

It was now dark enough for him to walk through the woods to the pasture fence. From there, he could see the cabin where the man lived. It wasn't long before the cabin lights were out. He made his way across the pasture up a trial that led to the big barn. From there, another path led to the woman's house. He stood in the trees and watched her house and waited for her lights to go out. He waited an hour and walked up onto the front porch and picked the lock and slowly opened the front door. The door, to his dismay, squeaked like crazy. *Damn these old houses,* he thought. He waited silently for a few minutes to see if he heard any sounds.

She heard the squeak of the front door. Juan had offered to put WD40 on it and make it quiet, but she said absolutely not. She wanted it to do what it just had done. She opened the drawer of her bedside table and removed a snub nose .38 revolver. She crept to her door and waited. Her heart was pounding, and her hands were shaking.

The man decided it was safe to move on. He walked into the hallway that led to her bedroom. She peered around the corner of her door and could see his silhouette in the hallway. She almost gasped out loud. Instead she turned into the doorway and fired two shots. The first she knew was high but the second found its mark and the man was down.

She flipped the switch to the hall light and saw the man dressed in all black lying on his side and not moving. She slowly walked to him and stood at his feet.

She could see he had gray hair, but she could not see his face. She was thinking what she should do when he quickly rolled over and shot her in the forehead. He shot her with a .22 caliber pistol equipped with a silencer.

He was shot in the shoulder and he needed to stop the bleeding. He also knew the sound of her two shots would certainly arouse the man in the cabin. He didn't have to wait long until he heard the man coming into the house calling, "Ms. Andy, Ms. Andy, are you all right?"

The man stepped into the doorway of one of the rooms off the hallway. The hall light was still on, and when Juan turned the corner and saw her on the floor, he ran towards her, shotgun in hand and bent over to check on her. He never heard or saw the .22 as it punctured the back of his skull.

The man found a bathroom and the items necessary to dress his wound. The last thing he did before leaving, was to pin the note on her gown.

"SHE WAS WARNED NOT TO TALK"

Chapter 75

It had been a never-ending night for Harry. He had paced. He had prayed. He was looking for peace. He was looking for closure. The tension just seemed to keep building. Andy was becoming relentless. The look on Betty's face, the tone of her voice and the sincerity of the words she spoke grabbed his heart like a vice. As the sun started to peak over the horizon of the lake, he looked to the sky and said, "Thank you, Lord." He waited until six and could wait no longer. He dialed the number. She answered with a sleepy "hello."

"Harry, are you okay?"

"Yes, I think. I am sorry to wake you. I've been up all night."

"What's wrong, are you in pain?"

"Not anymore. I've got to go to L.A. for this mini-series event. They wanted to know if they should have an escort for me or would I be bringing one. Betty, will you be my escort? Before you answer, will you be my permanent escort?"

"Oh, Harry."

Chapter 76

It was after five in the afternoon when Clay had gone to the farm to find out why both Andy and Juan's phones deferred callers to voice mail. When he saw the crime scene, he broke down. He had dropped to his knees and cried as he had never before. It took ten minutes to regain his composure and call his office to report what had happened.

He was furious that the SOBs would take such vengeance. He remembered his conversation with Andy about just dropping the whole thing, and now his guilt felt like it was crushing his head. He could not collect his thoughts. When his team showed up, he wandered down to the barn and began to weep again. He was not an emotional man; therefore, fighting to get his emotions under control.

When the work at the house was completed, Deputy Canady found Clay at the barn to inform him the bodies had been removed and they were all ready to leave. Clay told him he would join them back at the office later.

Clay hung around the scene for about a half hour after before he finally left. He pulled into Harry's driveway and parked next to Betty's car. He rang the bell and Betty came to let him in. As soon as she saw him, she knew something was wrong.

As soon as he entered and saw her, he had to fight back the tears. She called Harry to join them. When Harry arrived, Clay choked, then set his jaw and told them Andy had been murdered. He explained the situation at the farm, including the note that was pinned to her gown. They were both in shock. Betty began to cry. Harry was stunned and sat silently. He told them he was pretty sure she had hit the intruder with her .38. They both told Clay they would be there for anything he needed and Clay left.

Betty and Harry embraced, and she whispered, "I hope this is not bad to say, but I am so glad you called me this morning and not after this happened. Is that bad of me?"

"No, I was thinking the same thing."

Epilogue

It had been eighteen months since Andy's murder. Clay's feelings of guilt for not just dropping the DEA thing as Andy had suggested were subsiding. Her murder had shocked the little lakeside town, and old-timers said her funeral was the largest they could ever remember.

Jack Winstone had hired a team of lawyers and convinced the DEA and prosecutors that he had been duped and was innocent of any crime. He had ceased all operations in South America. Despite the pleas of his girls, neither Jack nor his two daughters attended the funeral.

Harry and Betty had attended the Hollywood mini-series premiere and came home via a stopover in Las Vegas as Mr. and Mrs. Harry Blake. His sons were ecstatic and even Millie and Sallie seemed to be happy for their father.

On this night the Blakes were entertaining the newly married Clay and Ruth Hardaway. Ruth had received a wedding gift from an undisclosed location south of the border, of a golden box of gold coins which she promptly passed on to Harry.

They dined on lamb stew in honor of an old friend. The gold coins were back on the table where they had always been, and where Harry said they belonged.